"We could marry. In name only," West hurried to add.

"Marry?" Her lips tightened in surprise. "I just told Bertram I wouldn't be marrying for the foreseeable future—in name or not."

West glanced down at her hand, which he still held. "I know, but it would be a marriage of convenience. A business arrangement. A way to make a go of this on our own, while still keeping things proper. You and Hattie would have the house and I'd bunk in the barn."

It wouldn't be as if she and West were actually married. Not like her and Chance had been. Vienna squelched a shudder at that thought.

"So what you're saying is, if we do this, you'd get your dude ranch and I'd get a home?" The question sounded far more frank than she'd meant it, but she wanted to be certain she understood his motives before she made her decision.

A flicker of emotion that she couldn't identify crossed his face. "Yes, I'd have my dude ranch and you'd have a home." He withdrew his hand from hers, leaving her feeling a bit cold in spite of the sunshine.

Stacy Henrie has always had a love for history, fiction and chocolate. She earned her BA in public relations before turning her attention to raising a family and writing inspirational historical romances. The wife of an entrepreneur husband and a mother of three, Stacy loves to live out history through her fictional characters. In addition to being an author, she is also a reader, a road-trip enthusiast and a novice interior decorator.

Books by Stacy Henrie

Love Inspired Historical

Lady Outlaw
The Express Rider's Lady
The Outlaw's Secret
The Renegade's Redemption
The Rancher's Temporary Engagement
A Cowboy of Convenience

Visit the Author Profile page at Harlequin.com.

STACY HENRIE

A Cowboy of Convenience

HARLEQUIN® LOVE INSPIRED® HISTORICAL

Recycling programs
for this product may
not exist in your area.

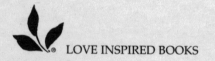

LOVE INSPIRED BOOKS

ISBN-13: 978-1-335-36971-0

A Cowboy of Convenience

www.Harlequin.com

Printed in U.S.A.

To…give unto them beauty for ashes,
the oil of joy for mourning, the garment of praise
for the spirit of heaviness; that they might be called
trees of righteousness, the planting of the Lord,
that he might be glorified.
—*Isaiah* 61:3

To all of the Love Inspired Historical team and readers

Thank you! It's been an honor to be a part
of this experience with you.

Chapter One

Near Big Horn, Wyoming, July 1901

Vienna Howe didn't immediately take note of the knocking at the door. From inside the ranch house kitchen, she thought the pounding sounded more like the distant *thwack* of a hammer than anything else. She blew a breath upward to disrupt the blond hairs sticking to her damp forehead, her hands covered in pastry dough. The wranglers at the Running W Ranch never turned down her food—especially not dessert.

"Who's at the door, Mommy?" Two-and-a-half-year-old Harriet, known as Hattie by everyone on the ranch, looked up from where she sat at the nearby table, pretending to feed her baby doll. The doll had been a gift from Vienna's employers, though Edward and Maggy Kent had been and always would be her dear friends, first and foremost.

The thudding noise repeated and this time Vienna cocked her head to listen. "Is that the door? I thought the boys might be fixing a fence." She grabbed a towel to wipe off her hands and headed for the door.

"I wanna see who's there." Gripping the doll about the neck, Hattie trailed her through the dining room and into the front hallway.

Remembering her apron at the last minute, Vienna untied it, hung it on the nearby hall tree and smoothed her hand down the front of her wrinkled white blouse and long skirt. She opened the door to find the sheriff standing there. Not the one from the nearby town of Big Horn, either. Sheriff Tweed, from seven miles away in Sheridan, looked relieved that someone had at last answered his knock.

"Just startin' to wonder if no one was around, after all," the man said as he removed his hat.

Vienna shot him an apologetic smile. "So sorry to keep you waiting, Sheriff. I was baking in the kitchen."

"That's all right."

When he didn't say anything more, she added, "I'm afraid my daughter and I are the only ones here. Edward is in town, and Maggy and Mrs. Harvey are gone on official detective business." In addition to helping her husband run their successful horse ranch, Maggy Kent operated her own small detective agency with the help of the Kents' head cook and housekeeper, Mrs. Harvey.

"I saw Mr. Kent earlier, which is how I knew you'd likely be here, Mrs. Howe."

She blinked in surprise. "You're here to see me?"

"Mommy, what does he want?" Hattie tugged on Vienna's skirt, reminding her of her daughter's presence—and the little girl's rapt attention.

At that moment Westin "West" McCall, the ranch foreman, strolled across the yard toward the porch, a ready smile on his face. "Howdy, Sheriff. What can we do for you?"

"Howdy, McCall." The sheriff smiled back. "I'm here to speak to Mrs. Howe."

West glanced at her, his expression and honey-brown eyes as wary as the emotion now churning in her stomach. "Everything all right?"

"Not to worry, son," the sheriff said, turning back to Vienna. "But I'm afraid I need to speak with Mrs. Howe in private."

Vienna scooped up Hattie and walked past the sheriff. "West, do you mind watching her for a few minutes?"

"Not at all." The man gave Hattie a gentle smile as he took her from Vienna and set her on her feet again.

The little girl gazed up adoringly at him. "You can help me feed my baby, Mr. West."

"Now remind me what her name is again," he asked as he led her in the direction of the corral.

"Hattie! Like me…"

Vienna felt both gratitude and pain watching the pair of them. While she was thankful her daughter had honorable male figures in her life such as Edward Kent, the wranglers and most especially West McCall—Hattie's favorite by far—she still grieved and worried over her little girl's lack of a father in her life.

"Come on into the parlor, Sheriff," she said, waving the lawman inside. Once he stepped into the house and followed her into the room, she motioned for him to take a seat on the sofa.

He declined with a shake of his head. "I won't be long, but *you* might wish to sit down, Mrs. Howe."

"All right." Her heart pulsed faster with dread as

she sank onto the sofa and folded her hands demurely in her lap. "What is it you wish to tell me?"

The man shifted his weight, his gaze more on the hat in his hand than on her. "There's no easy way to say this."

She gave a stiff nod, though he wasn't looking at her, then swallowed hard. "Is it something to do with my aunt?" After the death of her parents, she'd lived with her aunt and uncle, who had represented Sheridan's high society for many years. Her uncle had passed away two years ago, at which time her aunt had gone to live with Vienna's cousin in Buffalo.

"No, it isn't about your aunt." The sheriff finally looked her directly in the eye. "It's about your husband, Mrs. Howe. I learned earlier today that Chance is…well, he's dead, ma'am."

Dead? Vienna blinked in surprise before staring down at her hands, waiting for some emotion to push through her shock. When it came, it felt more like resignation than sorrow.

Chance Howe hadn't been her husband in the true sense for the past three years, which he'd spent in the Wyoming territorial prison for arson before being released just a few days ago. And before that… A shiver that had nothing to do with the sheriff's news and everything to do with her five-year, turbulent marriage tripped up Vienna's spine.

Reflexively the memories brought a flash of fear, but she reasoned it away. She'd been safe from Chance for a long time now, and that wasn't about to change, especially if he was no longer among the living.

"How did it happen?" she asked.

Sheriff Tweed looked away again. "He…um…got in

a fight in Sheridan after a card game. The other man had a revolver. I was told it was over quick, no suffering on his part."

"I see." And she did. The drinking, the gambling, the temper—they'd been Chance's companions long before she'd married him. Unfortunately it hadn't been until after their wedding that she'd learned that tragic fact.

The man sent her a contrite look. "I figured you'd want to know right away."

"Yes, thank you for your trouble." Vienna rose to her feet.

Placing his hat back on his head, the sheriff moved toward the open parlor door. "No trouble, Mrs. Howe. What'll you do with your ranch now?"

She hadn't set foot on the HC Bar Ranch since the night she'd finally found the courage to leave Chance in order to provide a stable home for their unborn child. Chance had owned the place outright before they'd married, so there'd never been a mortgage to be paid. Vienna had half expected he'd gamble away the place someday. Thankfully that was no longer a possibility. Perhaps that was one blessing to come out of his time in prison—it had kept Chance away from the card tables. Though Vienna couldn't help wondering what sort of state the ranch was in after three years of neglect.

"I...I'm not sure," she answered honestly.

While she loved living and working at the Running W and was grateful for the safe haven it had provided for her and her daughter, she still longed to have a home of her own again, something to pass down to Hattie. That longing had first sprouted inside Vienna when her parents had died and she'd been forced to sell their floundering ranch. And it had only increased after she'd gone to live with her aunt and uncle, in a home that never truly felt like hers.

The sheriff dipped his head in acknowledgment as he stepped out the front door. "I'm sure there's time enough to decide. The funeral'll be tomorrow."

"Oh, of course." Should she attend? Would she be expected to say something? Panic clawed at her throat at the thought of addressing a crowd, especially if she had to talk about Chance, until Sheriff Tweed spoke again.

"I took the liberty of speakin' to the pastor myself. He'll conduct a short service at the grave site at the cemetery in Sheridan."

Vienna didn't have to conjure up her relieved smile. "Thank you, Sheriff."

"These things are never easy, 'specially under the present circumstances."

He'd been the one, along with Edward and West, to come to her rescue that awful night when Chance had kidnapped her after she'd left him. Few knew the real reasons for Vienna separating from her husband prior to his arrest and most of them, with the exception of Sheriff Tweed, lived at the Running W.

After asking what time she needed to be there for the funeral, Vienna bid the man goodbye. She shut the door and returned to the kitchen. But even the thought of making pastries didn't fill her with her usual calm and delight. She covered the dough with a towel, stashed it in the icebox, and headed outside through the back door.

The afternoon felt warm, but a nice breeze kept the air from being too hot. Vienna glanced in the direction of the corral. Hattie sat on the top rung of the fence, while West stood beside her, holding her in place so she wouldn't fall. As if sensing Vienna's presence, West turned his head in her direction. She pointed toward the mountains to indicate she needed a walk. With obvious understanding, he dipped his chin in a nod.

The wordless communication between them had been one of many things Vienna had appreciated about their friendship, both prior to her marriage to Chance and then again since coming to the Running W. There'd even been a time when she'd thought—hoped, really—that she and West were becoming more than friends. But she'd been wrong.

Vienna pushed aside recollections of the past as she slowly walked toward the Big Horn Mountains. The pastures, fields and trees, cloaked in their summer greenery, never grew old to her. She'd moved to this area with her parents at the age of eleven, six years after the tragic death of her older brother, and had quickly fallen in love with the wild beauty of the land. Her appreciation for ranching, though, had never fully developed. She still preferred gardening, and more recently cooking and baking, than she did riding or caring for horses.

Did she want to keep the HC Bar, then? Vienna plucked up the long stem of a wildflower and ran it along the tall grass growing beside the horse trail. Moving into town and opening a café or a restaurant sounded more appealing to her than running a ranch. Besides, she couldn't operate such a spread by herself. That had been one of the reasons she'd sold her home after her parents' deaths. If her brother hadn't died as a child, perhaps the two of them could have managed the place together. But at sixteen years old, and an orphan, Vienna had had little choice except to leave.

The thought of selling yet another property, even if she'd only lived at the HC Bar for two miserably unhappy years, filled her with a physical ache. She wanted—no, needed—to give Hattie the sense of home and purpose she herself had lost. And she couldn't do that if she stayed at the Running W. This was someone else's dream, someone else's land. She was simply borrowing security and stability here; she hadn't yet created them permanently for herself and her daughter. And a café or a restaurant… A business like that would be hers, yes, but would it give her the same sense of permanence that came from standing on her own land?

"Help me know what to do, Lord," she murmured out loud as she came to a stop, her eyes rising to the mountain peaks.

She'd managed to keep the little remaining money she had from the sale of her parents' home hidden from Chance and she had saved most of her wages from working for the Kents as their assistant cook. It might be enough to reestablish the HC Bar as a working ranch again or to do something else if she sold it. But which path should she take?

Tossing aside the flower, Vienna spun around and walked briskly back the way she'd come. Chance's death might have been a complete shock, but she had enough faith to believe there was purpose and timing in it, too. And while she might not have all the answers yet regarding her future, she did know one thing for certain. As much as she hated the thought of leaving this place and its people or of being entirely on her own, with a child this time, it was time to go.

* * *

West McCall threw another glance in the direction Vienna had gone on her walk. He'd wanted to press her for information about Sheriff Tweed's news, but the pensive look on her pretty face when she'd exited the house had told him that she needed some time to herself first.

This undercurrent of protectiveness for Vienna wasn't new, and it had only grown stronger when she'd come to live at the Running W three years ago—and then when West had learned her scoundrel of a husband was bound for prison. And now that protective instinct included taking care of the little girl he held firmly in place on the fence post next to him.

He'd thought Hattie Howe fairly cute when she'd been a squirmy, bright-eyed baby with a healthy set of lungs he could often hear clear down at the bunkhouse. But the moment the little girl had taken to following him around and calling him "Mr. West," he'd been a goner. The kid had wormed her way into his guarded heart, which no one, not even her mother, had completely breached in years.

"What's the new horsie's name?" Hattie asked him.

West pushed up the brim of his hat. "Don't know that Mr. Kent has named her yet. What would you name her?"

"Um…" The little girl peered up at him with large green eyes that matched her mother's. "How 'bout Hattie?" A triumphant smile lit her face.

Pressing his lips over a laugh, West pretended to think the suggestion over. "You don't think that'd get a bit confusing? We already have Hattie the girl and

Hattie the doll." He tipped his head toward the toy she still held under her arm.

"But it'll be Hattie the horsie," she countered with an arch look. "So it's different."

How could he argue with that? he thought ruefully. Hattie began kicking her shoes against the fence, sending the new horse skittering away at the loud, repetitive sound.

"Remember what I taught you about makin' noise around the horses?"

She squinted up at him, then brightened. "We have to be real quiet." Bringing her pointer finger to her mouth, she made a loud shushing sound.

"That's right," West said with a chuckle. "Which means no kicking the fence, especially with a new horse around."

Her brow furrowed as she glanced down at her feet. "I'll tell them to be quiet." Then she shushed her shoes.

West laughed fully this time, and Hattie joined him a moment later, even though he suspected she didn't know what they were laughing about.

"There's Mommy." She wiggled in his grip, indicating she wanted to get down.

Sure enough Vienna was walking back toward them. West lifted Hattie off the fence and set her on her feet. The little girl darted across the yard to greet her mother.

"Mommy, there's a new horsie, and I want to name her Hattie. And my feet weren't bein' quiet so I had to shush them. Like this." She repeated the quieting action, her narrowed gaze on her black shoes.

A faint smile lifted Vienna's lips. "That's wonderful you're learning to be quiet around the horses, Hattie."

"Mr. West teached me."

Vienna looked at him, a mixture of appreciation and regret in those beautiful green eyes. They reminded him of a pair of jade earrings his mother used to wear. The color of the stones mirrored the exact shade of Vienna's eyes.

Did his mother still own those earrings? It had been more than ten years seen he'd last seen them or their owner. The reminder threatened to pull him toward darker thoughts—ones he typically buried under an easygoing demeanor and plenty of hard work.

"Mr. West has been a wonderful friend and teacher to you, Hattie," Vienna said as she glanced away.

Has been? A feeling of foreboding settled in his stomach at her use of the past tense. Maybe it had only been a slip of the tongue…or maybe whatever news the sheriff had brought her meant something in their lives was about to change. Though he hoped not.

"You all right?" he asked in a low voice, falling into step beside her and Hattie.

Vienna nodded. "Hattie, will you go pick those wild-flowers by the stable there? I'd like to put some on the supper table for the Kents tonight."

"All right, Mommy. But you gotta hold Hattie for me." With that, the little girl shoved the doll at her mother before racing toward the small stable that stood next to the ranch house.

When her daughter was out of earshot, Vienna turned toward him, her hands clutching the doll to her middle. "Chance is dead," she said without preamble.

"What?" West gaped in shock at her. "When?"

"Yesterday apparently. There was a…a fight and he was shot, though it sounds like he didn't suffer."

A desire to comfort Vienna filled him, a longing to reach out and take her into his arms as he'd done years ago—and then again the night he'd helped rescue her from Chance's crazy kidnapping scheme. But things had been more formal between them for a long time and he wasn't sure if Vienna would appreciate the comforting gesture or not.

"I'm real sorry, Vienna," he said, hoping she sensed his sincerity. While he despised Chance Howe for the way the man had treated his wife, he didn't fault Vienna for feeling grief over her husband's demise.

She offered him a thin smile of acknowledgment. "Thank you. I don't really know how I feel about it."

West could relate far better than she knew. How did one respond to loss when it had been preceded by so much conflict and harshness?

"I suppose I feel mostly sad, more for him than for myself or Hattie," she admitted. "He and I have lived apart for so long now that it's more like hearing about the death of a distant acquaintance than a spouse."

"I'm glad to hear he didn't suffer." No matter his anger toward Chance and his choices, West didn't like the idea of him suffering any more than the man already had. After all, Chance Howe had lost his wife and child long before he'd lost his life.

Vienna dipped her head in a slow nod. "Me, too."

"Will you tell Hattie?" West still didn't know how much Vienna had told her daughter about the girl's father and it wasn't his place to ask. He was their friend and possible protector but nothing more.

Gazing at her daughter who was filling her tiny fist with flowers, Vienna sighed. "I'll tell her soon. In some ways, it may be easier to explain that her father passed away than if he'd lived and I'd had to prepare her for him coming back here. Someday I'll need to tell her the truth of all of it, but not yet."

"Sounds wise to me." He matched her steps as she moved toward the house.

Her expression conveyed genuine relief. "I appreciate that. More often than not, I feel anything but wise."

"What will you do now?" Not that Chance's death was likely to have much of an impact on her. West already knew how little Vienna cared for ranching and how much she enjoyed working at the Running W—same as he did. Having his own spread was still his ultimate dream, but in the meantime, he couldn't ask for a better or more generous employer than Edward Kent.

Vienna stopped walking, and for a second, West didn't think she was going to answer his simple question. Then she darted a quick look at him.

It might have been short, and yet, it was long enough for him to see unmistakable remorse in her eyes. The sight set off a warning bell inside his head. He had a sinking suspicion he wasn't going to like what she was about to tell him.

"Hattie and I will be leaving the Running W soon," she said in a quiet but resolved tone.

West didn't feel one ounce of pleasure at knowing his suspicion had been correct. "Where will you go?"

"Back to the HC Bar. I don't know yet what I'll do with it or where we'll end up. But it's time Hattie and I found a home of our own."

Chapter Two

"McCall?"

West frowned, his arms resting against the door of the stall where the new mare stood eating. He couldn't keep his focus on his work. Instead, he kept thinking about Vienna's announcement earlier. Truth be told, he'd struggled to concentrate on anything the rest of the afternoon and evening.

"McCall? Did you hear me?" Edward asked in his slight British accent. "You look as lost in thought as Vienna tonight."

At the mention of Vienna's name, West straightened away from the stall and threw his employer a contrite smile. "Sorry, Boss. Where were we?"

"I asked after the new mare here."

West dipped his head in a quick nod. "Right. She seems to have settled in well. And I don't think she'll give us much trouble with breaking her in."

"Excellent." Edward moved away from the mare toward the open doors of the ranch's main barn. "What about the south pasture fence?"

"Nearly all fixed. We'll finish tomorrow."

He joined his employer outside where the first stars had begun to glitter overhead. The unimpeded view of their brightness in the vast stretch of sky never ceased to amaze him. It was one in a long list of things he cherished about living out west.

"How did Thurston do overseeing the fence project today?" Edward asked next.

The wrangler had been working at the ranch longer than any of the other young men, and West had been recently tasked with giving him more opportunities to lead. "Did real well. You gunnin' for him to replace me?" he half teased.

"Not right away." Edward chuckled. "But I know you still want to run a dude ranch of your own someday."

West had confided that dream to Edward about a year after coming to work at the Running W. His visits to a dude ranch in North Dakota as a young man had inspired his future plans as well as the pivotal decision to fully embrace a life out west. He'd been relieved and grateful when Edward, a man he fully respected, hadn't scoffed as some ranchers did at the notion of building a career helping wealthy guests experience Western life.

"Which is why," Edward added, "when the time comes, I want to be sure Thurston will be ready to take over as the next ranch foreman."

West expected Edward to head to the house right then as the man usually did. Not that he could blame him. If West had a wife and a baby on the way, he'd probably wish to spend every possible moment with his family, too. But while a family meant potential for great joy, as Edward had clearly discovered, they could also be the means of immense heartache. West had learned that sad, hard fact years ago—one was loved and important as long as they were doing what everyone wanted. Once the usefulness wore out, so did the strength of familial ties.

Rather than go inside, though, Edward loosely folded his arms and regarded West curiously. "You want to share what was on your mind earlier?"

"Just thinking," he hedged.

Edward glanced in the direction of the house. "Did you hear Chance Howe is dead?"

"Yep, Vienna told me earlier." West kicked at a clump of grass with the toe of his boot. "Did she tell you what she'll do now?" He didn't want to share her plan to leave the ranch if she hadn't yet told the Kents.

"She and Hattie will be moving back to the HC Bar."

West felt Edward's gaze on him as he stared hard at the ground. "I suppose that makes sense."

"Then what's the reason for your scowl?" the other man asked with a laugh.

Crossing his arms, West lifted his chin and did his best to school his expression into his usual relaxed one. "Just surprised. Vienna seems to really like working and living here. Hattie, too."

"I believe they did, that they do. However, Vienna wants a home of her own." Edward looked out across the ranch and pastures. "Now that Howe's gone, she can return to her home without any fear of him interfering."

West swallowed back an uncharacteristically sarcastic remark about the Running W being her and Hattie's home. Still, he wasn't surprised by Vienna's desire to have her own home. He'd known nearly from their first meeting, seven years ago, how important home was to her and how much she missed the one she'd had to sell after her parents had both passed away.

He'd wanted to tell her that earlier, but after revealing her shocking news, she'd retreated into the house. West had seen her later when she'd served dinner to the ranch staff, but there hadn't been a chance to talk privately with her again.

"You can still look out for them, you know." Edward's words intruded into West's thoughts. "They won't be far away."

Heat rose up his neck at the realization that his need to protect Vienna and her daughter hadn't gone unnoticed by his good friend. "I've never acted in a way that wasn't aboveboard, Boss. I promise."

"I don't doubt that for a minute, McCall. And I apologize if you think I was implying something to the contrary." Edward maintained West's gaze as he added, "You've been the perfect gentleman in honoring your past and present friendship with her."

The relief he felt at Edward's reassurance was short-lived. More than friendship had motivated West to watch out for Vienna since the night he had helped rescue her from Chance. It had only been a few days prior to that when he'd learned, to his shock and dismay, the kind of husband the man had been to Vienna.

But he couldn't share his true motive with Edward for wanting to protect Vienna—not yet, maybe never. To do so would mean giving voice to his ever-present guilt. Guilt that told him Vienna's unhappy marriage to Chance was all West's fault. After all, he'd been the one to encourage the match in the first place, and he'd be the one to make things right by her now, even if no one, including Vienna, understood why.

"It'll be strange, won't it, not having them here any-more?" he said as much in truth as to steer the conversation away from himself.

Vienna might have only been on the ranch for three years, but West could hardly remember what things had been like prior to that. He wasn't sure he wanted to imagine what it would be like not having her around anymore. Nodding, Edward looked toward the house again. "It'll be an adjustment, no question about that. And not simply because we'll need to find a new cook to help Mrs. Harvey. Maggy and I will miss them both." He shot West a sad smile. "Maggy, in particular, is having a hard time of it, though she understands Vienna's reasons for going."

West wasn't surprised to hear Edward's wife was struggling with the news. Anyone could see that the bond between Maggy and Vienna ran as close and deep as sisters. Which meant West wouldn't be the only one to grieve Vienna's departure when the time came, no matter how close the Howes' ranch might be to the Running W.

He hoped to visit there as often as he could, but it wouldn't be the same as seeing Vienna's soft smile every day or having the chance to teach Hattie something new about the horses and the ranch.

The reality of their leaving sunk deep inside him with that last thought, leaving West feeling hollow with loss in a way he hadn't felt in years.

The Kents' wagon rattled along the road from Sheridan to the ranch. Vienna sat in back, along with West who had been oddly somber since yesterday. She missed his usual smiles and laughter. Still, she'd been relieved when he, Edward and Maggy had asked if they could accompany her to the graveside service at the cemetery today. Mrs. Harvey had volunteered to watch Hattie, so the four adults had set off in the wagon shortly after breakfast.

The sunshine seemed to mock the reality of seeing Chance's coffin and listening to the pastor's short speech. The only other people present besides Vienna, the Kents and West were Sheriff Tweed and Chance's friend Gunther Bertram.

Not knowing the circumstances, the pastor likely hoped his words would bring all of them, especially Vienna, solace—but she wasn't a typical grieving widow. She needed comfort, yes, but more from the shock of how drastically life could change from one moment to the next than from sorrow over losing a husband she hadn't seen in three years—a husband she had left, hoping to never see again.

After the short service, as the other guests had visited quietly, she'd remained beside the open hole. "I'm sorry, Chance," she whispered, "that you were so troubled and broken. I realized shortly after befriending Maggy that I couldn't fix that for you. Only you could do that."

Tears blurred the freshly turned earth beside the grave as old memories and remembered pain filled her thoughts. She wrestled them back with the reminder that she was now forever free of Chance's mistreatment.

"I wish we'd both known that you were responsible for yourself. Maybe then things would have been different. Or maybe not." She sniffed back the salty moisture. "Either way, I've forgiven you and I'm grateful for the gift of our daughter that you gave me. She's beautiful and smart...and best of all...she isn't afraid or timid." Not like Vienna used to be. Not like she still felt sometimes. "Goodbye, Chance."

She'd felt sapped of all energy even before Bertram had approached her with condolences and news about her horses, which he'd apparently been caring for at Chance's request. West had thankfully interrupted, cutting the conversation short, and led her to the wagon. Once inside, she'd slumped onto the boards and had been lost in her thoughts ever since.

"Have you given any more thought to your idea about opening a café or restaurant?" Maggy asked, turning on the wagon seat to look at Vienna.

She shook her head. "No, not really."

"You want to open a café?" West's question sounded genuinely curious, but the look in his brown eyes told her that he was surprised and possibly hurt that she hadn't shared the idea with him sooner.

Vienna hurried to explain. "It's only something I thought of yesterday."

"I'd definitely come eat at any place you run, Vienna." Maggy smiled as she massaged the small of her back. Vienna could readily identify with the discomfort that came with being eight months pregnant. "I didn't think anyone could bake or cook as well as Mrs. Harvey, but you're now as competent in the kitchen as she is."

Vienna's cheeks heated with a blush, though she appreciated the sincere compliment. "Thank you. I didn't realize how much I'd come to love making food."

"So you'd sell the HC Bar and buy a place in town?" West lifted his knee and rested his arm on top. The casual pose belied the tension she noticed in the lines of his shoulders and jaw. Was he upset with her?

The thought brought remembered fear and an instant need to smooth things over, as she had so often done with Chance. But West wasn't a threat, she reminded herself.

She met his level gaze with one of her own and swallowed back her fear. "Honestly, I don't know what I want to do yet. I like the idea of running my own business, but I'm not sure I can picture me and Hattie living in town."

"If you open something in Big Horn rather than Sheridan, you'd be closer to the Running W," Maggy pointed out.

Having a café or restaurant in the small town a few miles from the ranch sounded more attractive to Vienna, too, though a larger town like Sheridan would likely mean more visitors. Either way, did she want to raise her daughter among the hubbub of town, large or small? Or would they both miss the sprawling openness of the prairie? They would certainly miss the people, especially the ones right here.

A lump filled her throat at the thought of leaving them and the Running W behind. And yet…it was past time she proved to herself and to everyone else that she was capable of being on her own.

While she'd been grateful for a roof overhead and food to eat after she'd lost her parents, Vienna had often felt frustrated at being beholden and dependent upon first her aunt and uncle and then her husband for nearly everything in her life. She'd greatly appreciated the opportunity to earn her keep with the Kents, but she still wished to live in and manage a home that was entirely hers.

"How much work does your ranch need?" The question came from Edward.

Vienna frowned. "I'm hoping not much, beyond some cleaning inside the house and a few repairs outside." If the ranch needed significant work to get it up and operating again, or at least in a fit state to sell it, that would likely require more money than she had.

"We'd like to help how we can, Vienna." Edward turned far enough around on the seat to send her a genuine smile. "Whether that's with getting settled in or assisting with repairs."

A fresh swell of gratitude rose inside her at all that he and Maggy had done for her. "I appreciate the offer. I thought I'd drive over to the ranch later today, when Hattie takes her nap, to see what the place looks like."

"I can drive you in the wagon if you'd like," West volunteered.

His earlier tension had seemed to drain away, to Vienna's relief. "That would be wonderful. Thank you, West."

He nodded. "I can help with any repairs, too—if the boss is all right with that."

"Certainly," Edward answered. "It'll be good practice for Thurston to manage things without you hovering over his shoulder."

Vienna offered West a thankful smile. "I'd appreciate the help."

When he smiled back, she felt her lingering shock and regret over Chance's death fade away. She was grateful for West's friendship—his presence had been a steady and welcome one to both her and Hattie the last few years. And she hoped it would remain so, wherever she ended up.

As she viewed the wooden arch of the HC Bar for the first time in three years, Vienna felt a clammy sweat collect beneath the collar of her blouse. She shifted on the wagon seat, causing West to glance her way. Not able to muster up a smile, she kept her face trained forward, toward the ranch in the near distance.

The last time she'd been here it had been summer, too. Chance had been drunk—again—and hurling insults and curse words at her like bullets. During the midst of the barrage, words from her new friend Maggy about worth and strength had pierced Vienna's mind and wouldn't let go. So, for the first time in the two years she'd been married, she finally stood up for herself. She told Chance that she was through, that she would no longer stay in a house with someone who treated her as less valuable than his precious horses.

Chance's retribution was swift, though not entirely unexpected. He landed a solid slap across her cheek before raging all over again. Vienna steeled herself for another blow, but it never came. Instead her husband marched out the door, disappeared into the barn and rode away a few minutes later.

Vienna waited by the window, her cheek smarting, certain Chance would be back at any moment. The moments stretched to minutes, though, before she realized the opportunity he'd unintentionally presented to her. If she saddled her own mount, she could make good on her vow to ride away from Chance and the HC Bar forever.

The lure of freedom propelled her into action. She went to the barn, which was thankfully devoid of any of their ranch hands, and prepared a horse, but dark thoughts threatened her progress. What if Chance returned before she could get away? What if she got away, but he tracked her down and dragged her back from wherever she went to finish his punishment?

Vienna froze beside the saddled horse. Her heart crashed so hard against her ribs that she could hardly breathe.

She shut her eyes and whispered a prayer. It wasn't like the others she'd offered in hopes of softening Chance's heart or becoming a better wife. No, this time she petitioned God for courage and any particle of strength she might possess in order to follow through with her plan—a plan that included providing her unborn baby with a safe and loving home. She also prayed she would make it away unharmed if possible.

With slightly calmer breaths but trembling hands, she'd mounted her horse and rode hard toward the one place she'd hoped she would be safe from Chance— the Running W Ranch, where Maggy was staying and West McCall worked as a foreman. She made it to the ranch without incident, and despite two other attempts by Chance to force her to come home, Vienna had been liberated both times. After that, she'd made a life for herself, and later for Hattie, at the Running W. A life of peace and happiness.

Did she really wish to leave that life now? she wondered as they passed by the HC Bar's corral. Was she capable of being on her own? Of being strong? Could she live in this place that held so few happy memories?

Her heart sped up with dismay when she viewed the

barn and house. Both buildings were in sore need of new paint, and tumbleweeds had taken up residence along their walls. Her once beloved garden was now a sea of weeds. The scene so accurately matched the bleak and lonely emptiness of her short marriage that her chest tightened, and she found herself flinching in preparation for some expected blow.

West's hand settled on her arm, startling her from her panic. Looking from his strong fingers to his face, she vaguely noted that he'd parked the wagon. He hadn't spoken much on the drive over, but then, neither had she.

"You're safe, Vienna," he said in a low voice, his brown eyes devoid of any levity.

They were the same words he'd murmured to her the night he'd helped rescue her after Chance's kidnapping. As they had then, they soothed her agitation and fear now.

"Yes, you're right." She exhaled slowly and rested her hand on top of his for a moment. Beneath the solid comfort of the friendly gesture, a strange sensation flittered through her stomach—not so unlike the one she'd felt when they had first met.

Vienna twisted on the seat, breaking his hold and ending the bizarre butterflies in her middle. While their interactions were only that of friendly propriety, she'd long thought West McCall handsome with his black curly hair and warm brown eyes. He was thirty, which put him at only five years her senior, and his easygoing personality and kindness were as recommendable as his good looks. The girl who successfully won West's heart would be blessed indeed.

A prick of regret followed such a thought, surpris-

ing Vienna. Setting aside the odd path her thoughts
had taken, she waited as West climbed down from the
wagon and circled around it to come help her. She could
do this—she could make something of this place.

"God hath not given us the spirit of fear," she reminded herself. It had become her favorite scripture.

"Let's give the house a closer look first," she said as
West assisted her to the ground. "Then I can figure out
what needs to be done to make this place livable again."

Chapter Three

⟡

West had never been to the HC Bar Ranch before now. Yet even knowing what a scoundrel Chance Howe had turned out to be, he was impressed at the man's extensive property. And to think, Vienna's late husband had owned all of this outright.

Still, the signs of neglect and absence were everywhere. The moderate-sized house featured dusty, cobwebbed furniture, a roof in need of new shingles and a back porch with missing boards. Vienna's earlier determined look lost more and more of its resolve as she led him through the house.

"Maybe the barn has fared better," she said with what sounded like false cheer.

West followed her around the broken porch boards and into the yard. But a gaping hole in the barn's roof and the scratching of tiny claws in one of the stalls told an unpromising story.

"I knew it might need work." Vienna's shoulders slumped. "But not this much."

He lifted his hand to touch her arm as he had on the wagon before remembering how she'd twisted away from him after a moment. Clearly she didn't wish for more than comforting words right now.

"There is a lot to do," he said, lowering his arm back to his side. "Both structures appear to be sound, though."

Vienna shot him a rueful smile. "Sound for whom, West? The mice?" She motioned to the stall where the scurrying noises hadn't stopped.

"Where are all of your livestock?" he asked as he glanced around the empty barn.

She retreated into the yard. "Gunther Bertram told me this morning at the graveside service that he and Chance had an arrangement that Bertram would care for the horses while Chance was…away. As far as the cattle we used to own, most of them were sold to pay off gambling debts. The rest may have been stolen or they could have wandered off as I suspect the milk cow and the chickens did. I heard Chance had to let our ranch hands go before he left, but I don't know if they took any of the animals with them or not."

West moved in the direction of the corral. The fence looked in decent condition. Beyond the house and barn, he spied several empty pastures. There were likely spots that needed fixing along their fence lines, though all in all the necessary repairs to the ranch weren't as significant as he'd expected after being deserted for three years.

One look at Vienna's expression told him that she begged to differ. "It's going to take some time and money, Vienna, but you can get this place up and running again. And you heard what Edward said earlier—there are people willing to help you do it."

He might not like the idea of her leaving the Running W, but he'd accepted it. If living here was what she wanted, then West would do all in his power to help her.

"It's not that." She folded her arms as if chilled, despite the pleasant temperature. "I want a home of my own, for me and Hattie. But even with all of the money I've saved, I don't think I have enough to pay for the repairs and buy more livestock. And even if I choose to give it up and move to town, if I don't fix up the place, it's hardly livable and unlikely to sell for a good price."

He felt the familiar squeeze of his heart at her predicament. "I have some money…" He'd been saving for years for his dude ranch, but he would gladly use it to help Vienna. He owed her that.

"No," she said, shaking her head. "I appreciate it, West, really I do. But I don't want to be a charity case anymore."

He frowned. "That's not how anyone sees you. Least of all me or the Kents."

"I'm sure you don't, but I want to do this on my own. Besides—" she gave him a knowing look "—I seem to recall you saying years ago that you planned to save all you could to have a ranch of your own someday. Is that still true?"

Nodding, West decided not to press her. "What will you do, then?"

"Well—" she spun in a slow circle, her hands resting on her hips "—I think I ought to finish my conversation with Bertram about my horses this afternoon, and sometime in the next while, I'll need to come back and clean the house. Once that's done and Hattie and I are moved in, I'll just have to see how many repairs I can afford."

As he trailed her back to the wagon, he glanced over his shoulder at the barn. He could easily repair the roof with materials he knew Edward would donate. Plus the Kents had several cats, any of which would solve the current mouse problem. Maybe he could convince Vienna to allow him to do that much. It would be a paltry attempt to appease his deep-seated guilt, but it was still a small chance to begin to make things up to her.

"The boys and I will sure miss your cookin'," he said to fill the silence between them as he drove the wagon toward Bertram's place. And while it was the truth, he couldn't say that what he'd miss most was her and Hattie.

Still, his words brought a tentative smile to her face. "I think I'm actually going to miss cooking for a crowd. The ranch hands at the HC Bar were responsible for their own cooking, so I never cooked for more than Chance and me. Maybe that's why running a café or restaurant sounds appealing."

"Maggy is right—your food is incredible. Any establishment you set up is sure to do well."

Her cheeks flushed an attractive shade of pink. "How do I know you aren't just saying that?" she teased, though her blush and the sparkle in her green eyes showed she appreciated his compliment.

He'd thought her beautiful from the first moment they'd met. And while he'd kept things between them appropriate and above suspicion ever since, he hadn't failed to notice that she'd only grown lovelier the last seven years. She'd also lost most of her timidity since coming to live at the Running W, which West had been relieved to see. Vienna wasn't weak, regardless of what Chance had made her believe about herself. She was strong and lovely and full of faith. Her blond hair had also once been silky to the touch, and he figured that hadn't changed, though he'd long ago lost the right to test that theory again.

"Is something wrong?" She threw him a puzzled look, which alerted him that he'd been staring at her and hadn't answered her initial question yet.

Clearing his throat, he faced forward again. "No, nothing wrong. And the promise of your cookin' after a long day working on the ranch isn't something I'd joke about."

"Thank you," she said with a light laugh. "Hattie is going to miss you and the wranglers."

West tightened his grip on the reins, making the horses toss their heads. *Only Hattie?* "We'll miss her, too."

"Is Thurston going to take over as foreman soon?"

He welcomed the change in topic. "Not sure." West still needed to save more money if he wanted to build his dude ranch and procure the necessary livestock for it. But with Vienna leaving now, the thought of staying at the Running W for much longer held less appeal to him.

When they reached Bertram's ranch, West helped Vienna down from the wagon. Several ranch hands eyed them curiously as they approached the main house. Bertram met them on the porch.

"Howdy again, McCall, Mrs. Howe." He removed his hat and held it to his chest as he added, "Like I said earlier, it's a real shame about Chance, ma'am. I'm sorry for your loss."

West sensed Vienna's tension from where he stood

beside her. Bertram clearly had no idea what kind of husband his friend had been.

"Once again, I appreciate that, Mr. Bertram. And thank you as well for coming to the service."

"What can I do for you?" the man asked as he clapped his hat back on.

Vienna's gaze flicked to the barn. "You mentioned this morning that you have Chance's…" She looked back at Bertram and raised her chin a notch. "I mean *my* horses."

"That I do." Bertram dipped his head in a nod. "Well, I got twenty of them, anyway, and a couple colts, too. Chance said I could keep three of the horses since I was carin' for the rest." He eyed Vienna as if unsure if she'd honor her late husband's promise or not.

She offered him a quick smile. "I think that sounds like a fair exchange. Can I see the other horses? I can't bring them home for a while longer, but I'd like to look at them."

"Home?" Bertram scratched at his jaw. "You're going back to the HC Bar?"

It was Vienna's turn to nod. "I am."

"Well, I'll be…" The rancher waved them forward as he moved toward the barn. "Chance said you didn't like ranching. Though that's a nice-sized spread you got there."

"It is," Vienna said, apparently choosing to ignore Bertram's first remark.

Inside the barn, the rancher showed them several of Vienna's horses before leading them to a nearby pasture to view the rest. West could see Vienna was as relieved as he was to find all of them looking hale and well cared for.

"They all look very fit, Mr. Bertram." Vienna offered him another smile. "Thank you for taking care of them."

Bertram flushed red. "It wasn't a problem, ma'am. I wanted to do my part to help Chance…and yourself." He turned to West, a flicker of wariness in his eyes. It was the same look the rancher had given West after he'd interrupted Bertram's conversation with Vienna at the cemetery. "Did you need somethin' too, McCall?"

"Nope. Just here to drive Mrs. Howe to and from the Running W."

His expression relaxed. "So you're really going to start up the HC Bar again, Mrs. Howe?"

"It's going to require some work and capital, but yes."

Bertram led them back toward his house. "You planning on doing it alone?"

"Most of it," she said, her tone slightly on edge, her shoulders tense.

If the rancher noticed the shift in Vienna's demeanor, he ignored it. "A ranch is a lot more than one person can handle, especially if that person is a woman on her own." He hooked his thumbs in his belt loops as if he was the authority on ranching and Vienna knew nothing about it. West barely resisted the urge to roll his eyes.

"Yes, I was raised on a—"

Bertram's words ran over hers. "Seems to me Chance wouldn't take kindly to no one looking out for his widow."

"I don't really—"

He leaned a little closer to Vienna as he continued. "I think there are those around here who'd readily agree with him, Mrs. Howe. Young bucks such as myself who might be willing to finally settle down when there's a pretty woman and a ranch in need of helping."

Was the man proposing to Vienna? West's gut churned with disbelief and intense annoyance. Vienna's face had lost all of its color.

"Of course any courting would need to wait a bit on account of Chance's only been gone a few days." He shot a glance at the sky and shook his head before he lowered his chin and grinned at Vienna, seemingly unaware of the awkward strain he'd created. "But my offer would still be good when your mourning was done, ma'am."

She visibly swallowed, her cheeks still pale. "I… um…thank you for your concern, Mr. Bertram." The rancher looked ready to crow until Vienna added, "However, for the foreseeable future, I have no plans to court anyone or to marry again."

Relief washed through West, sweet and liberating, though he hadn't really expected Vienna to take Bertram's proposal seriously. The thought of her marrying any of the local ranchers didn't sit right with him. It wasn't jealousy, though, he told himself. He had no claim to be jealous. It was more a feeling of tight uneasiness in his chest like the tautness in the air before a heavy storm.

"I see," Bertram said in a clipped tone, his brow furrowed. "No chance you'll be changing your mind, then?"

Vienna gave a firm shake of her head. "No."

"Still worth a try, I suppose." The rancher shrugged. "I'll keep the horses until you come to collect them."

It looked as if she tried to smile but failed. "Wonderful. I'll return in the next few weeks. Thank you."

West followed her to the wagon and assisted her onto the seat. She wordlessly settled her skirt around her feet.

"That was kind of Chance to give him three horses," he said as he drove away from Bertram's ranch. "The others look well."

She gave a wordless nod, silent anxiety emanating off her in waves.

"I don't blame you for being angry." He threw her a compassionate look. "His…uh…offer was rather unexpected."

Her laugh came out soft but brittle. "You think I'm angry at him for proposing? Shocked, yes, but I don't feel anger."

"Then what are you feeling?" he asked in confusion.

When she regarded him, he couldn't help noticing the depth of her jade green eyes. Why any man would treat her or any other woman so abominably West didn't know. Were he to ever marry, though like Vienna that wasn't in his foreseeable future, either, he would cherish his wife and treat her with the utmost respect and devotion—just as he'd hope she would do with him.

"I'm terrified, West."

He pulled his thoughts to the present. "Terrified?"

"Yes." She stared down at her hands, which rested decorously on her lap. "Now that Chance is gone and everyone knows his widow and the HC Bar are apparently up for grabs, how many other offers of marriage am I going to have to fend off?"

Her words pummeled him with all the force of a

horse hoof to the gut. He hadn't liked Bertram proposing to her, which meant he certainly didn't like the idea of every other single rancher or wrangler in the vicinity doing the same.

"So they wouldn't be welcome offers, then?"

She threw him an arch look, her eyes sparking with green fire. "No, they would not, West McCall."

"Just want to be clear," he said with a chuckle, feeling more than a little relieved to hear that her thoughts on the matter matched his own.

Pushing out a sigh, she fiddled with the cuff of her sleeve. "Most of them would probably mean well and they'd be right to think there is a lot of work to be done on the ranch, but I want to make a go of it on my own."

"Because of last time, with your folks?" He kept his tone gentle.

She glanced at him, her lips tipping upward in a soft smile. "You're probably the only one who understands why I want this so badly." That knowledge pleased him, though he wasn't entirely sure why. "But, yes, I couldn't keep our home back then and I don't want to lose another. This time I have some savings, and I have my daughter's future to consider, too."

"What about takin' out a mortgage on the place?"

Vienna appeared to consider the idea. "I don't think the bank would invest in the property as it stands right now, especially if I just turn around and sell it after making what few repairs I can afford."

"Then I guess the question is…" He paused and pushed up his hat brim. He didn't envy her position, though he wished there was more he could do to help her besides driving her around today and possibly patching up the barn roof. "What sort of home do you want for you and Hattie? A working ranch or a place in town above a café?"

Vienna didn't have an immediate answer. Instead, she shifted uneasily on the wagon seat, West's question repeating through her mind. *What sort of home do I want?*

"I love living out here," she said after a minute. Her gaze moved to the landscape they passed by. "I've always loved the openness of the countryside and being right in the middle of nature's beauty." She unclasped her hands and studied them. "And while I love cooking, I miss working with my hands in my garden."

West regarded her with kindness in his brown eyes. "You could probably still have a small garden plot in town if you wanted."

She could, but would it be the same? Chance had protested against using their money for anything other than necessary seedlings, so Vienna had set aside her desire to try her hand at growing flowers or medicinal herbs or more colorful vegetables than just carrots, corn and potatoes. Now that he was gone, she could experiment—at least once she had other things on the ranch under control.

"I think I want to keep the ranch."

The look of surprise from West matched the one that was surely on her own face. "You don't want to run a café anymore?"

"I do," she admitted with a laugh, "but even more than that, I want Hattie to keep experiencing life out here." She lowered her chin and directed her next words to her lap. "Is that completely foolish?"

He didn't respond, except to turn the wagon to the left and keep driving. After a few moments, she realized they were nearing the HC Bar again. But West kept silent until he parked the wagon beneath the archway.

"What do you see, Vienna?"

She smirked. "A ranch in need of a great deal of work and attention. Some of which I can pay for and some I can't. I don't even have enough money to buy new livestock, let alone employ the cowboys to care for them."

"Wrong answer." His teasing coaxed a smile from her—not unlike other times, both at the beginning of their friendship and since she'd come to live at the Running W. "You know what I see? I see the promise of a thriving ranch that any man or woman would be proud to call their own. I see it as a home. A place for Hattie to live and grow up where she can someday raise her own children." He let that sink in before asking her again. "So what do you see? Do you see it as a home?"

The picture he created in her mind so closely mirrored the one in her heart that she had to swallow past the lump in her throat to reply. "Yes," she half whispered. She could more easily picture this as her home than a place in Big Horn or Sheridan above a café or restaurant. "But how do I make it that way?"

It was as much a question for West as it was for God. She didn't want to fear the future, and yet, her options were limited. Once Maggy's baby came, the Kents' ranch house was likely to feel crowded—something Vienna had already been concerned about the last few months. She didn't want to be in the way of Edward and Maggy's growing family. But now, even if her savings weren't as large as she might have hoped they'd be before leaving the Running W, she had a place for her and Hattie to live, and the Kents could finally have their home to themselves.

"I have an idea."

Vienna shook her head. "I already told you, West, that I can't accept any more charity."

"I'm not offering charity."

Something in his voice and handsome face hinted at concealed enthusiasm but also wariness as if he feared she'd dismiss his idea. The thought that he distrusted her reaction saddened her. He'd been as good a friend to her as the Kents, and like them, West only wished to help her.

"What is it?" she asked gently.

He swiveled on the seat to face her. "What if we turn the HC Bar into a dude ranch?"

"A dude ranch?" Vienna couldn't help laughing, but the sound died away when she realized he was serious.

Nodding, West gazed past her to the house and barn in the distance. "This place would make the ideal location once we add housing for guests and just enough livestock to give them the ranching experience. There's nearby fishing and hunting and horse trails for riding. Plus Yellowstone National Park is close enough for overnight trips."

She couldn't recall ever seeing West so excited. But questions crowded her mind, the most critical one spilling from her lips first. "When you say *we*, what do you mean?"

"I mean me and you, Vienna." He clasped her hand in his, sending a ripple of feeling through her fingers and arm. Though from the look on his face, he wasn't even aware of his gesture, let alone its effect. "You can cook the meals, providing the guests with the best food in the country. And I'll see to the livestock and leading the excursions."

Vienna turned to look at the ranch, trying to see it through West's eyes. Only needing two people, at least at first, to run the place sounded far more doable than the large staff of wranglers she'd have to employ if she wanted a regular ranch for Hattie to inherit.

"It's perfect, really," West continued. "We'll combine our resources up front. That way no one's accepting charity." He shot her a playful grin that she answered with a chuckle.

Is this what I'm meant to do, Lord?

"Best of all," West added, "there aren't likely to be any more unwanted marriage proposals, since we'd be running the place together."

She had to admit she liked the sound of that. Bertram's not-so-subtle offer of marriage had been awkward and unwanted. But the stir she and West would create among the area's gossips, being at the ranch alone together, would certainly bring even more unwanted awkwardness.

"If we do this, the two of us, what would people say? I mean, I'm a widow, and well…" She waved a hand at him, her face flushing with embarrassment. "You're a bachelor cowboy."

The enthusiasm slipped from West's expression, and he frowned. "True. We'd want to do all of this proper-like."

"Yes." But what did that entail? Hiring more people so they weren't on the ranch unchaperoned? And yet, how could they afford to pay anyone wages and still have the money needed to start the dude ranch, even with their combined funds?

He cleared his throat and shot her a sideways glance. "We could marry. In name only," he hurried to add when she gaped at him.

"Marry?" Her lips tightened in surprise and frustrated confusion. "I just told Bertram I wouldn't be marrying for the foreseeable future."

West glanced down at her hand, which he still held. "I know, but it would be a marriage of convenience. A business arrangement. A way to do this on our own, while still keeping things proper. You and Hattie could have the house and I could bunk in the barn. You'd oversee the cooking and housekeeping, and I'd handle the rest."

The part about concentrating on the household tasks was more than a little appealing. Surely that would give her more time to resurrect the garden than she'd otherwise have as the ranch's sole caretaker. As West had pointed out, a dude ranch didn't require such a large volume of livestock, either—just enough to give guests the experience of what a ranch was like. And the less they spent on animals and the cowboys needed to care for them, the more money they would have for other things.

It wouldn't be as if she and West would actually be married. Not like her and Chance had been. Vienna squelched a shudder at that thought. Was she actually considering the idea?

"So what you're saying is, if we do this, you'd get your dude ranch and I'd get a home?" The question sounded far more frank than she'd meant it, but she wanted to be certain she understood his motive before she made her decision.

A flicker of emotion she couldn't identify crossed his face as he glanced down. "Yes, I'd have my dude ranch and you'd have a home." He withdrew his hand from hers, leaving her feeling a bit cold in spite of the sunshine.

"I do find the whole idea rather interesting." And she did. "Would our combined savings be enough to get a dude ranch going, though?"

West rubbed his chin. "I think so. It wouldn't be anything fancy to start, but as we got more guests, we could eventually expand." When he looked at her again, it was with as much undisguised hope as consternation. "You don't have to agree to any of it, Vienna. It's one solution to some of your problems and a plan that could benefit us both, but I don't want you to agree to anything you aren't comfortable with."

"I know, and I can't thank you enough for suggesting it, West." That he'd dreamed of owning a dude ranch wasn't news to her, but the fact that he was willing to include her in that dream in order to help her meant a great deal. "Can I have some time to think and pray about it?"

"Absolutely." He circled the team, then drove the wagon through the archway and back toward the main road. "If you'd like to see firsthand what a dude ranch is really like, we could take the train to the one I spent my summers at in North Dakota."

The thought of taking a trip filled her with as much excitement as nervousness. She hadn't left the area since coming here as a girl. It was a sound idea, though. If she was serious about this venture, she needed to fully understand what it would entail. And traveling with West would surely make the whole experience feel less intimidating.

"How much would it cost to travel and stay there?"

"Leave that to me," he said. "The Eaton brothers are old friends and I'd like to pay for our train tickets and guest fees."

Vienna twisted the button on the cuff of her sleeve. "How long would we be gone?"

"Six days ought to be enough time."

Six days? It sounded so long. "Will Edward let you have that much time off?"

West didn't hesitate to give a decisive nod. "I think so, especially since it'll be good practice for Thurston. If you and I decide to move forward with the dude ranch, the young man will need to take over anyway."

"All right," she said after a long moment, the frenzy in her middle increasing.

He raised his eyebrows as he regarded her. "All right to which part? Taking the trip to North Dakota or considering my plan?"

"Both." She laughed at his stunned expression.

"That's the best news I've heard in ages." He grinned at her, and his renewed eagerness succeeded in quieting her concerns and restoring her earlier optimism and calm. "God willing, I think this may be an answer to both of our dreams."

Chapter Four

"Don't think that I can't tell you're moving slower on my account," Maggy said, her belly leading the way down the drive of the Running W.

Vienna laughed but maintained her unrushed pace to accommodate Maggy's. She well remembered how her friend had kindly done the same for Vienna when she'd been pregnant with Hattie.

"I'm going to miss living here." She linked her arm with Maggy's.

A flash of sadness appeared in her friend's blue eyes. "We still have plenty of time before you leave. West only sent off that letter to his friends in North Dakota this morning."

"Do you think I'm crazy?" Vienna asked her.

The battle of anticipation and anxiety inside her hadn't stopped since she and West had formulated their plans yesterday. Which emotion was winning largely depended on the hour and the direction of her thoughts. This evening, with her regular duties completed, her nervousness had taken the lead.

"To start a dude ranch or travel to North Dakota?"

Vienna shot her a pleading look. "Both?"

"Then no to both," Maggy answered with a laugh. "I don't know that I would've pictured you running a dude ranch before now, but with the two of you as a team, I can see how it plays to yours and West's strengths and interests." She had said as much last night after Vienna and West had presented their idea to the Kents.

Vienna gave an absent nod. "What about agreeing to a possible marriage of convenience?" A confused sigh dropped from Vienna's lips. "Am I being foolish about that, Maggy? We both know how unhappy my first marriage was."

"True." Maggy's gaze moved to the ranch's iron archway as they walked beneath it. "But that doesn't guarantee a repeat in another marriage. That's conditional on the person you marry."

Her friend was right. After all, Maggy had found great happiness in her marriage to Edward. "Besides, it wouldn't be as if it were a real marriage," Vienna said in an attempt to reassure herself. "Not like you and Edward have, anyway."

"Still, you'll have a friendship to base your relationship on, even if it is in name only." An impish expression crossed her face and had Vienna bracing herself before Maggy added quietly, "And you never know, a marriage of convenience could turn into something more. After all, West McCall is kind, hardworking, handsome… Mrs. Harvey and I have been trying to find him someone to marry for more than a year now."

Vienna's cheeks flamed with heat. She couldn't disagree with Maggy's assessment of her potential groom without lying. But what if someone overheard them?

She glanced around and felt immense relief that no one—especially West—was walking nearby.

"It wouldn't be like that. This arrangement isn't a setup for eventual romance." She'd felt the fickleness of romantic love, for West in the past and then for Chance. Neither had yielded what she'd secretly hoped it would.

Maggy's eyes twinkled with mischief. "More unlikely things have happened."

"Are you sure you don't mind taking care of Hattie for me," Vienna asked next, deliberately changing the subject, "while West and I are in North Dakota?"

Maggy shook her head. "Not at all. It'll give you a chance to focus solely on learning what you can about dude ranching."

"I appreciate that." She gave her friend's arm a gentle squeeze. "I don't know what Hattie and I would've done these past three years without you and Edward and everyone else here."

Returning Vienna's squeeze, Maggy said in a slightly strained tone, "I don't know what we would have done without *you*. And I'm not just talking about your excellent help in the kitchen, either."

Her honest appreciation of their friendship made Vienna smile. From the moment she'd met Maggy, she had been in awe of the other young woman's strength and no-nonsense attitude. But Vienna wasn't the only one who'd grown since coming to the Running W. Maggy was still as courageous and matter-of-fact as ever, but her marriage to Edward had softened some of her blunter edges. She more readily shared how she felt with those she cared about. And Vienna felt blessed to be counted in that number.

"I'd still like to come visit often, me and Hattie. If that's all right with you."

Maggy stopped walking and threw her a narrowed look. "If you don't, I will be staking out your ranch." As Vienna laughed, Maggy steered her around and tugged her toward the house. "We'd better head back now. Otherwise Edward will have to collect me in the wagon, and you know how much I would hate that."

"Oh, I most certainly do," Vienna said with another laugh.

Things might be rapidly changing around her, but she could draw comfort from the knowledge that she had God and dear friends to see her and her daughter through anything.

The new mare nuzzled West's shirt as he led it out of the corral. "Nope, no carrots on me. You'll get your treat in a minute, though."

"You were right," Edward said, walking along beside them. He'd been watching West and the horse for the last while. "She doesn't appear to be much trouble to break."

West smiled at the horse. "She may be a bit stubborn still, but she's learning quickly."

"I believe it also helps that she has a talented trainer."

The compliment pleased him, and yet, it also brought a flicker of regret. This would likely be his last horse to train for some time. Because if things went well in North Dakota, West could very well be leaving the Running W for good.

"You sure you don't mind my taking the time off for this trip?"

Edward shook his head, not a trace of hesitation in the gesture. "No."

"Can I ask why?"

His employer led the way into the main barn. "You have a great opportunity before you, McCall, a chance to make your own way. I don't fault you for a moment for wanting to take it."

"It may not happen," he pointed out. "Vienna may decide after this trip to do something else with her ranch."

Opening the mare's stall door, Edward stood back. "Perhaps. But even if you don't end up setting out on your own this year," he added with keen perceptiveness, "it will happen eventually."

He was right, and they both knew it. But more than that, West was grateful that Edward respected his dream.

In some ways, their situations were alike. Edward Kent had also come from a wealthy family—though no one in the area, Edward included, knew West shared that similarity. The third son of an earl, Edward had left England for the United States eight years ago, eager to make a name for himself and establish a successful horse ranch—and the man had done both. However, unlike West's family, Edward's family hadn't disowned him for following his dream to create a different life than the one he'd known growing up.

"Thank you." West didn't feel the need to elaborate— Edward would understand that his gratitude extended well beyond the time off to go to North Dakota. The man had given him a job as foreman almost eight years ago, even though West hadn't worked in that sort of leadership position before. And he would be forever thankful for the experience and the friends he'd made during that time.

West led the mare into the stall, then backed away so one of the wranglers could brush the horse down. "She'll be a great horse."

"She will," Edward concurred. "Though we may need her trainer to return now and then to help break in some of the others. If he's willing, that is."

He grinned—as much at his boss's words as at Edward's confidence that running a dude ranch was most definitely in West's near future. "Of course, Boss."

"I'd pay you for the help." When West started to shake his head, Edward interjected, "I mean it, McCall. You have a gift. Besides, this way I can be of some assistance with helping your dude ranch get up and running, while also getting top-notch help with training some of my horses." He held out his hand to West. "What do you say?"

"I'd say thanks again," he replied, clasping the other man's hand in a firm, friendly handshake.

Ten days later

The train whistle pierced the morning air, a signal to all the remaining passengers that it was time to board. Vienna clasped Hattie to her once more, then stood to hug Maggy. She'd never been away from her daughter for an entire day, let alone six. The prospect had her rapidly blinking back tears. This trip was for their future, she reminded herself. Both hers and Hattie's.

"She'll be fine," Maggy reassured Vienna, taking Hattie's hand into her own. "We'll make cookies with

Mrs. Harvey and go exploring. It'll be great fun, won't it, Hattie?"

The little girl eyed Maggy with slight hesitation. "Can I sneak some of the dough like Mommy lets me?"

She'd been unusually quiet on the wagon ride to the station. That fact, along with Hattie's pinched expression, nearly had Vienna calling off the trip, in spite of all the arrangements West had made.

"Absolutely." Maggy grinned at Hattie. "And I might sneak some dough, too."

West came to stand beside Vienna. "We need to board the train."

"All right." She gave Hattie one more kiss. "I love you, sweetheart. I'll be home by the end of the week."

"With a special surprise for you," West added as he bent down and tousled Hattie's blond hair.

Her little mouth lifted into a full smile for the first time all morning. "A surprise for me, Mr. West?"

"A surprise just for you, Hattie girl." He straightened. "And that means your mother and I need to hurry and get on that train."

The little girl nodded with palpable enthusiasm. "Okay, Mr. West. Bye, Mommy." She waved to Vienna without an inkling of reluctance this time.

Giving her a wave back, Vienna hurried after West and up the steps of the train. "Thank you," she said as they moved down the aisle toward two empty benches.

"For what?" he asked, motioning for her to take the one that faced the depot. He sat on the opposite bench—close enough to continue their conversation but still maintaining enough distance between them to keep things proper as they traveled.

Vienna slid toward the window. "I appreciate you helping cheer Hattie up just now."

"It can't be easy leaving her."

She waved vigorously at her daughter and the Kents, who waved back, until they were lost from her view as the locomotive rolled forward. "I know she'll be fine."

"But..." West prompted gently.

The gnawing in Vienna's stomach that had started before breakfast stretched wider. "But I've never been away from her for more than a few hours. Now it will be six full days until we return."

"Tickets, please," the porter announced before West could reply.

Vienna withdrew her ticket and handed it to the young man.

"Traveling all the way to North Dakota?" He flicked a glance at West. "You and your husband?"

She gave a nod as he passed her back the ticket. "He's not my husband, though."

"No?" He studied her with new interest as he leaned casually against the seat back in front of Vienna.

What would he think if he knew Vienna was likely several years older than him and a mother and widow to boot?

"Let me know if you need anything, miss. I'd be more than willing to look out for you on your journey."

West loudly cleared his throat, jerking the porter's attention back in his direction. "Here's my ticket, young man." His gaze held more steel than friendliness as he presented the stub of paper. "And if the lady needs assistance, I'm here to help her."

"But she's not your wife," the porter stated with a frown.

Vienna might have chuckled at the confusion on his face if she hadn't felt so vulnerable—at saying good-bye to Hattie and at being the subject of the porter's interest. The idea of leaving the safety and familiarity of the Running W to embark on such a new and uncertain venture felt suddenly overwhelming. Surely she wasn't brave enough to do this. She would likely say or do the wrong thing. Doubt had her twisting her gloved hands together where they rested in her lap.

"Nope, she's not my wife," West answered in a level tone.

"Your sister, then?"

West shook his head.

"Sweetheart?" The porter threw a puzzled look in Vienna's direction.

The sight of the young man's bewilderment somehow broke the choke hold of her fear. She was here, wasn't she? Surely that was a step of bravery. Offering the man a polite smile this time, she spoke again. "He's a good friend and may possibly be my future husband and business partner."

"Ah, I see," the porter said, still eyeing them in a way that told them he didn't. Vienna suppressed a laugh. Then with a shrug of his shoulders, he tipped his hat to her. "Pleasant travel, folks."

As the young man disappeared through the door to the next car, West swiveled on his seat and looked her way, his head cocked in thought.

"What?" she asked, touching her hair where it was pinned up beneath her hat. Was there something amiss about her appearance?

One corner of his mouth lifted in a languid smile.

The kind that used to set her pulse tripping seven years ago.

Used to? her head argued. *Then why is your heart jumping about right now?*

"You've changed," he said at last.

Vienna ducked her chin and brushed a piece of lint off her skirt. "I have? How?"

"Saying what you did just now to the porter—all confident with no reticence."

Her cheeks grew warm. "Thank you, I think."

"It's a compliment, Vienna." He chuckled. "Your confidence is coming back."

Lifting her head, she glanced at him. "Back? I don't know that I was ever really confident before." Certainly not while she'd been married to Chance. Even before that, while living on her aunt and uncle's ranch, she hadn't felt much self-assurance.

"It was there." His expression held a trace of seriousness. "I saw it in you."

Something like regret emanated from him, though Vienna couldn't identify its source. "I was still shy, even before meeting Chance. Don't you remember the first time we met?"

Instead of prompting the smile she expected, West turned toward the window. "I remember everything about that day."

"Then you'll remember that you tried to talk to me three different times at that picnic before I finally said a word." She sniffed with amusement at the memory of her own timidity. How she'd ended up with someone like Chance—gregarious and impatient and the complete opposite of West McCall—she might never know. Then again, Chance's outgoing personality had meant that when she was by his side, she could stay quiet and view life from a distance. It hadn't been so bad at first until she'd realized that was exactly where her husband had wanted her to remain, indefinitely—in his shadow, with no voice or authority of her own.

Now the smile she'd been expecting appeared on West's mouth. "As I recall it wasn't a word you gave me. It was a laugh."

He did remember it well. She'd been as uncertain as she'd been flattered by West's attention, and when he'd made some joke about himself, she couldn't help laughing. After that, there was no longer any reticence at being around him. She'd felt seen for the first time since her parents' deaths—a feeling that expanded over time from camaraderie to friendship to…to love. For her, anyway. West hadn't come to the same conclusion about their relationship.

"So it will take all day to travel to the dude ranch?" she asked, changing the subject. It was better not to focus on the timeworn memories between them. Otherwise she'd dredge up old heartache, and she'd had enough of that to last a lifetime.

West studied her a moment, while Vienna stared innocently back at him. He might have once been able to read her thoughts, but just like her romantic feelings for him, that was long ago. "It'll probably be past suppertime before we reach the ranch."

"And they know we're coming?"

He grinned, breaking the tension between them. "They know. And what's more, they said they can't wait to show us around."

Excitement propelled West to be the first one off the train in North Dakota, though he did turn back to help

Vienna down the narrow steps and onto the depot platform. It was more than anticipation that their long day of travel was at an end. He hadn't been back here in eight years, and in many ways, it felt like coming home.

The Custer Trail Ranch had been a home of sorts to West, and Howard, Alden and Willis Eaton as well as their hired hand and horse doctor Alexander "Alec" Russell were like family. West had exchanged letters with Alec and Howard in the years since leaving North Dakota. But they couldn't compare to an actual visit back to the ranch that had been so instrumental in shaping his life.

"They'll have sent someone with a wagon," West reassured Vienna.

She looked tired, her forehead lined with weariness. "All right."

"West!" he heard a familiar voice call out.

He turned to see Alec striding toward them. Grinning, West met his best friend halfway across the depot, where they clasped hands in a hearty handshake before clapping each other on the back. "You came to collect us yourself?" He'd half expected someone with fewer responsibilities around the ranch to drive into town to fetch them.

"Howard insisted," Alec said with a matching grin. "So I didn't have to wrangle up an excuse, though I was prepared to do so when I found out you were coming. How are you?"

West nodded. "I'm well." Especially now that he was back here again, his dream of owning a dude ranch closer than it had ever been.

"Where's this prospective business partner of yours?" Alec glanced past West.

He led his friend over to where Vienna stood, the handle of her valise clutched between her hands. "Vienna, I'd like you to meet my good friend and the Eatons' right-hand man, Alec Russell. Alec, this is Vienna Howe."

"How do you do?" Vienna said politely.

Alec lifted his cowboy hat, revealing his dark blond hair underneath. "Ma'am." He threw West a puzzled look. "What about your business partner…"

"Vienna is my prospective business partner." He'd left off telling them he was bringing a woman to the ranch, not wanting anyone to read more into his and Vienna's relationship than was actually there. "She and I are thinking of starting up a dude ranch together." He hurried to add, "Vienna was recently widowed and is looking for a way to revive her ranch back in Wyoming."

His friend's blue-gray eyes still widened with obvious shock. "Well, there you go. A potential business partner and a pretty one at that. Not to mention rather brave if she's willing to work with you." Alec chuckled at his own joke.

Vienna blushed, but unlike with the train porter that morning, she didn't look uncomfortable at the flirtation. A tiny smile appeared on her pink lips as she ducked her chin. West felt a jolt of irritation shoot through him, though he wasn't sure why. It wasn't as if she was interested in his friend…was she?

"Where's the wagon?" West asked, eager to end the unsettling moment.

Alec pointed a thumb over his shoulder toward the opposite end of the train station. "Parked it out front. May I help you with your bag, ma'am?"

"Yes, thank you." Vienna relinquished her valise to Alec's care, then trailed them across the depot to the waiting wagon.

West quickly stowed his bag in the back so he could be the one to help Vienna this time. Offering her a hand, he assisted her onto the middle seat of the buckboard. When Alec took up the reins, West joined him on the front seat. As they drove away from the station and out of town, he couldn't help staring at all the farms that had cropped up in his absence.

"It looks so different from the last time I was here."

Alec nodded. "There's a lot more homesteaders now."

"When was the ranch built?" Vienna asked as she leaned forward.

Turning slightly toward her, Alec answered, "Howard started here in 1879. And he's built up a fine reputation for the place. Even Vice President Teddy Roosevelt counts the Eatons as his friends."

"Really?" Her tone suggested a touch of awe. "Does the ranch's clientele usually consist of famous people?"

Alec pushed up his hat. "Typically, the ranch's guests are from wealthy families back east. Like mine, for instance, or even Wes—"

"I've got a story to tell you about Roosevelt, Vienna," he interjected, cutting Alec off. He managed to maintain his usual unaffected air and easy smile, but that didn't stop the sweat from collecting beneath his collar and hat.

No one in Wyoming, including Vienna, knew where—or more accurately, what sort of life—he'd come from before leaving Pittsburgh for good. His family was every bit as prestigious and wealthy as

Alec's, but unlike his best friend, West had been cut off from his family and his inheritance after he'd decided to become a cowboy against his father's wishes.

Some of the old envy he'd once felt for Alec returned. It was partly the reason West had sought to find a job elsewhere, rather than staying on indefinitely with the Eatons. He had found it increasingly difficult to keep working alongside his best friend, witnessing constant reminders that Alec's family had not only accepted their son and his choice of employment but had encouraged him, too. They had even paid for Alec to attend college to become a veterinarian doctor, and now West's friend saw to the health of all the livestock on the Custer Trail Ranch.

Back home in Pittsburgh, West had seen how people reacted when they learned he was the only son of one of the richest men in the city. And he'd hated it. He wanted to be known for his own character and successes—not forever wondering if someone wanted to get to know him or hire him based solely on where he'd come from or how they could wield him for their own purposes.

That was why, when he'd left North Dakota for Wyoming, he'd chosen to keep his wealthy background to himself. He was no longer the heir to Lawrence McCall's great fortune, nor did West want or need it, so he wanted to be known simply for who he was—West McCall, a poor but hardworking cowboy and horse trainer.

"What's the story?"

Vienna's question broke through West's troubled thoughts about the past. "Right, the story." Alec threw him a curious look. Ignoring it, West turned to half face Vienna. "The story goes that one time while Roosevelt was staying in a hotel, he shared a room with several cowboys. In the middle of the night, he was woken up by some men holding a lantern and a gun aimed directly at him."

"How scary," Vienna murmured.

"He probably *was* scared until he heard the men say that he wasn't the one they were looking for." West smiled, warming to his story. "Then they turned to his bedfellow and told the cowboy to come quietly. Which the man did."

Vienna shook her head. "What did they want with him?"

"I believe he'd robbed a train."

Her mouth tilted up at the corners again. "A future vice president and a train robber sharing a room? I only hope we're as fortuitous to have such interesting guests if we have our dude ranch, West."

Our dude ranch. Why did those three words and the rare glimpse at Vienna's lighthearted side have the power to command his heart to speed up with anticipation?

"I guess time will tell," he drawled before facing forward again.

And wasn't that the truth? Time would tell if anyone found out about his true origins or if he and Vienna went forward with creating a dude ranch and the venture proved successful. But in spite of the risks, on all accounts, West was ready and willing to move forward with their plans.

After a late supper that was as delicious as one she and Mrs. Harvey might have made back at the Running W, Vienna was more than ready to go to sleep. She bid West good-night. But when he started to rise from the dining table where he'd been catching up with his friends, she waved him back into his seat. It was obvious how much he was enjoying talking with Alec and the Eatons, and she was glad for it.

When she'd once asked about his family, shortly after they had first met, West had told her that for all intents and purposes he was an orphan same as her. And while Vienna had been close to her cousin Lavina, who now lived in Buffalo, Wyoming, she'd found a new family with the Kents at the Running W, just as West had. Still, she was pleased to see that he had others in his life here in North Dakota who, like Edward and Maggy, could also be called family.

"I'll see you at breakfast," she said to West.

He nodded. "Good night, Vienna."

"Good night."

She was led to a nice room on the second floor of the big house. After hearing the story of Roosevelt and the train robber, she was more than relieved to discover she was the room's only occupant.

Thanking her hostess, Vienna shut the door and readied for bed. It felt strange that she only had herself to care for tonight, rather than getting Hattie ready for bed, too. A wave of missing her daughter brought a lump to her throat as she knelt beside the bed to pray. She thanked the Lord for her and West's safe arrival, for the kind welcome and hospitality of the Eatons, for West's friendship and for the help of the Kents, who in caring for Hattie had made this trip possible for Vienna. She asked that her daughter would be watched over and that she would know what to do about their future. Then before ending her prayer, she pleaded, as she always did, for strength and courage.

Vienna blew out the lamp and climbed into bed. But in spite of her travel-weary body and a longing to sleep, her mind was jumping about like a jackrabbit.

She'd liked what she had viewed of the Custer Trail Ranch in the dusky evening light earlier. The two-story main house, which featured logs on the bottom half and siding on the top, appeared spacious and comfortable, with living and dining rooms on the first floor. A peek into the former had revealed plenty of books for reading and even musical instruments for playing.

Tomorrow Alec had promised to show Vienna around the grounds—well, her and West both. Overhearing his friend's invitation to Vienna, West had asked to come along, saying he needed to reacquaint himself with the place.

Vienna smiled into the dark at the memory. It seemed West didn't want her touring the ranch alone with Alec. There'd also been that moment at the train station when she'd smiled at Alec and had caught what looked like jealousy in West's brown eyes. Did he think she liked his friend?

Alec was nice-looking, with his dark blond hair and blue-gray eyes, and she had appreciated his compliments. But she didn't fancy him or any other man. A recollection entered her thoughts of how her heart had tripped faster when West had given her a smile on the train and told her that she'd changed.

That didn't mean she fancied him again, she told herself as her smile drooped. Her reaction to him likely only stemmed from the old feelings of attraction she'd once felt. He might be handsome, kind and hardworking, but anything other than friendship in their relationship would be strictly business-related. Even if they married for convenience.

Not for the first time, a shudder ran through Vienna at the thought of being married again—even in name only. How naive she'd been when she had married Chance. She hadn't really known him and whatever warning signs she might have noticed she'd credited to comparing him too much with West. Then there'd been all the hiding and secrets regarding Chance's many vices.

She blew out a steadying breath, rolled onto her side and shut her eyes. Her marriage with Chance was over; it was a thing of the past. And even if she did choose to marry West for convenience, she wouldn't have to fear that he was keeping secrets from her. She might not know yet what do about her ranch, but she did know West McCall—and he wasn't hiding anything.

Chapter Five

West was up before breakfast the next morning, eager to see the ranch in broad daylight. He also didn't want to miss Alec's tour with Vienna. Because he wanted to see the changes the Eatons had told him about last night, of course—nothing more. It wasn't like he was worried that Vienna fancied his best friend. Although, if Vienna did like Alec, would she still be willing to consider converting the HC Bar into a dude ranch in partnership with West?

He frowned as he finished pulling on his boots and stood to collect his hat. Better not to meddle in matters of the heart, especially where Vienna was concerned. West had erroneously tread that path once before. He wouldn't put himself or her through that again.

No, he thought, clapping his hat on his head. *I'll let things play out as they're meant to this time.* It wasn't as if Vienna had made up her mind yet about the dude ranch, anyway. She could still choose to do something else with her house and property, which may or may not be influenced by a certain blond cowboy.

West wouldn't petition the Lord for things to go

his way, either. He'd done that once before, on a matter as dear to his heart as having a dude ranch, but it hadn't materialized as he'd wanted. Experience was often a stern teacher, and it had taught him well. The safest course, the surest way to avoid disappointment or heartache, was to quit asking God for those things he deeply desired. Instead, he'd work hard toward reaching his dreams, but if they didn't materialize now or in the future, he'd experience less pain for not having asked for them in the first place.

Leaving the building dubbed the "dude pen," where he'd slept last night, West strolled toward the main house and into the dining room. There were already people seated at the table—likely guests who wanted to eat before they headed out on a full-day's ride.

He was halfway through clearing his own plate when Vienna walked in. She was dressed in a white blouse, a brown vest and a matching brown split skirt for riding. Her hair hung down her back in a simple braid instead of the elaborate coiffure from yesterday. And while West had liked her traveling look just fine, there was something undeniably attractive about the simplicity of her attire and hairstyle today.

Her mouth pinched tight as she surveyed the crowded room. West recognized the shy, nervous look. It was one he'd seen often whenever she dealt with new people. This morning, though, she squared her shoulders after a moment and lifted her chin, bringing more than a flicker of pride to him. It was like he'd told her on the train—Vienna had gained strength and confidence in the past few years; she just didn't always identify it in herself.

"Sleep well?" he asked when she joined him at the table.

Vienna nodded. "I didn't think I would, but I slept better than I have in ages." She sampled a bite from her breakfast plate and murmured approval. "I don't know if my cooking will be able to compete."

"It doesn't need to compete because there's no competition. Your cooking is excellent."

Pink flooded her cheeks before she asked him, "Is it nice to be back?"

"Yes," West admitted with a smile. "It's grown a lot since I left the ranch, which also helps me picture what a place like the HC Bar can become in time."

She nodded thoughtfully. "Do you think we'd eventually need a house this size?"

"Depends on how well things go." He pushed his empty plate aside and rested his arms on the tabletop. "If we do decide to expand, you've got plenty of land to do it. We can start with one guest building and the two extra rooms upstairs inside the current house. I was thinking we could eventually add on to the house, too, make the parlor and the dining room larger."

Her green eyes crinkled with amusement. "That would be nice."

"That's only *if* you decide you want to do the dude ranch." Embarrassment had heat creeping up his neck over getting carried away with his plans again.

Vienna reached out and briefly touched his hand. "It's all right, West. That's why we're here. To talk and see and plan. Then we can both pray and decide what we're going to do."

"Me decide?" He already knew his answer—he wanted a dude ranch, whether that was with Vienna or not. Though he hoped it would be with her. He'd begun to picture it that way, the two of them working alongside each other.

She blushed again, her gaze dropping to her breakfast. "I mean about all of it." She lowered her voice to little more than a whisper as she added, "Not just about the ranch but about marrying for convenience, too."

"Right." How could he have forgotten about that part of the deal? Or maybe he hadn't *forgotten* as much as put it out of his mind for now. Not that he had any real qualms about such an arrangement. It would allow him to help Vienna as they ran the ranch together and it would certainly protect her from any more unwanted proposals or bullies disguised as husbands. He'd get to maintain his daily friendship with her and Hattie, too. And it wouldn't hurt to be attached himself. He'd fended off more inquiries over the years about his plans to settle down than he cared to remember. Being married would keep any further matchmaking by those around him at bay.

However, was he being selfish to ask Vienna to marry him, even if it was in name only? She didn't seem to want another marriage, at least not the kind she and Chance had shared. And it would still be her choice to marry for convenience. But what if someone came along whom she might come to fancy, someone she might want a real marriage with?

As if mocking his uneasy thoughts, Alec appeared, an extra hat in his hands. "You ready for your first day on a dude ranch, ma'am?" He plunked the hat onto Vienna's hair.

"I believe I am," she said, chuckling as she resettled the hat and glanced up at Alec.

West couldn't tell if she was merely being friendly or if something more motivated her reaction to his best friend. He shifted uncomfortably in his seat. What did he really know about women or love anyway? He'd once thought Lucile French, his former fiancée, had loved him. At least until he'd stopped following the course she and West's father had mapped out for his life. After that, the girl couldn't leave him behind fast enough and his father had written West out of his will and the family.

"Are you all right, West?" Vienna's brow scrunched with concern as she studied him.

He hadn't been careful enough about hiding his thoughts. What he needed was to push them aside entirely. He was only courting disappointment by dwelling on the past. His life might have turned out differently than he'd once envisioned, but it was still a good life—a life West would choose all over again, even if he could go back.

Forcing his lips upward, he nodded as he stood up from the table. "Let's have the grand tour, Alec."

"The Custer Trail Ranch can accommodate between fifty and sixty guests," Alec explained as they paused beside another of the buildings used as guest quarters.

Vienna shook her head in disbelief, her startled gasp sounding more like a squeak. She didn't have any misgivings about cooking for a small army that size. No, it was the thought of all those strangers around that had a flash of timid nervousness rising into her throat. What if some of them turned out to be like Chance? People hiding vices behind a slick smile and a false notion of wealth and charm?

"We won't have that many to begin with," West said. With his arms crossed casually across his chest, he stepped to her side, facing the building as she did. "And they're more than likely to be upper-crust folks from back east like those at breakfast. Not drifters or regular cowboys."

She glanced at him as a rush of relief washed through her at the reminder. "I still find it hard to believe that people are interested in traveling so far to come stay at a place like this."

"For decades now, the eastern elite have been clamoring to experience what we have to offer out here." He threw her a smile. "It's a way of life they can't quite comprehend but want to see anyway."

A cloud passed over his face as it had in the dining room earlier. But given the way he'd ignored her question then, she guessed he'd do the same now so she didn't bother asking.

"How does one go about finding these elite guests?" she asked instead. "Do we advertise in the newspaper?"

West exchanged a quick glance with Alec, though Vienna couldn't tell what it was meant to communicate. "In-person visits to those you know or referrals from friends is the typical way to find guests. That's because the dude ranch owner usually asks those interested in coming for references before agreeing to host them."

"You mean someone travels back east to meet with people?"

West nodded. "Usually in the winter when business is slow. But I'm hoping Howard might help us out now by talking with some of his already established clients."

"Why not just use your…" Alec let his voice trail

when West gave him a hard look, though the cowboy's expression remained puzzled.

West interrupted the tense silence to ask a question of his own. "How many horses did you say they have here now, Alec?"

The other man seemed to shrug off the odd exchange as he smiled. "Somewhere between five and six hundred."

"Five or six…" Vienna's mouth fell open. While she liked what she'd seen of the dude ranch so far, everything seemed so much larger and grander than anything she and West would be able to afford.

Alec waved them forward. "Let me show you the windmill."

"It wasn't always like it is now," West said, falling in step beside her. "The Eatons didn't start having paying guests until the 1880s. They've been building their business ever since."

Vienna glanced at the ground. "Our place would be so much smaller, West. Would it be enough to draw in guests? What if no one is interested in coming?" Even if she chose this path, without guests, the dude ranch would be a failure, and she'd be back where she started in trying to secure a livelihood for herself and Hattie.

"Most things take time." His confident tone urged her to look at him. "If we want to do this, Vienna, I know we can. We'll start out with what we are able to, and then we'll keep growing from there."

His reassurance peeled back her doubts. And he was right. She couldn't compare their hopeful start to the Eatons' end result after decades of work. "It is pretty amazing what they've created here." Her gaze moved to the windmill ahead of them.

"I couldn't agree more," West said, grinning at her.

Alec showed them the windmill and large tank that supplied water for the ranch. After that, he led them past the various outbuildings and eventually to where they would saddle up some horses for a ride. They weren't the only ones doing so, either. A number of other guests were preparing for horse rides of their own.

Once she'd settled into the saddle of her roan gelding, Vienna nudged the horse to follow after West's and Alec's mounts. The sun shone brightly as the three of them left the ranch behind, making her grateful for the hat Alec had loaned her. She might still prefer whipping up something in the kitchen or kneeling in the warm earth of a garden to horseback riding, but she thought she could understand the appeal to city folk of striking out across the fields with little to obstruct one's view.

The farther they rode, the more she felt a lightening of the pressure and uncertainty regarding the future. A forgotten sense of well-being flooded through her. The only damper was not having Hattie here in this moment. Not for the first time, Vienna wondered how her little girl was faring back in Wyoming. It felt strange, though not entirely unpleasant, to have her only focus be observing her surroundings, instead of cooking for the Running W staff and keeping an eye on Hattie.

When they stopped the horses sometime later, Alec helped her to the ground. "You ride quite well, ma'am." His bluish-gray eyes were lit with approval that made her blush.

"Vienna's an exceptional rider," West interjected as if Alec had insulted rather than complimented her.

She didn't know whether to laugh or not at the challenge in the men's locked gazes. "Thank you both. But I still largely prefer walking to riding."

"How come?" Alec asked.

West looked as if he was about to answer for her, but Vienna signaled him with a shake of her head that she was fine. "My father was thrown from a horse and killed when I was almost sixteen. My mother died of illness shortly after that."

"I'm so sorry, Mrs. Howe."

She offered him a reassuring smile. "I appreciate that. It was a long time before I could muster up the courage to ride a horse again."

"But you did." West's low remark was likely meant to carry to her ears alone.

Gratitude tumbled into her heart at his words. She always felt stronger in West's company than she did with anyone else. It had been that way nearly from the beginning of their friendship. She'd missed his confidence in her bravery while she'd been married to Chance. That experience had nearly stripped her completely of strength, at least until she'd met Maggy, a strong woman in her own right and certainly the bravest one Vienna knew personally.

With West at her side, though—as a business partner and husband, even in name only—Vienna could surely keep being a little braver and conquer her lingering fears about her own abilities to run a business. The fact that she and Hattie would have West around to help was another strong reason to pursue the dude ranch idea.

Please, help me know if this is what You want me to

do, Lord, she prayed when she, West and Alec finally headed back toward the ranch.

She'd asked if they could cut the ride short so she could shadow those who worked in the kitchen. She wanted to get a better feel for what it was like cooking for wealthy guests instead of humble wranglers. After that, Vienna hoped to be closer to having an answer about her future. They had only four more days to figure things out, but she had every confidence that they would.

"How come you haven't told Vienna about your family?" Alec demanded.

It had been two days since their tour of the ranch, and he and Alec had just returned from accompanying some guests on a long ride.

West helped him lead the horses into the barn. "There hasn't been a lot of time." But the answer sounded pitiful to his own ears, even if it was true.

Vienna had spent the better part of each day working in the main house, learning all there was to know about cooking and housecleaning for guests. West had been equally as busy, going on rides, asking the Eatons endless questions about starting up a dude ranch and assisting Alec with whatever needed to be done.

A part of him wished he and Vienna could stay longer so they could take one of Howard's pack trips to Yellowstone National Park, but he understood her desire to get back to Hattie. Truth be told, he'd missed the little girl, too. And he still needed to come up with a surprise to bring home for her.

"I don't just mean while you've been here," Alec

countered. "Why didn't you tell her years ago when you first met?"

As he considered how to answer the question, West removed the saddle from one of the horses and began to brush the animal down. "It's because I wanted to be seen for who I was right then. Who I am now. Not where I came from or who I used to be as the son of a banking tycoon. I figured if people knew about my family, they wouldn't see me for me. They'd only see the money and prestige, which I have no claim to anymore."

"Those are some fair points." Alec went to work brushing down his own horse. Friendly quiet stretched between them for another minute or so before Alec cleared his throat. "I don't know that I ever said it all those years ago, West, but I was sorry that your family treated you the way they did."

Familiar regret and anger stiffened West's shoulders. His fingers tightened their grip on the brush until he forced them to relax. "Thanks. I appreciate that."

"Now look at you." His friend waved his brush at West. "Your life is everything you wanted it to be. You get to start your own dude ranch, just like you always told me that you would."

One corner of West's mouth kicked up. "If Vienna agrees."

"By the look of things, I think she will."

West hoped so, but as usual, he was careful not to let that hope spill over into his prayers.

"She doesn't seem bothered by the marriage of convenience part, either. Though I'll admit I was surprised to hear that was your idea."

Ducking lower, West pretended to be more focused

on the horse than on the conversation. "I don't see why not. It benefits us both."

"True, but I didn't think you'd ever consider marriage again. Not after..."

Alec didn't need to finish his sentence and West was relieved when he didn't. His broken engagement to Lucile was far in the past. He'd been hurt when she'd ended things between them, but a part of him had felt grateful, too. He hadn't shared with her his growing ambition to live a life out west or to own a dude ranch until that dream had become too large to keep inside himself.

When he'd finally told her, Lucile had burst into tears, which soon gave way to angrily hurled words. Unbeknownst to West at the time, she'd gone straight to his father to confess what she'd learned. Lawrence had been outraged. When West refused to give in to their alternate plans for his life and career, Lucile ended their engagement and his father dismissed him from the family home. West still wondered if they'd both expected him to come crawling back. However, he was nothing if not a McCall—and his father hadn't gotten to where he was without raw determination and hard work. West had inherited both of those qualities from him.

"That's the beauty of a marriage of convenience," he said, straightening so he could see Alec over the horse's back. "Love doesn't factor into it. It's a business arrangement, pure and simple."

Alec gave a thoughtful nod. "I guess that makes sense, so long as you both know what you're getting into."

"Which we do."

"Good." His friend paused, his mouth drawing into a line. "Speaking of marriage and the past, I've been meaning to tell you—"

Before Alec could finish, another cowboy strode into the barn, requesting his help.

"I'll finish up," West volunteered.

"Thanks."

As his friend followed the other fellow out of the barn, West wondered what he had been about to say. Was Alec going to confess a fondness for Vienna? West shook his head. No, the man had said his statement was connected to something about the past.

Shrugging, he finished seeing to the horse beside him before moving on to the next. Whatever Alec had meant to say it could wait until later. West had left his past behind—it had no power over him now.

Chapter Six

Vienna held her breath and pressed closer against the outer wall of the barn. It wasn't until the two men had exited the building and passed by her without apparently seeing her that she breathed a sigh of relief. They hadn't caught her eavesdropping. Not that she'd meant to eavesdrop. She'd come to the barn, excited to tell West what she'd helped make in the kitchen today, when she'd heard him saying something about their plan for a marriage of convenience.

Curious, she'd stopped outside the open barn doors to listen, only to hear West say, *Love doesn't factor into it. It's a business arrangement, pure and simple.*

She'd been so taken aback by his words and the adamant tone with which he'd spoken them that she had turned and stumbled away. When another cowboy approached the building, she'd feigned interest in something in the distance until he'd disappeared inside.

Now she didn't know what to do. Walk away or go inside and confess to West she'd overheard him? Her cheeks flushed at the latter thought. Besides, what had she been expecting? That West had proposed a marriage of convenience because he secretly harbored a fondness for her?

Fanning her warm face with her apron, Vienna hurried back toward the main house. West's remark shouldn't have come as such a shock. After all, his feelings hadn't mirrored hers seven years ago, and there was no reason to believe anything had changed for him since then. Besides, it wasn't as if she even wanted a real marriage again—with him or any other man.

Except why the needling of pain in her chest, then? They were friends, yes, and may very well become business partners. And yet, crazy as it might seem, had she expected more? Hoped for it, even?

She wanted to deny it, but she couldn't. The ashes of her old feelings for him must have been stirred to a flickering flame at West's suggestion of marrying, whether in name only or not. Or maybe it had happened after her conversation with Maggy who'd suggested something more might come from such an arrangement. But Vienna could bank those feelings once and for all. Especially now that she knew West's view.

If I choose that path, she thought, tilting her chin upward and glowering at the ground ahead, *I must realize it's a business relationship, pure and simple. Love will never be a part of that arrangement.*

With her thoughts back where they needed to be, she returned to the kitchen. But as she sampled the dish she'd meant to share a bite or two with West, Vienna felt something akin to grief settle like dust deep inside her.

Tired but happy, West left the barn and went to wash up before supper. He was looking forward to seeing

Vienna. During his ride today, he'd come up with several trail possibilities to take guests on rides back at home. His mouth rose higher at the thought of Wyoming being home. A week ago, he likely would have said that the Custer Trail Ranch still held that distinction for him. But now, even with one full day left here, he was already excited about getting back. It was the same feeling he'd once had about North Dakota each time he'd had to return to Pittsburgh.

"Westin McCall!" a high feminine voice declared with a note of surprise.

West shook his head, certain he was hearing things. Thoughts of Pittsburgh must have conjured up Lucile's voice…

"Is that any way to greet a dear family friend?"

This time he felt sure he wasn't just imagining his ex-fiancée's purring tones. But why in the world would Lucile be here? Jerking his gaze from the ground to the porch, to assure himself the woman was still more than a thousand miles away, West ground to a sudden stop.

There she stood, staring innocently down at him, her cowgirl clothes spotless, her imperial eyebrows lifted. "Hello, stranger."

"Lucile?" Her name came out garbled as if his tongue had forgotten how to say it. "What are you—"

She sauntered forward and smiled. "Doing here?" she finished. "Why I'm getting a taste for…what was it you once called it…the call of the Western life? This is what Walter wanted to do for our five-year wedding anniversary trip."

His mind was moving at the rate of molasses like it did in a nightmare. Lucile was married and here at the Custer Trail Ranch for an anniversary trip. West shut his eyes, hoping when he opened them he'd find he was waking up from a nap in the dude pen.

That wasn't the case, though. Lucile was still there when he looked.

"Darling?" A mustached gentleman whom West hadn't noticed until that moment stepped up beside Lucile. Like Lucile's outfit, this man's riding clothes screamed money. "Are you going to introduce me?"

"Of course, Walter." Lucile latched onto his arm. "This is Westin McCall, an old family friend. Westin, this is my husband, Walter Atwater."

As if oblivious to the tension coating the air, Walter offered West his hand to shake. "Any friend of Lucile's... Wait, are you related to the Pittsburgh McCalls? As in Lawrence McCall?"

"Pleased to meet you," West managed to get out through his gritted teeth as he shook the man's hand. He deliberately ignored the question.

But, unfortunately, Lucile wouldn't let it lie. "Why yes. Westin here is the one and only son of Lawrence McCall."

"Don't believe I've seen you around town," Walter said, giving West an apologetic smile.

Lucile's laugh, though soft and tinkling, grated against West's ears. "You wouldn't have, darling. Westin left Pittsburgh before you came and has been hiding out, here and there and who knows where, for years."

It took every ounce of willpower for West to remain stoic and not react to her baited comment. He didn't need to prove anything to Lucile—not anymore. Let her think what she would about him embracing the life he had. As long as she didn't go spilling his past to someone like Vienna...

Vienna! He had to get to her before Lucile did. And by the looks of things she and her husband were about to join everyone for supper.

"If you'll excuse—"

He cut off his words with a panicked growl when he saw Vienna exiting the house. "Oh, West, there you are. Supper's about to be…" She glanced at the three of them staring back at her, and her cheeks grew suddenly pink. "I'm sorry. Am I interrupting something?"

"You know *Westin* here?" Lucile asked Vienna, her gaze narrowing. Her calculated look increased the dread souring West's throat.

Vienna gave him a questioning look, but he couldn't offer her anything more than a grim expression. "Yes. But he goes by West."

"You shortened it to *West*? Oh, how quaint. And fitting." She gave another tittering laugh. "I am Lucile Atwater and this is my husband, Mr. Walter Atwater."

Returning the gentleman's nod, Vienna still eyed them with blatant confusion.

"And you are?" Lucile pressed.

"Vienna Howe."

Lucile's gaze swept up Vienna's dress and spotted apron to her disheveled braid. "How do you know Mr. McCall, Miss Howe?"

"It's actually *Mrs.* Howe," Vienna said with a regal look of her own that made West momentarily proud. "Though I am a widow now."

"Oops, my apologies. I simply assumed…" Lucile covered her mouth with her hand, but she didn't appear the least bit contrite.

Vienna offered her a smile, though West could tell it was strained. "That's quite all right, Mrs. Atwater."

She nodded politely and started toward the door. "I'll meet you inside, West."

His relief that Lucile hadn't squealed on him about his family or past lasted only a moment. When she reached the door, Vienna paused and turned back to face them, her expression curious.

"How are you and Mr. McCall acquainted, Mrs. Atwater?"

Moving fast, West climbed onto the porch and gently took Vienna's elbow in hand. "We can cover the incidental details later. I'd like to get some of that delicious supper before it's all gone."

"I've known Westin practically my whole life," Lucile announced with false innocence. "Our families are old friends back in Pittsburgh. Westin was part of our circle, too, until he decided to forego his father's millions and become a cowboy."

Vienna's face paled as she tugged her arm from his grip. "Y-your father's...millions?"

"Why, yes. Didn't he tell you?" Lucile tossed them a wide-eyed look. "As the only son of a banking tycoon, Westin stood to inherit a great deal. He was even slated for a grand future in politics after he worked in banking for a few years, of course."

The unmistakable hurt in Vienna's green eyes speared West to the core. "Vienna..."

"I think we ought to go on in and eat, Lucile," Walter suggested.

Lucile swept past them on Walter's arm. "Lovely to catch up, Westin. A pleasure to meet you, Mrs. Howe."

As they disappeared through the door, Vienna turned away from him, her arms folded tightly against her bodice. "I don't think I'm ready to go in, after all."

"Vienna, please."

She stared down at the ground, though she didn't move. "Why didn't you tell me?"

"What? That my father was rich?"

"No," she said, shaking her head. "I mean not just that. You had a family, too, and yet, you led me to believe you were an orphan like me."

West swiped his sleeve over his damp forehead. Working earlier with the horses hadn't brought up as much sweat as Lucile's sudden intrusion had. "I wasn't lying to you. I am an orphan, Vienna. My father—" he spat out the word "—disowned me more than ten years ago, forbade me from contacting my mother and sisters, too, after I told them that I didn't want to go into banking or politics. That I wanted to be a cowboy."

"Still, you should have told me the truth, West." She spun around and pinned him with a hard gaze.

West wanted to slip through the floorboards and disappear. He'd promised himself he would never be a source of pain for her—but that's exactly what he'd become by keeping silent about his past. "You're right. I should have. And I'm sorry I didn't, Vienna."

"Didn't you trust me?"

The question made him flinch. "It had nothing to do with trust. I thought of telling you countless times, but the longer it remained inside, the easier it was to keep there."

"You hid something from me."

She didn't need to add "like Chance did." West still heard the words as plain and clear as if she'd spoken them aloud. And they tore at his guilt, spilling it open all over again.

"I promise it wasn't out of malice." How could he

help her understand without inflicting more pain on himself? "The first couple of years I was too angry to even speak of them. Then when that faded, I came to accept I was on my own. Just like you. I found others to be my family, and it was nice to finally be known for myself, not who I was related to."

Her shoulders slumped. "I guess I can understand that." She shot him a glance that radiated compassion but also hurt. "But you still should've told me, West."

"I know, and I'm sorry." He nodded toward the door. "Would you like some supper now?"

Vienna shook her head. "No. Maybe in a bit. I—I need to do some thinking."

"About?" he asked, though he figured he already knew.

"The dude ranch...us..."

He nodded with understanding, though inside he felt like someone had plunged a fork into his heart. Every part of him wanted to blame Lucile for the damage to his and Vienna's plans. But he couldn't do it. He was the one to blame. His choice to keep silent and to hide something important from the one person he'd vowed to look after would be the cause of injury if their plans died right now.

Still, that didn't keep him from glowering in annoyance at Alec when the cowboy ambled out the door the next moment. "There you two are," Alec said, glancing past West to where Vienna had started across the yard. "Aren't you coming in to eat?"

"How long have you known Lucile was coming to visit?"

His friend crossed his arms in defense, though his expression appeared slightly sheepish. "I only found out this morning. That's what I tried to tell you earlier in the barn." When West kept silent, Alec relaxed his stance. "Did you see her?"

"I did," he ground out. "And what's worse, she met Vienna. With the delightful news of my upbringing."

Alec ran a hand over his bristled chin. "I'm sorry to hear that, West."

"What were Howard and the others thinking to allow her to come while I was here?"

His friend shrugged. "I don't know that they knew it was her who was coming. It isn't like she goes by her maiden name anymore. She's an Atwater now. Besides, I don't know that they remembered the two of you were once engaged."

West supposed that made sense. And while he'd confessed his familial and engagement woes to the Eaton brothers after coming to stay at the ranch permanently, he might have kept the name of his fiancée to himself. Which meant only he and Alec knew.

"How'd Vienna take it?" Alec nodded in the direction she'd headed.

"Not well. She accused me of hiding my past from her. And she's right."

Pulling off his hat, he stared at the worn, dusty brim. He'd had this hat ever since making the West his permanent home. It was probably past time for him to purchase a new one. But he didn't think he could part with it. Every inch was visible proof of how hard he'd worked at a life and a job he loved.

"Does that mean your deal is off?"

It was West's turn to shrug. "I hope not. But I don't know."

"You know you're always welcome here," Alec said,

clapping him on the shoulder. "It's been like old times having you back on the ranch."

He managed a quick smile. "It's been nice to be here."

"But?"

His friend headed into the house and West followed. "There are people I care about in Wyoming, and I'm so close to having my own place. Don't you ever wish you owned all of this instead of working it for someone else, even for people as good and generous as the Eatons?"

"Some days," Alec admitted. "Although, I don't think that ranching and horse doctoring is what I aim to do indefinitely."

West stared at him in surprise. He hadn't expected that Alec might leave here, too. "Since when?"

"Since my father started asking me in every letter what I plan to do with my veterinarian knowledge in the future." He grimaced. "He thinks I ought to do more than work on horses and cows or the occasional wounded dog."

"What would you do, then?"

Alec shook his head. "Don't know yet. I'm not even sure where I'd want to set up a practice. *If* I set up a practice."

West almost envied his friend. After all, it was clear that whatever Alec chose to do, his family would support him. Still, West was grateful that he knew his own heart well enough when it came to the future. Even if Vienna decided not to partner with him on the dude ranch, he would still find a way to eventually make it work on his own.

He squeezed into an empty chair between two

guests, which was thankfully nowhere near Lucile and her husband. As he ate, though, West couldn't help glancing in their direction. Why had Lucile agreed to come to the Custer Trail Ranch for an anniversary trip? Had she somehow learned West would be at the ranch, too? Was she actually there to poke at his healed wounds?

There was only one way to find out. When Walter lingered at the table, West got up and trailed Lucile into the living room.

"Darling, would you mind asking…" Her question ended on a squeal when she turned away from the bookcase and saw West standing there. The reaction was a crack in her poised veneer, and yet, it made her seem more human, too. "What do you want, Westin? Can't stand to see me happy and well-matched after what happened between us? Are you planning to tell Walter the sort of woman he's really married to?"

West fell back a step in disbelief. "Why would I do that?"

"Because I broke your heart." She glanced away before adding in a near-whisper, "And because you broke mine, too."

He'd hurt *her*? West shook his head, his confusion mounting. "I didn't throw you off. It was the other way around."

"You broke our plans."

Our plans—hers and his father's. "They were never *my* plans."

"You could've eventually been mayor or a senator." The earnestness of her expression was the most open West had ever seen it. Maybe being married to Walter had softened her.

"I could have, but that wasn't what I wanted."

Her bitter sniff rang with all too much familiarity in his ears. "Still as stubborn as ever, I see. And not willing to trust those who knew what was best for you."

"Knew what was best?" he echoed, irritation rising inside him. The people who'd supposedly "known what was best for him" were the same ones who'd cut him loose when he chose to do what felt right to him.

She lifted her nose in the air. "Yes."

"Are you running Walter's life and career, then?"

A flash of pain passed over her porcelain face before her expression hardened. "Perhaps I am. Which he, at least, appreciates in a wife and companion. He's also one who is destined for great things."

"I'm sorry, Lucile." It took great effort to push the apology from his mouth, but once he did, he felt better. "I'm happy for you."

Her hazel eyes widened, then narrowed with surprise. "You are? Why?"

"Because," he said with sudden understanding, "I don't hold any resentment for you."

And he meant it. Their brief conversation had been more than enlightening for him. While West had come to see himself as a person of value even without a family or inheritance, he recognized that Lucile didn't have that same strong belief about herself—back then or now—which was likely why she'd thrown his past in his face in front of Vienna. Lucile seemed to be trying to find her worth and confidence through someone else.

That realization brought West a measure of peace. Now he could completely shut the door on what had happened so long ago.

A nagging voice whispered there was still the matter of his family, but West ignored it. Surely understanding Lucile and her actions would be enough to bury the past.

"You always were too kind," she mused, her lips curved up in a smile.

He smirked. "And that's a bad thing?"

"In some professions." She spun back to the bookshelf and plucked out a volume. "I promise I didn't know you were here, *West*." She directed her statement more at the book in her hand than at him.

West knew her well enough to know she spoke the truth. "It was rather a shock to me to find you standing there myself."

"I didn't ruin things, did I?" she asked, turning to face him. "Between you and that widow woman?"

Ah, she thought there was more to his and Vienna's relationship than simply friendship. "No, not in that way."

"Oh good." Lucile looked genuinely relieved. "I admit I might have been the tiniest bit nasty." She held her finger and thumb close together to indicate how much.

West had to scramble to hide his shock over her owning her earlier unkind behavior. With him, Lucile had always felt the need to stand her ground, never backing down or admitting wrongdoing. He couldn't help concluding that marriage to him wouldn't have likely produced such a positive effect within her that marriage to Walter had clearly brought.

"Mrs. Howe and I are not together. At least not as anything more than friends."

One eyebrow shot up as if she was offended on Vienna's behalf. "Whyever not? She's pretty and clearly enjoys the same kind of life that you do."

"I..." How to explain, when one of the people who'd underwritten his deepest frustrations regarding love and relationships was the one doing the asking?

Lucile waved away the single syllable. "You don't have to explain. If I were you, though, I'd examine my heart, West, and see whom it longs for."

"Is that how you feel about Walter?"

A sincere and soft smile graced her lips. "I do."

At that moment her husband entered the room. "Everything all right, Lucile?" He glanced between her and West.

"Everything is perfect, darling." She moved to his side and pressed a quick kiss to his cheek. "West and I were only reminiscing and now we're all caught up."

West nodded agreement. He'd charged in here, angry and ready to throw out accusations at her. Instead they'd both extended an olive branch to the other, and that left him feeling lighter. At least until he remembered Vienna's reaction...

"Will you and Mrs. Howe be joining us on the pack trip to Yellowstone?" Lucile asked him.

He barely managed to arrange his face into a neutral expression, though inside he was reeling at the knowledge Lucile French Atwater was going on a pack trip. "No, we head back to Wyoming the day after tomorrow."

"Oh, that's too bad." She seemed to be sincere.

Walter smiled fondly at her before looking at West again. "Is there anyone you'd like us to deliver a letter to when we return to Pittsburgh?"

"No, thanks," West said, knowing the man's inquiry

was an innocent one. Walter couldn't have known that any letter West sent would be returned immediately as his early ones had. "Everyone is doing well, though?" He directed the question to Lucile.

She nodded. "They are all well."

"I'm glad to hear it."

Curling her arm through Walter's, she steered her husband toward the door. "If you'll excuse us, West. Good night."

"Good night."

West sank into a nearby armchair as they exited the living room, feeling suddenly tired but also relieved. He'd faced his past and helped set things right between him and Lucile. It was an unexpected success he'd express gratitude for in his prayers tonight. He just hoped things between him and Vienna—whatever her decision about the dude ranch—might end up being resolved as affably.

Chapter Seven

After her walk around the ranch, Vienna stood beside the corral fence and watched the windmill turning around and around. Just as her thoughts were doing. She'd made peace earlier with West's comments about their marriage of convenience and the nonessential requirement of love in such a relationship. However, to be confronted with the reality that he had hidden his past from her... She folded her arms against a fresh wave of hurt.

She didn't want to enter into an arrangement—even in name only—with someone who deliberately kept secrets from her. Vienna had traversed that same awful path with Chance; she wouldn't voluntarily do it a second time.

Which brought her right back to where she'd been after leaving West on the porch. What was she to do now? Go forward with the dude ranch and their convenient marriage? Or not?

Footfalls sounded from behind. Was it West or someone else? Half of her hoped it was him; the other half wasn't sure she was ready to see him yet.

When she turned, she was surprised to find Alec approaching her.

"Evening."

She nodded in acknowledgment before she faced the windmill again.

"I heard you met a friend of West's from back in Pittsburgh."

Vienna cringed at the memory of Lucile's haughtiness. "I did, yes."

"And you found out some things about West's past."

He didn't phrase it as a question, but she gave another nod anyway. "I never knew all of that. About him growing up wealthy."

"Is that what's bothering you the most? That he used to be wealthy?"

She pushed out a sigh. "No. It isn't that." Her aunt and uncle may not have been as wealthy as it sounded like the McCalls were, but Vienna wasn't unfamiliar with the upper class, either. "I don't like…secrets."

"Bad experience in the past?" Alec asked perceptively.

Her smirk resonated with more bitterness than humor. "You could say that." Remembered pain filled her thoughts. "My late husband was a well of secrets that eventually destroyed him and our marriage."

She was relieved when Alec didn't press her for more details. "What will you do now?" he asked instead.

"I don't really know," she said, lifting her shoulders in a shrug.

"Do you still want to partner with West?"

"Yes…and no."

Stillness drifted through the air between them for

several long moments before Alec cleared his throat. "I don't claim to know all of his reasons for not sharing his past with you. And I can't say that what he did was right. But I know this—West McCall is an honest man."

Vienna gazed out across the corral as Alec's words sunk in. As much as she wanted to contest them, she couldn't. She'd known West for seven years—Alec had known him even longer—and she'd never had any reason to suspect him of hypocrisy. On the contrary, he had always shown himself to be honorable and trustworthy. There had been no subtle warnings of a darker side to him as she now recognized there had been with Chance. If she needed any greater proof of West's true character, she only had to look at the way he'd watched out for her and Hattie, including offering her his dream and help with the dude ranch.

"You're right," she finally conceded. Turning, she offered him a smile. "Thank you, Alec. You're a good friend to West."

He smiled back. "So are you." His blue-gray eyes held a question. *Was friendship all that there was between her and West?* Vienna looked away to avoid answering.

"I guess I'll head back to the house now."

Alec fell into step beside her as she walked. "I wish you all the best in deciding what to do. I'll be praying for you and West."

"I appreciate that."

When he stopped a moment later, she did the same. "If you change your mind about a marriage of convenience and running a dude ranch…well, I'm not just West's friend. I'd like to think I'm yours, too, Vienna. You are a remarkable woman."

The hopefulness in his expression made her blush. She had little doubt what he was hinting at with his talk of friendship and his compliment. Unlike Bertram's veiled proposal, which had left her disturbed, Alec's left her feeling almost flattered. Still, her answer was the same.

"Thanks, Alec. I do consider you a friend." She tempered her next words with a genuine smile. "Someday, you'll make some girl a wonderful husband."

"But that's not you." He appeared slightly disappointed but not angry.

She shook her head. "I'm sorry, no. I've had my fill of romance. If I marry again, it will be for convenience to West so we can build a business together. That's all I need."

Alec dipped his chin in a nod of acceptance as they continued toward the house. But Vienna couldn't help wondering why her words regarding no romance in the future had rung a bit hollow in her ears and heart.

Hat in hand, West waited in the kitchen doorway the next morning for Vienna to take notice of him. "Morning," he said, when she finally looked his way.

"Morning." Her smile was brief, but it wasn't insincere.

An awkwardness he hadn't felt in a long time descended over him. It didn't help that several of the other women in the kitchen were pretending not to overhear their exchange.

"Can you take a short break?" he asked quietly.

West had waited in the living room last night for her to come back from her walk. Except when she had, she hadn't been alone. West had felt a stab of real jealousy when she'd entered the house with Alec.

He'd hoped to talk with her, but she'd excused herself to see if there was any supper left. The confusion in her jade eyes had told him that she wasn't ready to continue their conversation yet. With only one day left on the ranch, he hoped she was ready to talk now.

"Go on, Vienna," Howard's wife said. "Thank you for your help, but you're still a guest here."

Untying her apron, Vienna draped it over a chair and unrolled her sleeves. "Where to?" she asked as she trailed him outside.

"I thought we might take a ride."

"Another one? With Alec?"

West shook his head. "No, just you and me this time."

Something akin to pleasure—*or was it concern?*—flashed in her gaze before she nodded. "All right. Let me go change first."

"I'll meet you in the barn."

He was relieved to find that most of the other guests had already departed for the pack trip to Yellowstone, along with Lucile and her husband, or were busy elsewhere on the ranch. A quiet ride and a private place to talk were what he'd been hoping for. He hadn't fallen asleep easily last night. Instead, he'd spent several hours tossing, turning and praying. Each time the words had risen to his tongue to ask God for things to go the way he hoped and wanted, he'd worked to swallow them back down again.

"Your friend Lucile came into the kitchen early this morning," Vienna announced after they'd saddled their horses and ridden away from the ranch.

Apprehension had West gripping the reins too tightly. He commanded his fingers to relax. "What did she say?"

"No need for panic." Her smile was uncharacteristically impish, reminding West of Maggy. "She actually apologized."

He couldn't keep his jaw from going slack. "Lucile?" He'd been surprised by her apology to him the previous night, but after their tangled past, those words had truly needed to be said in order to clear the air. For her to apologize to Vienna, a woman who was practically a stranger to her…apparently Lucile really was changing.

"Yes, she expressed remorse over her behavior last night and said not to hold it against you for too much longer that you hadn't shared with me about your family."

Cautious hope rose inside him until she asked, "Was she only a friend, West?"

"No." He adjusted his hat, up and down. "We were actually engaged."

"Ah." Vienna faced forward. "She's quite beautiful, and I imagine her family is every bit as wealthy as yours."

He couldn't deny either. "You're right, but I don't feel a single moment's regret that she ended our engagement. I wish her and her husband only happiness."

Did he only imagine her exhale to be one of relief?

"Vienna." He waited for her to glance his way. "I'm sorry again for not telling you about my past. It wasn't right to keep it a secret from you, but I didn't set out to deceive you."

Her shoulders rose and fell with a long breath. "I

know. I was surprised and angry, but I mostly felt afraid."

"Because of Chance," he ventured.

She nodded slowly. "I don't want to experience that kind of heartache again."

"I don't want you to, either." His guilt nudged at him, but he shoved it aside.

"Thank you," she said, shooting him a grateful smile.

They rode on in silence after that, but it wasn't strained. West felt so relieved to have things resolved between them that he almost laughed out loud. Vienna might still choose not to go forward with the dude ranch, but it wouldn't be because of his own poor choices.

When they reached a meadow of wildflowers, West stopped his horse. Vienna did the same with hers. He dismounted, then helped her to the ground.

"It's so beautiful," she murmured, her eyes on the flowers.

West took in her enraptured expression. "Yes, it is." She'd mentioned Lucile's beauty, but he wondered if Vienna recognized her own. He certainly wasn't the only man to notice. His thoughts turned to Alec, and West frowned. That had been his other mental and emotional wrestle last night—getting to where he could be okay if Vienna's feelings matched that of his best friend.

"Is this what city folk want to see?"

It took him a moment for his head to understand her question. "You mean the meadow?"

"Yes, but also the untouched beauty and the close-ness of nature."

West chuckled with appreciation. "Absolutely. That and riding off on a horse without encountering another human habitation for miles. Or seeing the mountains and hills and the sky so wide and clear you feel like a tiny speck. And yet, at the same time, you feel important because you know God created all of this grandeur for His children to enjoy."

"If I wasn't already a Western girl myself, I think that speech would have sold me on this way of life."

He exchanged a smile with her, though his fell away quicker than hers. "Have you given more thought to the dude ranch idea?"

"I have," she stated matter-of-factly but with no hint at what she'd decided.

West blew out his breath, steeling himself for bad news. Maybe this time next year he'd have enough money to buy a small plot of land himself, something he could keep growing.

"We never did talk about what to give Hattie as a surprise."

The change in topic had him jerking his gaze to hers in confusion. "No, I guess we didn't. I suppose we could find something in town."

"That would be nice, but I thought of one thing."

He couldn't tell from her solemn expression what she was thinking. "What's that?"

"Well…" She paused, clasping her hands together. "I would like to give her the gift of a home—a legacy, really—and a father figure. Even if that's in name only."

West's heart jolted at her words. "You mean…"

"Yes." Her smile rivaled the sunshine gleaming down on the meadow. "After thinking and praying about it most of the night, I believe we should start our dude ranch." She added with a blush, "As well as go forward with our marriage of convenience."

He still couldn't believe her answer. "You're sure?"

"Quite." Vienna watched him a moment. "Are *you* sure?"

West grinned. "Quite."

When she laughed, he had the strangest urge to gather her in his arms, swing her around until she was breathless with happiness, then kiss those pink lips of hers... But the notion made no sense. She might be beautiful, kind, smart and strong, but Vienna was his business partner and his friend—nothing more.

He settled for scooping her hand in his, though even that brought a twinge of feeling to his chest. "We're going to give people the best dude ranching experience in all of Wyoming."

"You really think so?"

His grin returned. "I do. It'll take time and money and work. But we can do it."

"We can do it," she repeated, her eyes sparkling with jade-colored lights.

West wished they had some punch or lemonade so they could toast to the future. In lieu of that, he lifted Vienna's hand to his mouth and placed a quick kiss on the back of her hand. "We've got a great future ahead of us, Vienna."

"Yes, we do," she said, sounding slightly out of breath.

He released her hand and motioned to the horses. "Should we head back?"

She nodded.

After helping her onto her horse and mounting his

own, West couldn't stop grinning. His dream was finally coming to fruition. He was going to have a dude ranch, and Vienna and Hattie were going to have a home. Their future stretched out before them just like the sky overhead—bright and clear and free of any clouds.

Once the critical decision about the dude ranch had been made, Vienna didn't want to delay going forward with their marriage of convenience. Part of her reasoning was practicality—if she and West were already married when they returned home tomorrow, they could move into the ranch house at the HC Bar and get started right away with the repairs. There wouldn't be any wedding fuss, either. That was something she didn't want, given this was only a business arrangement. Still, her greatest reason for moving forward right away was so she wouldn't be tempted to change her mind.

What had seemed like the right thing to do during their leisure horse ride to the lovely meadow began to feel rash and unsettling an hour or so later. She needed to be brave—for herself and for Hattie—so she decided it would be best if they procured a license and were married by a judge in town before they embarked on their return journey to Wyoming.

West had looked downright shocked when she'd told him her plan, and he'd asked her more than once if she was sure. Despite the flurries of panic in her middle, Vienna had been adamant. If she was to marry again, she wanted it done sooner than later—and in a ceremony completely opposite of the one she'd shared with Chance.

She'd asked West if he wanted the Eatons to be present at the ceremony with the judge, but he'd declined inviting the brothers and their wives, stating this was simply part of his and Vienna's business arrangement and not an official wedding. Vienna was a little relieved to know there wouldn't be a crowd of people to witness her likely nerves. Only the judge, West and Alec who would be driving them back to town.

Vienna couldn't eat a bite the next morning. One of her hostesses took pity on her and gave her some tea that helped soothe her stomach a little. After saying goodbye to everyone, she and West joined Alec in the wagon.

The conversation between the two men only registered in her head when one of them asked her a direct question. Otherwise, Vienna simply stared at the landscape, her gloved hands strangled together in her lap.

She'd been nervous the first time she had gotten married. Only that had been more a hopeful nervousness. Now she could easily see what she hadn't been able to—or hadn't wanted to—back then with Chance.

Stop, she told herself. *This is completely different. West is a good man and this is only so we can run the dude ranch together.*

Nothing was required of her, except to agree to the marriage, take West's name as her own and fulfill her end of the ranching responsibilities.

Easy as pie.

Her brave words were just that, though—words. They couldn't fully silence her deep fears. Was she being foolish to do this? It was the only solution if she wanted a dude ranch and thereby a home for her daughter. And yet, she'd told herself long ago that she would never marry again.

Vienna mentally shook her head. No, she'd vowed not to let herself *fall in love* with another man again. That was a different matter entirely than marrying a second time, especially when it was merely a means to an end.

Please help me see this through, Lord.

If only she were strong like Maggy, who'd built a new life for herself as a detective after her horrible first marriage—or like West, who'd given up so much to go after his dreams. But Vienna wasn't strong like them. If she were, she likely wouldn't have married Chance in the first place or stayed with him as long as she had. There was only one area where she could claim strength—and that was with Hattie. She could do this for her daughter.

Clinging to her resolve, she straightened on the seat, relieved to see they'd reached town.

She waited in the wagon as West, accompanied by Alec, took care of procuring the needed marriage license. In no time at all, she found herself standing beside West in the judge's chambers, Alec acting as witness from the corner near the door.

Sweat collected on her gloved palms and along the edge of her high collar. The small room seemed devoid of even the slightest bit of air and smelled acridly of furniture polish.

"Do you, Westin McCall," the judge intoned in a slightly bored tone, "take Vienna Harriet Howe to be your lawfully wedded wife…"

After answering in the affirmative, West threw her

a smile. It was brief and barely creased the edges of his mouth, but it was enough to anchor Vienna.

She exhaled a calming breath and focused on the judge as he turned to her. "Do you, Vienna Harriet Howe, take Westin McCall to be your lawfully wedding husband…"

Less than two minutes later, West produced a ring from his pocket. Vienna removed the glove of her left hand so he could slide the thin band over her ring finger. The slim weight of the ring felt both familiar and strange. She'd removed Chance's ring the day after he'd received his prison sentence. It was at the bottom of her trunk back at the Running W. She'd forgotten she would need to wear a new ring as West's wife.

She was now Mrs. Vienna Harriet McCall—at least in name.

"You may kiss your bride," the judge said, his voice more animated this time.

Vienna stared in panic at West, realizing too late that they hadn't discussed this part. Hadn't told the man that this wasn't a real marriage ceremony, at least not to them.

West gazed reassuringly back at her, then leaned forward to kiss her cheek. The contact was as short-lived as his earlier smile, but Vienna still felt her pulse trip with happiness and her breath catch in her throat. Just as it had yesterday when West had kissed her hand in the meadow.

"Congratulations," Alec said with a smile when they turned around.

Vienna had to cough before she could say, "Thank you."

"Always thought it would be you before me." West's

warm brown eyes shone with teasing as he shook Alec's hand.

They bid the judge good day and returned outside to head to the train station. Just as before, Vienna sat in back, while West took the front seat next to Alec. She kept looking at the ring on her finger as if that would somehow solidify the reality in her own mind of what she and West had done. They were actually married now.

When they reached the station, West helped her to the ground and Alec came around the wagon to bid them goodbye. "It was a real pleasure to meet you, Vienna." He lifted his hat to her.

"You, too, Alec. Thank you for everything." She extended her hand toward him. "If you ever find your way to Wyoming, you can stay with us, free of charge." A flicker of surprise shot through her at how easily the *us* had fallen from her lips.

Alec smiled as he shook her hand. "I might just do that."

"You promise?" West asked after the two best friends had clapped each other heartily on the back. "We'd love to have you."

The cowboy nodded. "I'd love to come. If only for your cooking, Mrs. McCall."

A blush flared across her cheeks, at the compliment and the reminder of her new married name. Would she get used to it? Or would it always inspire such a reaction?

"Goodbye, Alec," she said.

He waved at them before they turned and made their way to the train, West carrying their bags. Once they'd boarded the train, Vienna slipped into an empty bench.

Through the window, she saw Alec offer another parting wave, which she returned. It was nearly the same scene she'd experienced six days ago. However, when West joined her on the bench, Vienna realized this train scene wasn't similar to the other one at all.

Vienna had left Wyoming as a widow, feeling nervous about the future. She'd be returning, still nervous about the future, but now she was a bride. She was married to the man seated next to her, whose warmth pushed welcomingly at the chill she'd felt all morning.

Neither spoke a word until after the porter came through their car to collect their tickets. This young man didn't give Vienna more than a passing look before his gaze lowered to her ringed hand, which she'd forgotten to cover with the glove still clutched between her fingers.

"Have a pleasant journey, ma'am. Sir." Then with a tip of his hat, he moved on.

She tried to pull her glove back on, but her hands were trembling too much to accomplish the simple undertaking.

"Let me," West volunteered.

Taking the glove from her, he held it out. She slipped her fingers inside as he tugged the glove onto her wrist. Vienna's racing heartbeat belied the simplicity of the everyday task. "Thank you," she mumbled. She started to pull her hand back, but West held it gently in his.

"You ready?" he asked in a low voice.

Vienna instinctively knew what he was really asking—was she ready for the future, one that included a dude ranch and the two of them together?

Was she? She couldn't say she felt excited or courageous in this moment. In some ways, she felt more jumpy now than she had when she'd left Wyoming. And yet, this time, she wasn't facing the future all alone. It would be her and West and Hattie. The thought calmed her, even though West's touch on her hand still felt pleasantly confusing.

"I'm ready," she said with more than feigned confidence as she nodded.

Chapter Eight

West let Vienna exit the train first in Sheridan, though he felt sure she wouldn't have let anyone, including him, keep her from disembarking ahead of everyone else. The moment the depot came into view, she was on her feet and prodding him to move into the aisle.

Smiling, he watched her drop to her knees and embrace Hattie. The tenderness between them also brought a surprising spark of envy. The two of them had each other. But who did he have in his life who loved him as unconditionally as Vienna and Hattie loved one another?

It took work to keep his smile in place as he approached the mother-daughter pair as well as Edward and Maggy. "Howdy."

"Welcome back," the Kents said in unison before looking at each other and laughing. Edward lifted his wife's hand and kissed it with obvious tenderness.

The envious spark inside West became a tiny flame. He might be married himself now, but his relationship wasn't what the couple before him shared and enjoyed.

"How did everything go here?" he asked, pushing aside the fruitless comparisons.

"It went well," Edward answered. "Thurston is over his nerves, and the new mare is proving to be quite the little horse."

Maggy joined in the conversation as Vienna stood, her arm still around her daughter. "Hattie and I had a fun time, too. Didn't we?"

"Uh-huh. We watched the horsies and made cookies and I ate some cookie dough." She glanced up at Maggy. "But not as much as Miss Maggy did."

Vienna looked as if she didn't know whether to laugh or scold her. But Maggy chuckled. "You're right, Hattie. I did eat more cookie dough, and that's because the baby wanted some, too." Her hand rose to her belly as her expression softened.

"Did you bring me a surprise, Mr. West?" Hattie asked, turning expectant green eyes on him. "Did you? Did you?"

West went down on his knee so he could be eye level with her. "I sure did, Hattie girl."

"What is it?" She clapped her hands, her excitement too much to contain.

Grinning, he opened one of the bags at his feet and withdrew the toy he and Vienna had managed to grab during one of their stops. In the frenzy of getting married before leaving North Dakota, they'd both forgotten about finding something tangible to bring home to Hattie. West had been as relieved as Vienna looked when they'd stopped at a town that had a mercantile just down the street from the train station.

"It's a pony of your own," West answered. He lifted

the intricately carved horse for Hattie to see. It had wheels beneath its hooves and a string attached to its painted bridle. "See, you pull it around like this." Setting the horse on the platform, he tugged the string, making the horse roll past his knee.

Hattie squealed with delight. "My own pony! Thank you, thank you."

"You're very welcome."

As she scooped up the horse, he stood and found himself the beneficiary of Vienna's smile. The kind of smile that radiated pleasure and gratitude—for him. A moment later she gave him a questioning look. West recognized what it meant. It was time to share their other surprise with her daughter and the Kents.

"We have one more thing to share," Vienna announced.

West picked up their bags and moved to stand next to Vienna. Edward and Maggy exchanged a confused glance.

"For me?" Hattie asked, squinting up at West and her mother.

He cocked his head. "Sort of."

"You see, Hattie. Mr. West and I..." She paused and glanced at him, the color rising into her cheeks. "Well, you see, this morning, we decided to..."

Maggy was watching them shrewdly. "Did you two..."

"Did they what?" Edward stared blankly at his wife.

Leave it to the detective to read between the lines. "You got married, didn't you?" Maggy said with a note of triumph.

"We did." Vienna nodded as she visibly exhaled. "It

seemed the most sensible thing to do, once we decided to go forward with the dude ranch."

West noticed Hattie still appeared confused. "You gots married, Mommy?"

"Yes, sweetheart, we did." She crouched once more beside her daughter. "Remember how I told you that we'd be moving back to the ranch that me and your daddy used to have? And how the place needs a lot of work to look nice again? Well, Mr. West is going to help us—as Mommy's new husband."

The little girl appeared to think that over. "Does that mean I have a new daddy?"

"Yes," she said, though her voice held a note of hesitation as she straightened and looked at West, as if asking his permission.

He reached down and hoisted Hattie into his arms. "That's exactly what it means, Hattie girl."

"Can I call you Daddy West, then?"

The inquiry hit him square in the chest but not in an unpleasant way. He might be able to kiss the hand or cheek of her mother and resist the knocking it stirred inside his heart. But West was no match for the little girl watching him with a rapt and hopeful expression.

Surely there was no harm in Hattie using the name, even if his and Vienna's marriage was only a business partnership. He could still be a father figure to the little girl as Vienna wanted.

At Vienna's nod of approval, he grinned at Hattie. He might not have ended up with everything he'd once dreamed of or wanted. However, the friendship of this good woman standing next to him and the adoration of her daughter was a close second.

"Daddy West it is."

* * *

"I can't believe you got married today!" It wasn't the first time Maggy had shared a similar sentiment since they'd all arrived back at the Running W.

Mrs. Harvey took another sip from her teacup. "Where's the groom tonight?" she asked, her rich English accent lacing the question.

"Probably down at the bunkhouse," Vienna answered, her face every bit as warm as the tea in her belly.

Hattie had fallen asleep earlier in their shared room upstairs, her doll and pony tucked beneath her arm, but Vienna had felt too antsy to sleep. After all, it wasn't every day a girl got married, even in name only.

When Mrs. Harvey had offered to make her and Maggy some tea, she'd gladly accepted. This would be the last night the three of them drank tea together before bed. After tomorrow, Vienna wouldn't be sharing the same house with her dear friends anymore.

"I imagine there aren't many grooms who get married in the morning," Maggy mused, "and then spend the night back in a smelly bunkhouse with their bachelor friends."

Vienna swallowed another mouthful of tea. "It isn't like that. He won't be living in the house at the HC Bar, either. We're business partners, who now share the same name to keep things respectable."

"We understand, love," Mrs. Harvey said with a kind smile. "And won't be teasing you about it any longer. Will we, Maggy?" She threw her employer a loving but pointed look.

Her friend's expression turned instantly contrite. "Sorry, Vienna. I'm still a bit shocked and I'm tired and

the baby seems to think my ribs are there for kicking."
All three of them chuckled. "But that's no excuse. I'm
proud of you actually."

"You are?"

Maggy nodded. "You've changed so much over
these past few years. Why, look at how you've taken
charge of your future since hearing about Chance. Now
you're married to a good and decent man, even if it's
in name only, and you're about to start a dude ranch.
If you ask me that is bravery."

The compliment echoed the one West had offered
Vienna on the train ride to North Dakota. Only his had
pointed to the strength that already existed inside her
before she'd married Chance. Was that true? Had she
had some strength inside her all along? Was her current
path evidence of that? She wasn't sure, but she hoped
both West's and Maggy's words proved true.

"Thank you," she said over the emotion filling her
throat, "to both of you."

Tears swam in her eyes as she regarded the precious
faces of these two women—one like a sister, the other
like a mother. They'd helped her when she'd been at
her lowest; they'd shared in her joy over the birth of
her daughter; and they'd championed and encouraged
her every day for the past three years. Could she really
stand to say goodbye?

"I refuse to cry now because then I won't be able
to stop." Even as she said it, though, several tears slid
down Maggy's cheek. "We're going to miss you dearly,
Vienna."

Mrs. Harvey reached out and squeezed Vienna's
hand. "You'll still come to see us, right, love?"

"Of course. And you're always welcome at the HC

Bar." She smirked as she lifted her teacup to her mouth again. "Well, at least after I've cleaned the house. It's not suitable for any company right now." She'd been so busy with her regular duties at the Running W, as well as her decisions about the future and the trip to North Dakota, that she hadn't yet returned to the HC Bar to clean and ready the house.

Maggy shook her head. "You won't have to do it by yourself."

"I won't?" She set her cup back down without drinking.

"I've already arranged a housecleaning party for tomorrow morning. We'll have the place neat as a pin in no time."

Vienna tried to smile. "That would be…wonderful."

"It'll be all right," Maggy reassured.

She wasn't surprised that her friend had detected the nervousness building inside her at the thought of a large crowd in her home, even one that consisted of other women.

"It's just some of our friends from town and a few of their children."

Vienna let herself relax. It would be nice not to have to tackle the initial housework alone, and one of the older children could keep Hattie entertained so the little girl wasn't underfoot.

But her calm evaporated like the steam from the tea when Maggy added, "I wonder what they'll say when they find out you're married again."

"You got married, McCall?" Gunther Bertram declared, his hammer poised in midair over the section

of roof they were repairing on the house at the HC Bar.
"To Mrs. Howe?"

Heated embarrassment rushed up West's neck.
"Yes…two days ago." He wanted to say more, explain
the circumstances, but he and Vienna had agreed that
it might be best for their business if only the Kents and
Mrs. Harvey knew the marriage was in name only.

"Well, how do you like that?" Bertram threw a
scowl at him. "She turns me down less than two weeks
ago and now you're saying…" He waggled the hammer at West. "That not only did she decide to up and
get married after all, but she decided to marry *you*."

Edward cleared this throat as he scooted toward
them. "It may not be as black-and-white as all that,
Bertram. And regardless, Vienna needs our help fixing the roof today."

Relief flooded through West when the other man
blew out a resigned breath and lowered his hammer.
Not that he'd really feared the rancher would hit him.
He guessed Bertram was feeling the sting of injured
pride than real anger. But he was grateful for Edward's
assistance nonetheless. Especially since appealing to
Bertram's desire to help Vienna seemed to assuage
the man's ire.

"I had no idea you were even sweet on Vienna,"
Douglas Kitt piped up from his spot on the roof. "Sweet
enough to up and elope, huh?" The man grinned at
West.

He didn't know these men as well as Edward did,
though he'd spoken to them around town or at church.
Unlike West, they were part of the area's elite group of
ranchers who often dined together or with their wives
at the Sheridan Inn. Though, West supposed, that *did*

include him now that he and Vienna would be running the HC Bar Ranch together. Still, he didn't have much of an appetite these days for getting dressed up and eating a fancy meal. That was something he didn't miss about his life back in Pittsburgh.

"McCall and Vienna have known each other for a long time," Edward explained, clearly taking West's silence as discomfort over Kitt's remark. His conclusion wasn't too far off from the truth.

Bertram pushed up the brim of his hat and eyed West. "That's right. Weren't you two friends until Chance came along and stole her heart?" He sniffed with amusement as if he'd shared something clever.

"Something like that," West muttered, the reminder pricking painfully at his memories—and his guilt. Why couldn't they all just work in silence?

Kitt paused once more in his hammering. "So you realized what you'd lost back then and went after it with gusto this time around. And speedily, too."

Grinding his teeth together, West managed to shoot the man a lazy smile, though everything in him wanted to protest Kitt's erroneous claim. He was grateful their potential guests would likely be strangers. That way his and Vienna's story and motives wouldn't be up for discussion by every person who set foot on the HC Bar.

"Just don't go letting her think she can boss you around as she pleases," Jett Preston called from the far side of the roof. It was the first time the man had added anything to the awkward conversation. "If you set your expectations now, they're more than likely to stick."

Kitt raised an eyebrow. "I don't know that it works that way with a second marriage, Preston. Vienna has already learned how to live with one husband. She can surely figure it out on her own with McCall here."

Rising abruptly to his feet, West tried to appear casual. "I'll be back. I told Vienna I'd keep an eye out for Hattie while I was up here. I'm going to see where the girl might have gone." He beat a hasty retreat down the ladder.

He was more than grateful for their help with the repairs—it would save him and Vienna time and money. However, he couldn't stomach another bit of speculation about their "courtship" or any more well-meaning advice relating to marriage.

Which made him wonder if Vienna was faring any better with the women.

On hands and knees, Vienna vigorously scrubbed the floorboards in one of the upstairs bedrooms. She'd been more than willing to let some of the other women clean her and Chance's old bedroom. Overhead she could hear the *tap-tap-tapping* of the men's hammers as they reshingled the roof. With all of the help, they'd be able to sleep in the house tonight—at least she and Hattie would.

"I didn't know she was even fond of Mr. McCall." The voice of Matilda Kitt floated through the open doorway where Vienna worked. "She never said a thing."

Vienna hung her head. It wasn't the first time this morning that she'd overheard or been directly told something similar. Matilda was more her friend than any of the other women here, with the exception of Maggy. But Vienna couldn't impart any additional details to her. Not when she and West had made the decision to keep the marriage-of-convenience agreement under wraps.

"I bet she was plumb scared of what to do for her and her girl," she overheard Josephine Preston, the sister of Gunther Bertram, state. "After that no-good husband of hers up and got himself killed."

She nearly laughed out loud that the unromantic Josephine had come closest to identifying the truth. With a shake of her head, she continued to make her way toward the door, cleaning the floor as she went.

"Still," Matilda added, "it's a pity she didn't get a real wedding in a church."

Was it? Vienna mused. Her last wedding in a church had preceded the most difficult two years of her life, though most of the townsfolk hadn't suspected anything was wrong until Chance had been convicted of arson. However, she couldn't stop the image that rose into her mind of herself clad in a white dress and West waiting happily for her at the front of the church, looking as handsome as ever in a three-piece suit.

Pushing aside the ridiculous picture, she finished cleaning the floor and climbed to her feet. Another room ready for living in, as well as ready for their future guests. Vienna managed a small smile.

She dropped her brush in the soapy water and lugged the bucket downstairs. In the kitchen, Maggy—in no physical condition to do any cleaning herself—was overseeing the work of two teenage girls. As Vienna came down the hall, one of them loudly proclaimed, "I still think it's so romantic that they up and eloped. If someone as handsome as Mr. McCall was in love with me, I'd elope, too."

Peals of girlish laughter followed the innocent remark, but Vienna felt no merriment as she paused in the hallway. Instead, she could feel a headache building behind her eyes. All this talk of romance, eloping and marriage had begun to grate against her good humor.

"That would be very shortsighted of you, Susan," Maggy said in a kind but firm tone. "How a man looks on the outside isn't an indicator of his heart or his integrity. You have to look at his actions, not just at his face or his words."

Murmurs of "yes, Mrs. Kent" echoed through the kitchen. Would they listen? Vienna wondered. If only someone had dispensed such wise counsel to her before she'd agreed to marry Chance. On the contrary, everyone back then had pushed her toward him. He'd been handsome, with charming words and what appeared to be a well-lined bank account. And so her aunt and uncle had encouraged the match. Would her parents have done the same, though? She liked to think they would have been wiser in what they observed about Chance. Either way, Vienna couldn't go back. What was done was done, and if she hadn't married Chance, she wouldn't have Hattie. And her daughter was such a blessing in her life.

"How are things going down here?" Vienna asked as she entered the kitchen.

She wasn't sure who looked more startled at her sudden appearance, the girls or Maggy. "We're doing well," Maggy said cheerfully after a moment. "We're nearly done washing all of the cupboards and the dishes."

"The parlor is cleaned and dusted," the girls' mother, Lola Winchester, said as she joined the group in the kitchen. "You have such a lovely home, Vienna."

Vienna set her bucket on the table. "Thank you."

"Are you going to keep ranching like you were doing before?" Lola picked up a towel to help dry the clean dishes.

"No." Vienna shook her head. "We're actually going to turn this place into a dude ranch."

The girls looked at each other in confusion before the older one asked, "What's a dude ranch?"

"It's a ranch that caters to those who want to spend a little time experiencing Western life but who don't want to settle out here permanently."

Lola stared wide-eyed at her. "So you just allow these people into your home?"

"Not exactly," Vienna said with a light laugh. "They pay for food and lodging and also for the use of a horse during their stay."

The younger of Lola's daughters still looked as baffled as her mother. "And there are people who *want* to come live on your ranch, for fun?"

Maggy laughed this time. "Yes, Mary. Believe it or not, there are a great many people back east who want to experience our way of life."

"When will you start taking in guests?" Lola asked next.

Vienna began putting the dishes back inside the newly scrubbed cupboards. "Hopefully in September. We'll need to build a guesthouse and purchase more livestock, but West thinks we can be ready for business by then."

"Well, look at that." Lola smiled brightly at her. "You found love a second time and now you have this new venture to start with your new husband. It's all so wonderful, Vienna. Pretty soon, I imagine there will be another little one or two tagging along after Harriet. Am I right?"

Vienna shut the cupboard, mortification heating the back of her neck. As she turned around, Maggy threw her an apologetic look.

"Speaking of Harriet," she managed to say in a voice that trembled only slightly, "I think I'll go see where she and your Lotty have run off to."

Mindful of those working on the back porch, she hurried down the steps and toward the barn. Tears of humiliation and frustration stung her eyes as she marched through the open doors of the barn. She appreciated everyone's help, but she could do without her and West's relationship being the sole topic of conversation.

"You all right?"

She looked up to find West leaning against an empty stall. "I will be." Glancing around the barn, she couldn't see anyone else working there.

"It's just me," he said perceptively. "Although, Lotty and Hattie are up in the loft playing with the cats Edward brought over."

Sure enough the sound of giggles floated down from the loft overhead. The innocent sound pushed back at Vienna's irritation and embarrassment.

"I was coming to see where they were." She took a step past West. Up close, she could see that he looked unusually tired. "Are *you* all right?"

He gave a casual shrug, then seemed to think better of the action. "Actually, I came looking for Hattie as an excuse to take a short break."

"From what?" she asked with a chuckle.

Crossing his arms, he leaned back against the stall

door again, his mouth curving up in a smirk. "All the marriage talk and speculations about you and me."

"West McCall!" She put her hands on her hips and feigned a scolding look. "Have you been listening in on the women's conversations?"

His eyebrows shot up with confusion at the same time he lifted his hands in surrender. "No, ma'am. I was talking about the men."

"The men have not been speculating about us and our marriage," she scoffed.

"On my honor."

She wouldn't have believed him before today, but now... "So you came out here to escape it?"

"Yep."

Vienna began to laugh. And once she started, she couldn't stop. At first, West watched her with a mixture of concern and bewilderment. Then after a few moments, he joined her.

"That's precisely the reason I came out here," she finally managed to say as she wiped at her wet eyes.

West cocked his head. "You're telling me the women were talking about the same thing."

"Uh-huh."

This time a full smile lit up his expression. "How long do you think we could hide out here?"

"I don't know." She laughed again, her earlier annoyance and discomfort all but forgotten in the wake of West's smile and their shared secret of commiseration.

Lotty and Hattie appeared at the edge of the loft. "See my kitties, Daddy West." Both of the girls held up the cats in their hands.

"Those are some fine-looking kitties, Hattie girl."

The tender look he sent her daughter left Vienna

feeling happy but wistful. There'd once been a time when West had looked at her with real tenderness. She'd been so certain back then that his feelings for her had matched hers for him, but she'd been wrong.

"You girls be careful up there," she said before turning to West. "I suppose we'd best get back."

He nodded. "Everyone might start to speculate where we've gone." His brown eyes sparked with amusement.

"True, and we don't need any more of that."

"No, we don't." They shared another laugh.

Vienna moved in tandem with him toward the barn entrance, though she felt suddenly reluctant to leave. It had been nice to talk to him, alone, as they'd been able to do in North Dakota.

"I'll see you at lunch, then?" she asked.

He gave her a half smile. "Wouldn't miss it."

She returned to the house, feeling lighter. Even when the conversation in the kitchen circled back around to her and West, she didn't mind so much this time. Maybe it was because she knew West was enduring the same with the men. Vienna's lips rose with a secret smile at that thought. Or maybe it was simply because she'd been able to see and talk to West when she hadn't been expecting to do so. Whatever the reason, she found herself humming softly under her breath as she worked to finish putting the house to rights.

Chapter Nine

T hat night the *pitter-patter* of rain against the bedroom window woke Vienna. She rolled over and peered
at Hattie asleep beside her. Thankfully the rain hadn't
woken the little girl. Vienna attempted to settle back
to sleep until she remembered West out in the barn.

While the house had been cleaned from top to bottom, the roof newly shingled and the porch fixed, there
hadn't been time today to repair the large hole in the
barn roof. Was West getting soaked in the loft?

She tried to tell herself that he could manage the situation himself. But the thought of him wet and shivering wouldn't leave her thoughts. Besides, where was he
to go? They'd already agreed that she and Hattie would
sleep in the house, while he bunked in the barn. He
likely wouldn't ask her if he could come inside, even
with the leaky barn roof.

With a sigh, she threw off the covers on her side
of the bed and patted to the chair in the corner. She
slipped her feet into her shoes and grabbed her robe.
After tying it around herself, she fetched a shawl,
too. She made her way through the quiet house to the

kitchen. There she lit a lamp and set it on the table. The smell of damp earth filled her nose as she stepped out the back door.

The rain fell steadily beyond the porch, creating puddles in the yard between the house and the barn. Pulling the shawl over her head, Vienna dashed forward, doing her best to avoid the largest of the puddles. She scrambled to open the barn doors, until finally, she was out of the wet weather. Still, a shiver ran through her at the cool temperature in the building. With only the two horses inside that Bertram had brought over earlier, the vast space, devoid of more animals, wasn't much warmer than outside at the moment.

"West?" she called softly as she pulled the shawl off her head. "Can you hear me?"

A shadow appeared almost immediately overhead, which told her that he hadn't been sleeping. "Vienna? What's wrong?"

"N-nothing." Embarrassment had her pulling the damp shawl around herself. "I…um…heard the rain and wondered if you were all right in here."

He didn't answer right away, his pause filling with tangible confusion. "I'm fine, thanks."

This was getting them nowhere, and she wanted to hurry back to the warmth of the house.

"Is the roof leaking into the loft?"

Another long pause followed her question before she heard him exhale in obvious defeat. "A little. But it's fine."

"West, you can come inside the house."

"But I thought—"

She shook her head, though he couldn't see her. The cold was beginning to creep beneath the hem of her robe. "I know what we discussed, but that was before it started raining. The guest bedrooms are clean and ready for use."

"Are you sure?" he asked with evident hesitation.

Was she? Vienna straightened her shoulders against the foolishness that threatened to make her go back on her word. "Yes. And…" she added, as much for herself as for him, "we are married, so there is nothing improper about you using one of the perfectly decent bedrooms that are available inside our house."

"All right. I'll come down."

Should she wait for him or return to the kitchen on her own? In the end, West made the decision for her. He scrambled down the ladder so quickly she didn't have time to make up her mind before he was standing next to her, his bag in hand.

"How long were you planning on staying up there, wet and cold?" she demanded, one hand on her hip.

Even in the dim light, she couldn't miss his smile. "Until morning. I've slept through far worse on pack trips and roundups."

"Then why are you so eager to leave now when you weren't a moment ago?"

He stepped closer, his breath warming her cheek. "Because when a kindhearted, pretty woman comes along to tell you that, yes, you can sleep inside a house rather than a barn with a leaky roof, it's an easy decision."

"As it should be," she countered, trying to ignore his compliment and the way her heart had started jumping against her ribs from more than the exertion of having run across the yard.

Turning on her heel, she headed toward the door

as she drew her shawl back over her hair. "Just know that it's every man or woman for themselves from here to there."

The last thing she heard before she raced back into the rain was the deep, pleasant laughter of West from behind.

West slipped from the porch into the kitchen after Vienna. He set his bag on the table, then removed his hat and shook the rain off it. "It really is coming down out there." He'd felt a little cold and damp trying to sleep inside the drafty barn, but now that he was truly wet, he couldn't stop shivering. He wasn't the only one, either. Vienna's shawl and robe hadn't withstood the rain any better than his clothes had.

"You're all wet, too," he said. Reaching for her, he rubbed the sleeve of her robe.

Her eyes widened, and in the lamp light, they looked the color of a deep green lake. "I'm all right."

"Now who's being stubborn?" He gentled his teasing with a smile.

Instead of returning it, she stepped back. "You can borrow some of Chance's clothes," she said without meeting his eye. "Since the ones in your bag are probably wet, too."

"Mind if I start a fire first?"

She shook her head. "You can start one in the stove or in the fireplace in the parlor. I'll go get the clothes."

West opted for the fireplace. He moved into the parlor and found the wood inside the nearby crate had been replenished. The entire house looked fresh and homey. Though when he was sitting at the table with Vienna and Hattie earlier in the evening, sharing the supper their friends had provided, he couldn't help wondering when he'd feel less like he was intruding and more like he belonged there. The place still felt far more like Vienna's than theirs together. Even if she had said "our house" just now.

Once he had a fire lit, West took a seat in one of the nearby armchairs and lifted his hands to the growing flames. His tremors of cold slowly began to subside.

Having already resolved to respect Vienna's wishes about where he slept, he'd been determined to stay his course in the barn, no matter how long and dreary the rainy night proved to be. So he'd been awestruck when Vienna had shown up to invite him in.

His mouth rose in an amused smile as he recalled the way she'd looked standing there. Almost ethereal with her blond hair and light-colored robe, save for her hand on her hip. He chuckled to himself. As far as he was concerned, she was the perfect mix of unpretentiousness, strength and occasional playfulness.

"Here are the clothes," she announced, walking into the room. She'd changed her robe while she'd been upstairs. This one was blue.

West straightened in his chair and accepted the bundle she handed him. "Thanks. And thank you for the chance to sleep out of the rain."

"You're welcome." She fell back a step. "You can take the bedroom to the left of the stairs. I put an extra quilt on the bed."

He nodded his appreciation, certain she would head back to her and Hattie's room now. The thought brought a twinge of sadness—it was the same emotion he'd felt when they'd left the barn earlier in the day, after sharing their private joke about all the neighbors' marriage talk. He'd had more private conversations with Vienna the past couple of weeks than he'd had in a long time. It reminded him of how much he had always enjoyed talking with her. With Vienna, he could simply be himself—she didn't judge him or try to wield his actions to fit her own purposes.

"That feels nice." When he lifted his head, he saw she was gesturing toward the fire.

Would she stay and talk? Jumping up, he tugged the second armchair closer to the warmth. "Have a seat," he said, gesturing to the chair.

"I think I will."

"I'll go change, but I'll be back."

At her nod, he walked casually from the room, but he was anything but slow swapping his wet clothes for the dry ones. He didn't want Vienna changing her mind about lingering in the parlor in his absence.

Contentment wound through him as he returned and found her still sitting there. Resuming his seat, West asked, "What does Hattie think of sleeping here?"

"She wasn't sure about it at first." Vienna bent forward and held her hands toward the flames. "But I think she was so tired after running around all day that she fell right to sleep without complaint."

West studied her out of the corner of his eye. She looked fatigued but happy. "You care a great deal for her, Vienna, and Hattie knows it."

"Thank you." She glanced down at her hands. "It hasn't been easy being both mother and father to her."

He leaned back against his chair. "No, I can't imagine it has been. But you don't have to do it alone anymore."

"I can't tell you how wonderful that sounds." The

admission was stated so softly that West wasn't sure she'd meant to say it out loud.

Turning to look at the fire, he mused on the unpredictable turn his life had taken. He wouldn't have thought even a month ago that he'd be married to Vienna, living at the HC Bar and preparing to start a dude ranch.

Vienna's question revealed her mind was running down a similar track. "Do you think we'll have enough money to start building a guesthouse?"

After supper and dishes, while Hattie had played with her toy pony, he and Vienna had discussed their pooled finances. They'd decided to set aside enough money to see them through the next two months without any income. What was left over would cover the repairs to the barn roof and the fences, new paint for the outer walls of the house and the barn and feed for the horses they'd bring back to the ranch from Bertram's place.

"I was thinking about that," he said, matching her posture of leaning toward the fire. "I'd like to see if the bank would let you—let us—take out a loan against the ranch. If they did, that would give us enough money to build a guesthouse and buy more livestock."

She swiveled her head to look at him. "You think the bank would do that?"

"I believe so. Especially if we get the rest of the ranch looking as nice as the inside of the house does right now. Plus, we have a solid plan for how we'll pay the bank back once the guests start coming."

Nodding thoughtfully, Vienna stared at the flames again. "Will we find enough people who want to come here?"

"Sure," he said with confidence. They had to. If not, he'd need to come up with some other way to earn a living. The extra money he'd get for helping Edward train horses now and again would help, but he had more than himself to look after now. He needed to provide for Vienna and Hattie, too.

"Once we get the rest of the place back on its feet," he continued, "I'll write to Howard and see if he's made any progress on finding people who are interested in trying out a dude ranch in Wyoming."

A sudden smile appeared on her lips. "Mary Winchester couldn't believe that there are people who want to experience life on a ranch, for fun." She laughed lightly, and the carefree tinkling sound warmed him even more than his dry clothes and the fire.

"I'm living proof of that." West clasped his hands loosely together. "Although in my case, it became more permanent."

Her next question took him by surprise. "Did you ever miss your family after settling out here for good?"

"Yes."

The word slipped out before West could stop it, but it was the truth. The days had turned to weeks and then months with no response to his letters. He'd prayed nearly every night for his father to change his mind, to accept West's choice and still let him be part of the family. But it hadn't happened. It was then that he'd learned not to petition the Lord for what he wanted—it was too painful when it didn't come to fruition.

"There are still moments I think about them, my mother and sisters especially, and I miss them all over again," he admitted.

Vienna shifted, sitting back against her chair. "How many sisters do you have?"

"Three."

"Are they older or younger?"

West felt a pinch in his chest at talking about them. "One older. Her name is Cordelia. She was already married when I headed west."

"And the other two?"

"Anita comes after me and Lydia is the baby of the family. Anita is twenty-four now and Lydia is twenty, which means they're probably both married, too, maybe even with children of their own."

Sadness enveloped him at the thought. He would have liked being an uncle, teaching his nieces and nephews about ranching as he planned to keep teaching Hattie. Too bad their first guests couldn't have been his parents and sisters and their families.

"I still miss my family," Vienna said quietly, the admission laced with grief.

He turned to look at her. "I can't imagine losing your father to that accident and then your mother to illness so soon after that."

"It was a difficult year." She fiddled with the tie of her robe. "My brother, Anson, would have been thirty this year."

"Do you remember much about him?"

The firelight caught the shimmer of unshed tears in her eyes. "A little. I was only five when he passed away, but I remember he was a kind older brother, even at ten years old. To me he seemed fearless and quick to laugh. Kind of like you." She shot him a small smile, which West returned. "I remember how excited he was that our cousin Lance got to spend the whole summer with us that year. None of us had any way of knowing they would both take ill and pass away."

"Did you get sick, too?" West couldn't remember if she'd told him that part of the story before.

Vienna nodded. "I did. But I wasn't as gravely ill as Anson and Lance." She looked stricken when she glanced at him, reminding him of other moments after they'd first met. "I don't think my aunt ever got over letting Lance come to stay with us that year and not being able to say goodbye to him before he passed away."

"And she held that against you and your parents." That part he did remember.

She gave a slow nod. "It often seemed that way, especially after I moved in with her and my uncle. But our relationship wasn't really strained until after my cousin Lavina married and moved away."

West had come to the area a year later and had been intrigued by the sweet, shy girl he'd finally made laugh at a town picnic. Having been parted from his own family, he'd felt instant compassion for Vienna when she'd shared how she was living with relatives after having lost her brother as a child and both parents as a youth.

"It's late," Vienna said as she rose to her feet. "I think I'll head to bed."

He probably ought to get some sleep, too. "I'll bank the fire."

"All right." As she came around behind his chair, her hand alighted on his shoulder—as delicate and wary as a tiny bird. "Thanks for everything, West. You've always been a good friend to me, and I want you to know that means a lot, especially now."

Almost unbidden, his hand rose to cover hers, but she withdrew it before he could and hurried toward the doorway. "You're welcome," he murmured. Then he added more loudly, "Good night, Vienna."

"Good night."

He sat for a long time after that, staring into the hearth, until the fire burned itself out and all that remained was ashes. The coolness in the room settled inside him, along with a feeling of sorrow. He could probably attribute his melancholy to talking about his family and the empathy he felt at hearing Vienna speak of hers. Still, as he stood and finally headed upstairs to the guest bedroom, he wondered if it could be something more.

West had never really planned to marry, but now he was to a quiet but remarkable woman who had been his friend for a long time. Yet something about the way Vienna had expressed her gratitude for his help and friendship had sounded rather…final, as if friendship was all they could ever have. It was that realization that made him want to mourn something he wasn't sure he'd ever had a chance at in the first place or had any right to hope of having in the future.

Chapter Ten

The three of them headed to church in the Howe wagon the next morning. Vienna was used to her and Hattie accompanying the Kents and the rest of the Running W staff to services. Before that, she'd gone alone, since Chance had refused to join her, save for Easter or Christmas. It felt odd, and yet nice to have a man driving her and her daughter to church today.

And a handsome man at that. Not that she hadn't seen West dressed up before, for church or for the occasional social function in town. Still, that was before he'd been her husband, even in name only. That was the only reason she could think of to explain the nervous flurries in her middle this morning. Or last night in the kitchen when West had rubbed her arm and peered intently into her eyes. Or when he'd listened willingly and with compassion as she talked about her family.

This growing awareness of him made little sense to Vienna. Nothing had changed between them. They were still just friends, even if they were married in the eyes of the law. She'd needed to remind herself of that fact the night before. That was why her expression of gratitude for all of West's help had been as much about thanking him as it had been a reassertion of what their relationship was and what it wasn't.

Her well-meaning words to him and herself had almost been for naught, though, when he'd reached for her hand where it rested on his shoulder. In that moment, Vienna had panicked, retreating upstairs as quickly as she could. Then she'd lain awake for some time afterward, going back and forth between congratulating and berating herself for not letting him hold her hand.

"Mommy, can I get down?"

Vienna yanked her thoughts to the present and realized they were already at the church. On the other side of her daughter, West watched Vienna with an amused look. "Yes, of course, Hattie," she said quickly. Too quickly.

"I'll help you." West climbed down from the wagon seat. He caught Hattie when she jumped to him, and then he carried her around the wagon to assist Vienna.

Once he'd helped her to the ground, she expected him to head straight into church as he'd always done. Instead he placed his hand on the small of her back and guided her inside the building—as a real husband might do.

News of their "elopement" had clearly preceded their arrival. It felt to Vienna as if the entire congregation poured out of the pews to surround her and West, who still carried Hattie. Smiling, West nodded appreciation to the well-wishers. Vienna tried to smile, too, but the ringing of "congratulations" in her ears and the press of people made her feel light-headed after a few moments.

"It's all right," West whispered to her, his brown gaze intent on her face, his hand firm but comforting against her back. "Just keep walking. We're almost to our seats."

At last they filed into the pew where the Kents and some of the other Running W staff members were already sitting. "Seems we've caused quite the ruckus, *Mrs. McCall*."

Warmth filled her cheeks, but it wasn't only shyness in the face of all the attention. It was hearing West call her by her new last name. His last name. *Their* name. They were the McCall family now, as far as anyone was concerned.

Thankfully, West had placed Hattie between them on the bench, which gave Vienna the perfect opportunity to hide her blush as she busied herself with straightening her daughter's dress.

"How come I couldn't bring my pony with me?" Hattie pouted.

Vienna smoothed back her blond hair from her forehead. "Because ponies have to stay home from church."

"But we have two horsies outside."

She glanced at West who she could tell was fighting a laugh. "True, but they aren't allowed inside, either."

"You do have your doll, Hattie girl," West pointed out. "And I think she'll listen much better to the preacher than your pony would."

The little girl moved the doll from the crook of her arm to her lap. "Shh, Hattie. You have to listen."

Vienna exchanged a smile with West before training her attention toward the front of the church and not on her kind, handsome, lawful husband seated close by. But that proved more difficult than she would have anticipated, especially later in the service when he bent to listen to something Hattie murmured in his ear and he placed his arm along the back of the pew behind them. His fingers came to rest lightly against Vienna's shoulder, much as hers had on his shoulder last night.

To her dismay, she felt more than cold when he withdrew his arm sometime later. She felt disappointment.

What was he doing? West mentally shook his head. He needed to stop looking for excuses to touch Vienna and pay more attention to the service. But he hadn't been able to stop himself from offering Vienna comfort earlier when they'd come into the church and been heralded with greetings from most of the members of the congregation. The fright in her green eyes had solicited his compassion, especially knowing how much she disliked being the center of attention.

As far as putting his arm around her... He'd done that partly to show Vienna that she didn't need to be afraid of him. Fear was the only explanation he'd come up with for why she'd practically sprinted from the parlor last night after they had talked.

Did she think he'd turn out to be like Chance? The thought had his jaw tightening. West hoped not, and his friendliness in putting his arm behind her would hopefully convey that.

Plus, he couldn't help noticing earlier the way several of the bachelor cowboys and ranchers were eyeing their pew and Vienna, in particular, with barely concealed jealousy and disappointment. That had been the other reason West had chosen to put his arm around her. He wanted to show everyone else how proud he felt that Vienna had picked him. That they were together.

Except you're not really together, his head argued. *Not in the way they think.*

Frowning, he lowered his arm from the back of the pew to his side—where it belonged. He was altogether too distracted today. It wasn't as if he hadn't sat near Vienna in church dozens of times over the past three years.

Only this time, she wasn't just a friend or another member of the Running W staff. This time she was his wife.

West stared straight ahead, willing the pastor's words to breach his chaotic thoughts. Vienna had made it clear, especially last night, that they were friends and nothing more. They had a dude ranch to start, and he didn't need to go complicating that venture or court-ing inevitable disappointment by pushing at the line of their established friendship. He was helping her—and repaying his debt of guilt for encouraging her to court Chance—and she was helping him, too, plain and simple.

His mind made up once more, West could finally concentrate on the sermon. The pastor was talking about love. But he wasn't talking about feeling love for one's fellow man but feeling the love of God for them. He read 1 John 4:19 from his Bible. "'We love him, because he first loved us.'" Then he asked if the audience believed that verse. Did they believe that even before they came to love God, He loved them?

West nodded along with several others around them. His family hadn't been particularly religious, beyond attending church services—unlike Vienna's parents who she'd said had lived their faith every day—but he'd had a belief in God ever since he was a child. He also knew God loved him back. At least as long as West was doing what God wanted, right?

The pastor's next words refuted his rhetorical question as if West had voiced it out loud. "Now you may wonder if God's love is conditional or unconditional," the man said, his kind gaze sweeping the congregation. "Does God only love us as long as we are doing what He asks?"

Shifting uncomfortably on the bench, West was rewarded with a curious look from Hattie. He attempted a smile at the girl, but it fell from his lips the moment he focused on the pastor again.

"Let's see if we can find the answer." The pastor turned the pages of the Bible. "We can find one if we turn to Matthew 5:45. Christ says here that the Father 'maketh His sun to rise on the evil and on the good, and sendeth rain on the just and on the unjust.'"

The man lifted his head and directed a smile at the churchgoers. "On the evil and the good, the just and the unjust. That doesn't sound like conditional love to me. It sounds like a Father in Heaven who loves us regardless of our choices, our mistakes, our successes or our failures. He loves us now and always, whether we choose to love Him back or not."

West found himself leaning forward, his arms on his knees. Why had he never heard this before? Or had he heard it and it was only now making sense to him?

"Now, before we go asking why should we follow God and love Him if He will love us either way," the pastor continued, "we need to remember that God blesses those who love Him. They are happier and find greater peace than those who choose to turn away from Him. But even if we do turn away, that doesn't mean

He stops loving us. He doesn't stop loving you..." The man's eyes seemed leveled directly on West. "And He never will. Because His love is unconditional."

The pastor ended his sermon a minute or two later and the notes of the closing hymn rang out from the organ, but West was too busy inside his own head to notice. God loved him, even if West didn't always do what he should or what God wanted? Could his Father in Heaven truly be so different from his earthly father?

His whole life he'd felt the conditional love of his parents, particularly Lawrence. Then later it was the conditional love of Lucile that West had felt. He'd naturally concluded that, like those closest to him, God only loved him as long as West was doing what he was supposed to do.

But if that isn't true... A feeling of liberation filled West from head to toe. If God loved him—right now as he was, flawed and imperfect but trying—could there be others in his life who would do the same? Who would love him unconditionally?

He glanced down at his hands that were somehow gripping the hymnal, though he didn't remember picking it up. An echo of pain poked at him anew as he recalled his family's rejection. No, there weren't likely to be others in his life who could love him simply for him.

What about Vienna, though? He studied her out of the corner of his eye, relishing as he often did her sweet soprano voice. But he already knew the answer. Vienna might like him for him, but she'd made it clear that anything beyond friendly fondness wasn't to be theirs. Besides, he wasn't sure if he could trust more than friendship from her, given that he was already doing what she wanted. She benefited from their marriage and their business plans as much as he did. But if he wanted something that didn't fit with her plans, would she still offer encouragement and support? Likely not.

Some of his feeling of relief diminished at the thought, but he remained distracted through the closing prayer and as they stood to leave. He might not have found—or was likely to ever find—that sort of unconditional, no-strings-attached kind of love that God showed for him, but that was all right. Then he felt Hattie tug on his suit jacket.

"What is it, Hattie girl?"

She held up her doll to him. "Hattie listened good during church, don't you think, Daddy West?"

As it did each time she said his name, a jolt of love and gratitude pierced West's heart. If nothing else, this little girl loved him unconditionally. He recognized that. And though he didn't quite understand why she'd taken to him, he was more than thankful that she had. Perhaps her unreserved adoration for him was both a gift and a reminder. There was at least one person in his life who loved him as purely as God did.

"She sure did listen good, didn't she? And so did you." He scooped her up to carry her from the pew, inspiring a squeal of laughter from the little girl and a genuine smile from her mother.

The Kents invited the three of them to the Running W for Sunday supper, and Vienna gratefully accepted the invitation. She and West hadn't yet had a chance to stock the cupboards at the HC Bar with food. For breakfast that morning, they'd eaten what was left over from the house cleaning party. Lunch had been more of the same.

After getting Hattie to lie down for a nap, Vienna had stretched out beside her. Her less than restful sleep the night before and the bizarre inner turmoil she felt over West had left her as exhausted as her daughter. Sometime later, a tap on the door woke her.

"Come in," she called softly as she sat up.

West poked his head into the room. Keeping his voice low, he said, "We probably ought to head over to the Running W for supper."

"Oh, right." A glance at the clock on the bureau revealed she'd slept longer than she'd intended. "I'll wake Hattie and we'll meet you downstairs."

He hesitated in the doorway. "I…um…like your hair like that."

"Like what?" Vienna touched her head, belatedly remembering she'd removed nearly all of her hairpins earlier.

His answering smile made her pulse quicken. "It looks pretty down like that or when you wear it in a braid."

"Th-thank you," she managed to reply. He noticed her hair?

"See you downstairs in a few minutes."

When he disappeared out the door, Vienna fell back against her pillow and covered her blushing face with her hands. How in the world was she going to survive the next week, let alone the rest of her life, with West as her business partner and husband when his compliments and smile already turned her insides to jelly?

"I can do this," she whispered fiercely to herself as she sat up again. She'd survived an abusive marriage, raised her daughter largely on her own so far and had agreed to turn her property into a dude ranch. She could certainly handle the kindness and praise from one thoughtful cowboy without feeling like a schoolgirl every time.

Determined, she stood, changed into a dress that wasn't wrinkled, and then purposely rearranged her hair up and off her neck. She woke Hattie next and brushed her daughter's hair before the girl went to collect her toys so they could head outside to where West and the wagon waited.

"Ready to go?" He smiled at her as he straightened away from the wagon.

If he noticed her hair was no longer down, he didn't mention it. To Vienna's relief. "Yes, we are."

"Do we have Hattie the pony?" he asked as he crouched in front of her daughter.

Hattie nodded and held up the toy horse.

"What about Hattie the doll?"

The little girl hoisted the doll in her other hand.

"Well, then…" He slapped his trousers and stood. "I think that's everything we need to head out." Vienna had to fight a giggle.

Frowning, Hattie peered up at him. "What about Hattie the girl, Daddy West? Did you forget me?"

"Never," he said in a slightly choked voice before picking her up and tossing her into the air. Hattie shrieked with joy as he caught her. "I could never ever forget you, Hattie girl."

He helped both of them onto the wagon seat, and soon he and Hattie were singing a song he'd taught her before the trip to North Dakota. As Vienna thought back over the scene she'd just witnessed and the sweet interaction between her daughter and West in this moment, she knew her resolve not to let him get too close was eroding faster than riverbanks in a flood.

Last time she'd fallen for West she'd been left alone and grieving before turning to the comfort of a man she'd barely known. This time she only hoped her heart would better weather any possible disappointment because whether she liked it or not West McCall was now in her and Hattie's lives for good.

Chapter Eleven

West wasn't used to eating in the Kents' dining room. He'd eaten the occasional supper here, as foreman of the Running W, but more often than not he'd eaten with the other staff in the mess hall adjacent to the bunkhouse.

It wasn't the formalness of the room or even having to eat in his Sunday suit, though, that had him eyeing the door. That had everything to do with observing Edward and Maggy throughout the meal. The way they looked at each other, the way their hands seemed to touch at every available opportunity, the way they laughed together at private jokes as if they were the only ones present.

Of course things wouldn't ever be the same between him and Vienna as it was for their happily married friends and former employers—theirs wasn't that kind of marriage. Still, that didn't stop a seed of discontent from sprouting inside him. And it wasn't just Edward and Maggy's interactions, either. Vienna seemed quieter than usual, but no matter how much West tried to draw her into the conversation for longer than a few moments, it hadn't worked.

"Mommy, I'm done," Hattie said long before the rest of them had finished.

West didn't feel very hungry anymore. "I'll take her outside."

"Are you sure?" Vienna studied him. Could she read on his face his real reason for ducking outside?

He nodded and pushed back his chair. "Come on, Hattie. Let's go see how Mr. Edward's mare is getting along." West helped her out of her seat, then picked up her toy pony and doll from the empty chair beside her. "Please thank Mrs. Harvey for me," he said to Maggy. "That was a delicious supper."

"You didn't eat much." He cringed at Maggy's forthrightness, though he shouldn't have expected any less from her.

With a shrug, he managed a grateful smile as he took Hattie's hand in his. "Doesn't mean I didn't enjoy every bite I did eat."

Thankfully no one else protested, and he led Hattie outside. Once past the porch, he let her run as far as the corral so she could expend the energy he'd seen building within her after having to sit still for so long. West greeted several of the wranglers by name, and they waved back. Being the Sabbath, no one was working in the corral today.

"Where are the horsies?" Hattie asked, when he reached her.

He crouched beside her and handed her both toys. "They're resting today. Just like God asks us to rest."

"Is that why Mommy made me take a nap?"

Chuckling, West took off his hat and plunked it on top of her little head. "Probably so."

"Where's the may you wanted to see?" She had to tilt her head back to see him from underneath the brim of the hat.

He straightened. "The *mare* you mean?"

"Yep." Hattie nodded, making the too-big hat tip back and forth.

"She's in the big barn."

With all of the horses either inside the barn or the pastures, he felt comfortable letting Hattie walk alongside him without holding her hand as he usually did. They headed into the barn and West led her to the mare's stall.

"Here she is."

He lifted Hattie—hat, toys and all—so she could see the horse better.

"She's pretty," Hattie exclaimed. "Can I feed her?"

West set the little girl back on her feet. "Sure, you can feed her. Let's go find some sugar cubes for her." When they found the cubes, he grabbed a few, then led Hattie back to the horse's stall. "Remember what I taught you? About feeding them?"

"Uh-huh." She passed him her doll and her pony, both of which he tucked beneath his arm. "I have to hold my hand really, really straight."

Nodding, he placed two sugar cubes on her outstretched palm. The mare had wandered over to the stall door to watch them. Hattie lifted her palm and kept it flat as the horse nipped the cubes out of her hand.

"It tickles," she said, giggling.

West smiled at her adorable laugh.

"Did I do it right, Daddy West?"

His smile deepened. "You did it just right, Hattie girl."

"What did you do, Hattie?" Vienna walked down the line of stalls toward them.

A flicker of delight shot through West at seeing her, though it couldn't have been more than twenty minutes since he and Hattie had left the dining room. Her demeanor seemed more relaxed, though.

The little girl grabbed the last sugar cube from him and held it, palm out, to the mare. "I'm feeding the horsie."

"Look at that." She put her arm around Hattie. "Did Mr. West teach you how to do that?"

Hattie frowned up at her mother. "Not Mr. West, Mommy. He's Daddy West now."

"You're right, sweetheart." She threw West a look he couldn't decipher, but she didn't seem upset by Hattie's insistence over his new title.

With the sugar cubes gone, Hattie took back her toys and skipped farther into the barn. West brushed the flecks of sugar off his hands.

"I appreciate all you've taught her, West." She fell into step beside him as they strolled after Hattie. "She's far less afraid of horses than I was at that age."

He glanced at her. "You were afraid of horses…even before your father's accident?"

"Silly, right?" Vienna gave a self-deprecating laugh. "Especially having grown up with them my whole life."

West shook his head. "It isn't silly at all. I didn't stop feeling nervous around horses until I was fifteen."

"You're teasing me," she protested, a line forming between her eyebrows.

"Nope. I'm serious."

She stopped walking and peered directly at him. "How is that even possible? You love horses."

"I do now." He folded his arms across his chest. "Growing up, my only experience with horses was that they pulled the family carriage around Pittsburgh. My father did buy us a little pony and cart to use when we were children, but I was taller than that horse by the time I was eight. The carriage horses were large and intimating, and the only time I tried to sit on one, I was bucked off. Could hardly sit down for a week."

Vienna started walking again. "So what changed?"

"The first time I visited the Custer Trail Ranch and saw the cowboys riding around on these tall, majestic horses, I decided I wanted to learn to ride one, too, not just admire them from the seat of a carriage." It was West's turn to laugh at himself. "But wanting to ride meant getting real close to these huge, powerful creatures again."

They exited the barn through the back entrance, Hattie still dashing ahead. "Hattie, don't go past the pasture," Vienna called after her daughter before turning to look at West again. "How did you overcome your fear, then?"

"Some wise counsel. I was told that horses aren't all that different from people. If you act scared, they'll feel it and act scared, too. If you can stay calm, though, even if the horses are afraid or you're tempted to feel afraid, then you can get through just about any situation."

She smiled at him. "Was it Howard Eaton that taught you that?"

"No." West glanced down. "It was my father."

Remembering the moment was bittersweet. Lawrence had seemed so proud of him when he'd finally learned to ride and later when West had shown a knack for working with horses. But the pride had dried up faster than a puddle in a drought when West chose to embrace that talent as an occupation.

"I didn't know your father visited the ranch in North Dakota."

When they reached the pasture, West rested his arms on the top rung of the fence. Vienna came to stand next to him. Hattie was busy plucking wildflowers nearby. "He was the one who came up with the idea for the two of us to visit the ranch in the first place. We went four summers in a row before…" He didn't feel the need to finish.

"I imagine that makes it doubly hard," she said quietly. "That he was the one who introduced you to this way of life and then cut you off for choosing it."

He settled for a simple nod as memories paraded through his head—some pleasant, like the times he'd gone riding with his father during those summers; some unpleasant, like the day West had been ordered to leave the family home and not come back.

"You have a gift, West."

He pulled his focus from the past to the earnest expression of the beautiful woman beside him. "You think so?"

"I know so," she countered with unusual firmness. "And as painful as all of that must have been for you, I'm glad your father encouraged you to learn to ride and that you decided to follow your dream." Her cheeks pinked as she lowered her gaze to the grass. "Otherwise, you might not have ended up here. Or would even want to start this dude ranch with me."

The reminder brought immediate reassurance. Vienna was right. While his father hadn't condoned his choice, it was because of Lawrence that West had discovered a love for horses and cowboying that he never would have learned any other way. He most definitely wouldn't have ended up in Wyoming, either, on the cusp of starting his own dude ranch, which would soon bring things full circle for him.

He also wouldn't have met Vienna and that would have been as much, if not more, of a tragedy as not choosing this way of life. Yes, his choices had come at a cost, a price. But as he glanced at Vienna again, he didn't feel an ounce of regret for having made them.

"So tomorrow we'll go to town for food and supplies?" Vienna asked, leaning back in the armchair.

Hattie was already asleep, but after tucking her daughter into bed, Vienna hadn't felt sleepy herself. She'd wandered back downstairs to find West seated in the parlor before a fire as he'd been last night during the rain.

It felt strange to be back at the HC Bar, with a man in the house once more. Thankfully West didn't inspire the anxiety within her that Chance regularly had. Although, if she were honest with herself, her friend and second husband did stir a different sort of nervousness within her. Or maybe it was the conflicting emotions she felt for him that were the real cause of the butterflies in her stomach. Was she really supposed to feel nothing, though, when she observed the tender interactions between him and Hattie? Or heard him confess to also being afraid of horses? Or learned how brave he'd been in choosing this life? A life that had led him here.

"...after we get back," West was saying, "I'll start repairing the barn roof and any fencing that needs mending."

Vienna reined in her thoughts to focus on the conversation. "I'll see if there's any hope of resurrecting my garden."

"What seeds do you want to get tomorrow?"

"Oh, all the usual vegetables."

Lifting his leg to rest it on his opposite knee, West threw her a questioning look. "That's all? When you said you liked working in your garden, I assumed you meant more than just vegetables."

"Well, yes. But with money a bit tight..."

He cocked his head, regarding her in that way that made her think he could see inside her head. "Vienna, would you like to grow something more than vegetables?"

"Yes," she said, training her gaze on her lap as she waited for the inevitable scoffing remarks about how she was being foolish. Ones she'd heard over and over again from Chance.

Silence yawned in their place before West asked her, "What kinds of things?"

"Some herbs, maybe, and flowers."

She caught his thoughtful nod. "I think that's a great idea. Especially the flowers. The ladies from back east would probably love to see what variety of flowers we can grow here."

"Y-you mean you're all right with me growing other things in the garden?"

His eyebrows rose in what appeared to be genuine

confusion. "Of course. Why would I object to that? The garden is yours to do with what you please."

"It's just that... Chance..." She pressed her lips over the name.

West bent forward, bringing his knees nearly to hers. "I'm not Chance, Vienna."

"I know that."

"Do you?"

A flash of irritation robbed some of her joy at the prospect of doing whatever she wanted with her garden. "I'm well aware that you are not like him."

"Good. Then there's no need to be afraid of me."

She reared back in surprise. "Why would I be afraid of you?"

"Just now, you looked like a man sent to the gallows before answering my question about the garden." He blew out his breath and glanced at his hands. "Then there's last night. After we talked, you bolted upstairs as if you were fleeing an angry mob."

Her mouth fell open but no audible sound came out. How could she explain? "I'm sorry, West. Little things like talking about the garden bring up old memories and I find myself bracing for a caustic remark out of habit."

"I'm sorry, too." A pained expression flitted across his handsome face. "And last night?"

Panic hobbled her tongue. She couldn't tell him that it wasn't him she'd feared when she fled the parlor—it was the strange transformation of her feelings for him that had frightened her.

"I was ready to get back to bed." It had been the truth, though probably not for the reasons he would assume.

He dipped his chin. "Fair enough."

"Besides..." She folded her legs up beneath her skirt and did her best to give him a level look. "I'm back in here tonight, talking to you, which shows I'm not afraid."

His mouth rose in that lazy grin that set her pulse skittering faster. "You're right." He shifted his gaze to the fire as he added in a quieter voice, "I'm glad. I like talking with you, like this."

Me, too. The words pushed for release against her lips. But Vienna feared saying them out loud would reveal too much of her inner turmoil.

She and Chance had never sat like this. At least not for long before he'd start complaining about something others or Vienna had done and she'd make the excuse of needing to see to something in the kitchen or upstairs.

But being here with West... This felt nice and comfortable and safe.

"We could make this a habit, then," she suggested. "Although we don't have to have a fire."

He sat back, his smile making another appearance. "Whether we have a fire or not, I like the idea of making this a habit. For us."

The warmth of his tone and the sincerity shining in his brown eyes reached out to embrace her, furthering the feeling of contentment that had settled over the room. "I'd like that, too."

She couldn't think of a better way to end the day than sitting here, conversing with West. Doing so would also require effort and bravery, though, especially if she hoped to keep her morphing feelings for him under control. But she could do it—she would do it. Because the alternative would lead her straight back to the sorrow and disappointment she'd once felt when West hadn't reciprocated her love. She wouldn't knowingly put herself in that position again.

For West, the next week and a half at the HC Bar passed quickly. He repaired the barn roof, assisted Bertram in bringing the rest of Vienna's horses back to the ranch, mended the trouble spots along the property's fences, painted the outside of the barn and the house and assisted Vienna in getting the garden planted. His days were busy with hard work, just as he liked them, but they were also filled with seeing the two people he liked best of all. Vienna and Hattie.

The three of them ate every meal together, and West had begun to give Hattie rides around the corral on the back of the older, gentlest horses. Each evening, he and Vienna met in the parlor to discuss how the day had gone, or their upcoming plans, or simply to talk. It was his favorite time of day.

True to her word, Vienna no longer acted as afraid of him, either. If anything, she'd fully embraced her role as fellow business partner. He'd noticed, though, that she hadn't rested her hand on his arm or his shoulder again. A realization that sometimes bothered him, though he couldn't reason why.

Not that he was complaining. He'd chosen to keep some distance himself by not putting his arm around her or rubbing her sleeve, even when she looked a bit cold. Things between them were as comfortable and friendly as ever, and for that, he was grateful.

With the house, barn and property looking almost new, it was time to head to the bank to see about a loan.

They dropped Hattie off at the Kents' ranch one morning, and then West drove Vienna to Sheridan.

He wasn't sure how she kept herself from bouncing right off the seat with the way her foot was tapping nervously against the floorboards. He might hide it better, but he was every bit as anxious. If the bank refused to give them a loan, they wouldn't be ready to open the dude ranch this year. Which would necessitate a delay in their plans and West finding other work to support the three of them.

"Maybe we ought to wait a little longer," Vienna said, throwing him a stricken look. "See what we can do on our own before we go to the bank."

He gave her what he hoped was a reassuring smile. "I don't blame you for wanting to wait, but we need the money from the loan to go forward."

"I suppose you're right." She blew out a long breath.

"It's all right to be nervous."

Vienna smirked. "That's easy for you to say."

"What? You don't think I'm feelin' a bit tense about this meeting, too?"

She lifted an eyebrow at him. "Are you?"

"Indeed I am," he said with a chuckle.

Her brow furrowed. "But you don't act like it."

"Either way, I'm still nervous." He smiled at her. "Just like you."

Chuckling, she shook her head. "And here I thought you were brave."

"I am."

"Except you just said you're nervous."

West turned his head to look directly at her. "Bravery isn't the absence of fear, Vienna."

"You mean…" Her expression appeared puzzled

again. "You think we can still be brave, even when we feel afraid?"

"*Especially* when we feel afraid." He trained his attention on the road again. "Don't believe me?"

She laughed. "I wouldn't say that. I just hadn't thought of bravery in that way before." Her foot's incessant rhythm began to slow. "I thought to be brave or strong meant you didn't feel fear at all."

"Think of Daniel. Do you think he felt a little fear right before being thrown into the lion's den?"

Vienna pursed her lips, drawing his attention to their perfectly bowed shape and pink shade. "I suppose he probably felt some fear."

"That would be my guess, too. But he didn't let that stop him from being brave." West forced his gaze from her lovely mouth to the horses' unattractive ears. "He trusted God was with him and that likely gave him the courage to face his fear and still move forward."

"Face his fear and still move forward," she repeated. "Which is what we need to do today, with the bank."

West chuckled. "Yep."

"Knowing that and doing it are still two different things," she admitted after a moment.

A desire to encourage her and bolster confidence in both of them had him clasping her hand in his and giving it a friendly squeeze. At least, he told himself the gesture only stemmed from friendliness.

"We can do this, Vienna."

Her green eyes had widened, but she nodded. "Yes, we can."

West released her to take the reins again, deliberately ignoring how nicely her hand fit inside his own. Or how pleasant it felt to have held it—even briefly.

To distract himself from his own convoluted thoughts, he started talking about what they might do with the money, if the bank granted them the loan. Soon Vienna joined in, adding her ideas to his.

When they reached town, West parked the wagon in front of the bank. He held the door open for Vienna, then followed her inside. They didn't have to wait long to meet with the bank manager.

He invited them to sit opposite his desk in two hard-back chairs. West got right to the purpose of their visit. Vienna had asked him the night before to take the lead on the conversation, though she did help answer the bank manager's questions about the history of the property over the last five years.

"You want to start a dude ranch?" the man asked, sitting back in his chair and resting his hands on the buttons of his vest. "Can't say I've ever heard that business proposal in these parts before now."

West, who'd removed his hat, inched forward toward the man's desk, eager to help him see the merit of their plans. "It's a sound business idea, sir. My friends in North Dakota have been doing it successfully for over twenty years."

"Hmm." The bank manager rubbed at his gray-whiskered chin. "And you think people will be interested in coming here?"

He and Vienna nodded together. "It's an ideal spot," West added. "Near the mountains and not far from Yellowstone National Park. We've got plenty of horse trails, fishing and, of course, all of the amenities that Sheridan has to offer folks who are visiting."

Drumming his fingers against the desk, the man eyed them thoughtfully but shrewdly. "If the man I send out to your property can verify the place is no longer in a state of neglect and is as valuable as you say…"

West's heart sped up, pounding as hard with hope as it did with apprehension. He knew whoever the bank sent would find no fault with the HC Bar. Which meant this was it, the moment they either blazed ahead with his dream—*their dream*, he thought glancing at Vienna—or they'd be forced to start over.

Something came to rest on his knee. Glancing down, he was surprised to see Vienna's hand sitting there. He wasn't sure if she'd hoped to reassure him or herself, but it didn't matter. He slipped his hand over hers without hesitation.

The bank manager suddenly climbed to his feet. "Mr. and Mrs. McCall, if everything checks out with the property, then the bank would be more than pleased to offer you a loan against your soon to-be dude ranch."

Had West heard him correctly? He turned to Vienna and saw the same shocked excitement on her face that he imagined was on his.

"Thank you, sir." West let go of Vienna's hand and stood. "We appreciate it."

The man shook West's hand, then nodded to Vienna. "My pleasure. Once our representative assesses the ranch, we can sign the papers."

"Thank you so much," Vienna said before West led her out of the manager's office and through the bank.

Outside, he stopped her beside the wagon. "We're going to be able to build our dude ranch, after all," he said, shaking his head in disbelief.

"The bank representative has to complete his visit first."

"True, but we both know he won't find any fault with the property."

"You're right." Vienna smiled at him. "I don't think I've ever seen you look this stunned."

"Aren't you?"

She laughed, her green eyes sparkling with happiness. "Yes. I'm also elated, and terrified, and so, so happy. We did it, West. We're going to get the money."

"Yes, we are."

The radiance in her expression and the memory of her hand on his knee prompted West to throw restraint to the wind. If only for a moment. He wrapped Vienna in his arms and swung her around.

"We did it!" he repeated loudly before setting her back onto the sidewalk.

Her breathless laughter, flushed cheeks and wide-eyed gaze had his heart racing far more than twirling her around had. They were standing close enough that West could see the various shades of jade and emerald in her eyes. He could feel the soft brush of her breath against his chin.

As it had earlier on the wagon ride into town, his attention wandered to her lips. It would be so easy to breach the distance between them and kiss her. It wouldn't be the first time, either. West had kissed her once, long ago. Right now, the memory of that sweet, tender moment filled his thoughts.

"We better get back," Vienna said, clearing her throat. She fell backward a step, widening the space in front of him. And just like that the strong pull between them fractured into stark reality.

This wasn't like last time, when West had kissed her

or had once loved her. Things were different now—and exactly as they both wanted them to be.

"Yes, we'd better go." He handed her up onto the wagon seat. "Edward and Maggy are going to want to be the first to hear the news."

That had her smiling again.

As they drove away from the bank, their earlier camaraderie settled over them once more. To West's relief. He didn't want to complicate their friendship. It was wonderful the way it was right now. Still, a nagging thought at the back of his mind had him wondering how much longer he would need to keep telling himself that fact before he actually believed it.

Chapter Twelve

Humming to herself, Vienna plucked up another weed and tossed it onto her nearby pile. She loved the feel of the sunshine on her back, her hands covered with the rich scent of earth. Dozens of shoots and stalks had already made their way up through the dirt, and she had clusters of flowers to grace the kitchen table.

She could hardly believe it was already August. The man from the bank had declared the HC Bar in top-notch shape, so she and West had returned to Sheridan to sign the bank papers, making their loan official. With the money, they'd purchased a milk cow, a small herd of beef cattle and the materials to build a guesthouse.

In the far corner of the garden, Hattie was spooning dirt and bits of weeds into a cracked bowl Vienna had given her to play with. Her daughter's doll and toy pony dutifully waited close by for their "supper."

"That's all of the weeding for today," Vienna announced. She stood and wiped her hands on her apron, her gaze moving past the barn to the nearly completed guesthouse. "Should we see if Mr.—" she amended her words before Hattie could protest "—I mean, *Daddy West* needs a drink of water?"

Her daughter hopped up, her make-believe meal forgotten in the excitement about seeing West. Not that Vienna could blame her. She, too, enjoyed any opportunity to see and speak with him. But most especially, she loved their time in the parlor each evening, after Hattie had gone to bed. Then they would talk about the day and exchange stories they hadn't yet shared with each other. There was always much laughter, thoughtful conversation and a collective sense of contentment during those nightly talks that Vienna hadn't experienced since her parents had been alive.

After filling a bucket at the pump, she carried the water and a ladle toward the guesthouse, Hattie skipping along beside her. Vienna could see that West was working on the roof today. They'd agreed to hire a man from town to assist in building the four-bedroom structure, but West had done a good portion of the work himself.

"West?" she called up to him when they reached the ladder propped up against the house.

A moment later his head appeared above the roofline.

"Daddy West, are you thirsty?" Hattie asked.

He grinned. "I was just thinking how nice a cool drink of water would taste right about now."

Climbing over the edge of the roof, he scaled down the ladder. Vienna scooped up some water with the wooden ladle and passed it to him. West drank it all, then handed it back.

"Do you want some more?" She could see the perspiration that had dampened his shirt and turned his dark hair even curlier than normal beneath his hat.

"Yes, thank you."

He drank a second ladleful and then another before taking off his hat and dumping a fourth over his head. Hattie snickered behind her hand.

"Oh, you think that's funny, do you?" West shook his wet hair, spraying the little girl with droplets of water. Hattie shrieked with merriment and tried to dart away, but he scooped her up.

"Toss me high, Daddy West."

He obliged, throwing her into the air and catching her with ease as Hattie laughed with delight. Vienna couldn't help smiling herself. She felt an underlying sense of gratitude these days—that her daughter had a father in her life and that Vienna herself had a good friend in West.

"How's the work in the garden today?" He placed Hattie back on her feet and collected his hat from where he'd dropped it.

Vienna set the ladle back inside the bucket. "It's going well. Always weeds to pull, but I'm reminding myself that means other things are growing, too." She shifted the bucket from one hip to the other. "How's the roof?"

"I'm nearly done putting the shingles in place," West said with a note of pride.

She hadn't realized he was so close to finishing. "That's wonderful, West."

"There's something I want you to see." He pointed his thumb at the ladder.

Vienna eyed the roof with a mixture of curiosity

and trepidation. She wasn't overly fond of heights. "Up there?"

"Yep. And it's worth it, trust me."

"I want to see, too, Daddy West." Hattie jumped up and down. "I want to see, too."

He crouched in front of her. "Another time, Hattie girl. Right now I want to show your mother something, all right?"

"All right," she conceded with a sigh. "Can I show you the stew I made when you and Mommy are done?"

Straightening, West smiled and set his hat on her head. "Absolutely. Where is it?"

"In the garden."

"Wait right there and I'll be over in a few minutes."

Her expression brightened once more. "Okay, Daddy West. I'll finish getting it ready."

"Am I going to have to taste it?" he asked Vienna in a mock whisper as he moved toward the ladder.

She laughed. "Probably."

"I'll go first." He climbed up the ladder, glancing back over his shoulder when he reached the top. "You coming?"

Vienna blew out a slow breath, bunched her skirt in one hand and stepped onto the bottom rung. "I'm coming."

Focusing on climbing carefully upward, she reached the edge of the roof before she knew it. West helped her onto the newly placed shingles.

"I just need to…" She felt light-headed as she looked at the ground. Scooting away from the roofline, she sat to catch her breath.

She sensed West sitting down beside her. "Does the height bother you?"

"Yes, a little." Vienna shut her eyes and breathed deeply.

"I'm sorry, Vienna."

Opening her eyes, she kept her gaze trained on his face. "It's all right. You didn't know. Now, what did you want me to see from up here?"

"Do you think you can stand?"

She shot him an arch look. "Stand?"

"It'll look more amazing if you can." He rose to his feet and offered her his hand. "I'll be right here to keep you safe."

Though she didn't like the idea of standing on the roof, she trusted West. "Fine." She put her hand in his and let him help her to her feet. "Okay. What looks so amazing that I had to…"

Vienna let her words trail out as she gazed in wonder at the ranch below. The newly painted house and barn, the pastures of livestock, the thriving garden where Hattie was playing—all of it looked so beautiful, so inviting.

"This is our dude ranch, Vienna." One of his hands clasped hers, while the other held her securely around the waist.

She shook her head. "It does look amazing."

"And I firmly believe there'll be others who think the same."

The dizzy feeling returned, though she wasn't sure if it was from standing so high up or from West's low voice in her ear. "It is beautiful. And now I would really like to be back on the ground."

"We'll get you there." West helped her into a seated position on the roof. "I'm going to climb down first, then you come behind me. Okay?"

She nodded and waited until he'd maneuvered his way over the roofline and onto the ladder before she inched toward the edge. There she turned around, in preparation for climbing down the ladder. She couldn't see where to place her foot, though.

"That's it," West instructed from below. "The first rung is right…there."

Her shoe struck the ladder and Vienna eased herself onto the rung. It was an easy, step-by-step descent from there, she reminded herself.

"You're doing great. Keep coming, nice and slow."

She appreciated West's encouragement, but it wasn't enough to overcome her sudden humiliation. How silly it must look that a grown woman was afraid of climbing onto and off the roof? Vienna's cheeks scalded with heat. She wanted the embarrassing situation over with—now.

In her hurry, her next step didn't connect so much with the ladder as it did with her long skirt. Vienna felt her foot slide against the fabric. She was slipping! A squeak of fright escaped her lips as she tipped sharply to the right. She scrambled to grab the ladder more tightly, but gravity was pulling her in the opposite direction.

"West!" she managed to call out before she lost her grip completely.

Instead of striking the ground, though, she landed against his chest, his arms beneath her trembling knees. She immediately encircled her arms around his neck and held on—more from fear over her fall than fear that he might drop her. After all, he'd caught her midair.

"Are you all right?" His question wafted warmly against her cheek.

She gave a quick nod, though her heart was still thrashing inside her chest. "Y-yes."

"You sure?"

Vienna turned her head to look at him, intent on reassuring him that she was fine, just shaken and embarrassed. But when she realized only a few inches separated his face from hers, filling her view with his brown eyes full of gentleness and concern, her reply faded from her lips.

She hadn't been this close to West since the day of the bank meeting, weeks ago, when he'd exuberantly swung her around outside. She'd even gone out of her way *not* to be this close to him, knowing it would only make her confusing, changing feelings all the more complex. And yet, there was nowhere else Vienna wanted to be right now, in this moment, than cradled securely in West's arms.

Especially when his gaze shifted from her eyes to her mouth, causing her pulse to trip for an entirely different reason than falling off the ladder.

"Daddy West?" she heard Hattie calling. "Are you coming to see my stew?"

A flicker of something—was it disappointment or relief?—shot through his eyes, and then he was setting her feet on the ground. "I'll be right there, Hattie girl."

"Thank you…for catching me." Vienna tried to smile as she reached out to steady herself against the ladder.

She must have not been convincing because West looked torn between staying with her and following after her daughter.

"Go on," she urged, waving him toward Hattie. "I'm fine. Really."

"If you're sure…"

She gave a decisive nod. The sooner he left her side the sooner she could get her feelings in check once more.

"I'm coming, Hattie." Throwing Vienna one more glance, he headed to the center of the yard. Hattie met him there and they walked hand in hand toward the garden.

Vienna sank onto the bottom rung of the ladder and fanned her flushed cheeks with her apron. That had been close—too close. And she wasn't thinking of her fall, either. What else was she supposed to feel when a kind, protective, handsome cowboy, to whom she was now married, gallantly rescued her and then looked as if he very much wanted to kiss her? If he'd closed those inches between them, would she have kissed him back? She didn't have to search long for the answer, and it made her cover her warm face with her hands.

It didn't matter how much she fought with herself. The truth lay before her, plain and simple. Vienna had gone and done what she had promised herself she wouldn't. She was falling for West McCall all over again.

By late afternoon, Vienna could see from the kitchen window that the sunshine had disappeared behind darkening clouds. It would likely rain within the hour, which meant she ought to call Hattie inside. She paused in her supper preparations, dried her hands on a towel, and stepped out onto the back porch.

"Hattie?" she called. "Time to come in."

When there was no response, she headed around the house to the garden. But Hattie's customary play spot stood empty. That meant her daughter was likely with West. Vienna didn't see him on the guesthouse roof, so she ducked inside the building—the smell of new wood and fresh paint filling her nostrils. The furniture she and West had ordered would arrive in another few weeks.

"Hattie? West?"

It didn't take Vienna long to peek into the empty rooms on both floors. Neither West nor her daughter was around.

"To the barn, then."

She heard singing as she neared the open door. West's strong tenor. Smiling, she entered the building to find him milking the dairy cow. The cow noticed her first and belted out a *moo*.

"Ah, so it's a duet you have going," she said as she approached the pair.

West swiveled on the stool, shooting her a sheepish smile. "Yes, but the ornery thing won't stick to her harmonies."

"Keep at it." Vienna glanced at the hayloft. "Is Hattie up there?"

He shook his head. "I don't think so."

"Have you seen her?"

"Not since after lunch."

A needling of worry pierced her good humor. "Maybe she's upstairs inside the house."

"I'll keep an eye out for her," West offered as he returned his focus to the milking.

Vienna nodded in gratitude. "Thank you." She considered staying and talking with him, but she wanted to find Hattie first.

Returning to the house, she made her way upstairs.

She could see that Hattie had been there—her toy pony sat askew on the floor. But there was no little girl and no doll.

She retraced her steps to the kitchen, then wandered through the rest of the house, and out the front door. The garden and yard were still devoid of her daughter. Vienna glanced in the direction of the road but saw no movement. "Hattie?" she called again. "Hattie?"

The first splatters of rain were her only answer.

Her provoking concern began to expand, but a growing anger attempted to mask it. If her daughter could hear her and simply wasn't responding... Vienna marched in the direction of the pastures, her hair and shoulders beginning to dampen with the rain. But she couldn't see Hattie anywhere.

The rain fell more steadily as Vienna's panic swallowed up her irritation. Something must have happened to her daughter. At the Running W, there had been plenty of people about to help keep an eye on Hattie. But here...it was only her and West. The ranch that had looked so inviting to her earlier from atop the guesthouse roof now felt like a death trap with possible dangers lurking around every corner.

She went back to the barn. "West, I can't find her," she said without preamble. "She isn't in the house or the garden or by the pastures. And it's starting to rain."

"Hattie!" he hollered as he jumped up from the milking stool. He scaled the ladder to the hayloft but shook his head as he descended it just as rapidly. "She's not up there, either." His voice held the same sharp note of concern that Vienna's had.

She began to knead her hands together, feeling helpless and overwhelmed. "I've checked the yard and the guesthouse too. Where do you think she went?"

"Wherever it is, we'll find her." He started for the barn doors. "I'll check the pastures again."

A shudder ran through Vienna at the thought of her daughter getting too close to one of the horses or the cattle. She trailed West to the barn entrance, but she stopped to glance back at the cow. "What about the milking? Are you finished?"

"No."

They needed to find her daughter, but she hated to leave the poor cow only half-milked. "I'll finish. Will you—"

"I'll find her."

Nodding, she watched him dart into the increasing rainstorm outside. She dropped her chin nearly to her chest and whispered a prayer that West would be successful where she hadn't been and that Hattie would be found safe.

She warmed her cold, trembling hands and took West's seat on the stool. To her relief, it took just a few minutes more to empty the rest of the milk from the cow's udder. Vienna carried the full pail into the kitchen and set it on the table. "Hattie? Are you in here?" Only silence reverberated in her ears.

Tears threatened, but she willed them back. "She's going to be okay," Vienna whispered to herself. "She's going to be okay." West would find her daughter.

But as she attempted to strain the milk and finish supper, her shaking hands would hardly cooperate. She fled the suffocating feeling in the house to wait on the porch. Except the feeling followed her. Her chest felt too tight, her breath too shallow, her fear too large.

"Please, Lord," she pleaded, her eyes trained in the direction she'd seen West go. "If possible, keep them both safe."

"Hattie!" West yelled, his hands cupped around his mouth to amplify his shout. "Hattie girl, where are you?"

The beef cattle and the horses were huddled in groups inside their respective pastures, giving him a clear view in nearly every direction. But he didn't see what he wanted—what he needed. Where could the little girl have gone? Had she really wandered this far away from the house and the yard?

Rain blew into his face, but he couldn't afford to keep his chin down against the elements. He swung his head from one side to the other, straining to see any movement, any sign of his little girl. For that's exactly what she'd become—even before he'd married her mother. Hattie was as precious to him as he imagined a child of his own would've been. And he couldn't bear the thought of anything happening to her.

"Where are you, Hattie?"

When he reached the far corner of the horse pasture, he wiped the rain from his face. Vienna would be worried sick, wondering why they weren't back yet. He'd expected to find Hattie much sooner, too. His fear morphed into desperation. He'd promised Vienna he would find her daughter. But what if he couldn't? Or what if he did, and something awful had happened? What if they lost her?

Icy dread pounded through him just as he'd felt once before—and in that moment, he was no longer standing in a rain-drenched field but the ornately decorated parlor of his home in Pittsburgh.

You choose that life, his father had said, his tone as sharp and cutting as a dagger, his brown eyes dark as flint, *and you will never see your mother and sisters again. Do you understand me? If you become a cowboy...* He spit the word out as if it were a foul epithet. *You will be lost to us, forever. You will have failed in your duty as my son.*

West clenched his hands into fists as he tried to fight off the strong memory. What if he failed Vienna in this critical moment just as he'd been accused of failing his father and his family back then? Would she reject him, too? Would she look on him with the same loathing or disappointment that he'd felt then from every person he'd once cared about?

Helplessness and defeat drove him to his knees in the sodden grass. "I don't know where else to look, Lord." He was careful not to ask directly that he find Hattie. Even if he'd started to believe God loved him regardless of what he did or didn't do, West still couldn't bring himself to ask for what he desperately wanted right now. "But You do. So if You could just..."

A whimper reached his ears. He jerked his head upward and peered hard through the rain. Had the sound been human or animal? The sob grew in volume and he no longer had to guess at its source.

"I'm coming, Hattie. I'm coming."

He scrambled to his feet and rushed in the direction of her cries. Halfway down the line of fencing that surrounded the horse pasture, he spotted her. She lay on her back, her doll clutched against her chest.

"What happened, Hattie girl?" West asked as he scaled the fence and dropped beside her on the grass.

He couldn't tell which drops on her face were tears and which were rain. "I…" She sniffled. "I fell…off the fence."

"Where does it hurt?" He couldn't see any visible signs of broken bones or blood, but that didn't mean she wasn't injured.

Her hand lifted slowly to touch her head. "Right here."

Rolling her carefully onto her side, he gently felt her head. His fingers touched a large goose egg. Hattie winced and moaned again. It didn't take West more than a few seconds to piece together what had happened. She'd likely tried to climb the fence alone, and when she'd reached the top, she had tumbled off the other side and hit her head. Which likely meant she'd suffered a mild concussion. He could only be thankful the injury wasn't more serious. If she'd been knocked unconscious, and he hadn't been able to hear her whimpering, there was no telling how long it would have taken to find her.

"I'm going to lift you, okay, Hattie girl? Then we're going to get you back to the house and out of the rain, all right?"

Her pale lips whispered, "Okay."

"Hold tight to your doll," he said as he carefully scooped them both into his arms. He kept her pressed to his chest as he walked along the pasture.

"It's Hattie…the doll."

He had to cough to get his next words out of his mouth. "My apologies to you both."

Her innocent reminder and the fact West had been

led to find her brought the threat of tears to his own eyes. *Thank you, God*, he prayed silently. He might not have asked for what he'd wanted directly, but the Lord had mercifully granted it anyway, and West was more than grateful.

Before he could open the pasture gate, he looked up to see Vienna running toward them through the rain. She must have been watching for them on the back porch.

"What happened?" she asked as she threw open the pasture gate. "Is she all right?"

West carried Hattie into the yard, and then Vienna closed the gate behind them. "She fell off the fence at the far end of the horse pasture. She hit her head pretty good."

"Oh, sweetheart." She hurried to Hattie's side. "Is that what hurts?"

Instead of answering, Hattie started to cry some more.

"I know it must have been really scary to fall like that." Vienna clasped her daughter's hand in her own. "You're going to be all right, though."

She opened the back door for them. West went inside and straight up the stairs, where he placed Hattie gently on the bed.

"I think she may have a slight concussion," he said quietly to Vienna. "Being out in the rain probably didn't help matters, either. She's likely to come down with a cold." *Hopefully nothing worse than that.*

West prepared himself to offer Vienna comfort. After all, her own brother had succumbed to illness as a child. It would be more than understandable if the sight of her own daughter, lying pale and lethargic on the blanket, brought up painful memories and old fears.

But Vienna straightened her shoulders and brushed right past him, her mouth set in a determined line. "I'll get her dressed in her nightgown, warm a brick for her feet, and see if her head needs any tending. In the meantime—" she glanced over her shoulder at him "—will you go for the doctor, West?"

It took him a moment for her request to breach his surprise. Apparently Vienna had no shortage of courage when it came to her daughter. "Yes…yes, I'll go for the doctor." He looked once more at Hattie and started toward the door.

"Oh, and, West…"

He spun back around.

"Thank you for finding her."

He nodded once. "You're more than welcome."

"I had every faith that you would." She rewarded him with a brief but genuine smile.

Warmth spread outward from his heart until he didn't feel wet and cold anymore. Vienna's green eyes glowed with gratitude. And something more? Could it be a flicker of the tenderness he'd seen in them earlier, after her tumble off the ladder? He'd been hard-pressed not to cross the hairbreadth space between them and kiss her in that moment. Only Hattie's cry had stopped him.

The little girl's whimpering did the same right then. Breaking eye contact with him, and ending the charged moment, Vienna turned toward her daughter and began to soothe her cries.

West studied them, then turned to leave. Only this time he didn't feel like an outside observer. His earlier feelings about Hattie as his own little girl returned as he hurried to the barn to saddle up a horse and go for the doctor. He was part of a family again and that felt every bit as good as finding Hattie and bringing her home.

Chapter Thirteen

Kneeling on the floor on the opposite side of the bed from where Hattie and Vienna sat against the pillows, West lifted his sock-covered hands. He was pretending they were puppets.

"Hello, I am Mr. Sock," he said in a nasally voice, opening and closing his hand as if it were a mouth.

Hattie giggled, her face looking less feverish today. As West had suspected, the doctor had confirmed that the little girl had suffered a mild concussion from her tumble off the fence. She'd also developed a cold from the exposure to the rain and had been confined to bed the past two days. And for a girl as energetically busy as Hattie, the time convalescing had been arduous and long. So West had come with an idea he hoped would help to lighten her boredom this afternoon.

"But *you* cannot be Mr. Sock." This time he used a deeper, slightly British voice for the other sock puppet. "For *I* am Mr. Sock."

West shook the head of the first puppet. "What can we do, then? We can't both be Mr. Sock."

Back and forth he went with the silly argument,

knowing how ridiculous he must look and sound. But seeing Hattie's green eyes shining with happiness and Vienna's smile growing ever wider made his humiliation worth it.

"Very well," the second puppet intoned at last. "I shall be Mr. Stocking and you shall be Mr. Sock."

Vienna clapped her hands. "Bravo, bravo."

"Tell another one, Daddy West!"

He scratched at his head with one of the socks. "Another one?"

"How about a story this time?" Vienna suggested, leaning back against the headboard, her arm looped around her daughter. They made a lovely picture sitting there together. Especially Vienna.

Ducking his head to keep his thoughts from showing on his face, West pretended to be thinking of a story. "All right, I have one." He lifted one puppet and began to narrate. "This is a story about a girl named Golden Hair, who was walking through the woods one day..."

He moved his arm along the edge of the bed as though the puppet was walking, and as he did so, he hummed in a high-pitched tone.

This time both mother and daughter giggled.

West went on to tell the story of the girl with golden hair who wandered into the home of three bears. He made sure to give each character his or her own unique way of talking. When he finished, he stood and took a bow. Hattie, grinning from ear to ear, clapped her hands as her mother had earlier. Only Vienna couldn't seem to stop laughing long enough to join in the applause.

"What did you think, Hattie girl?" he asked as he took a seat on the edge of the bed.

The little girl grabbed one of the socks off his hand and tried it on her own. "I liked Little Bear."

"And what about you, Mrs. McCall?"

Vienna started into another fit of giggles. "I think… my favorite…" she finally managed to get out in a breathless voice "…was…Mother Bear."

"Oh, you liked me, did you?" West said in the falsetto he'd used to portray Mother Bear.

Wiping at her eyes, she nodded and laughed again. He loved making them smile, but what he loved best of all, was making Vienna laugh. It was that same pure sound of merriment that had struck him hard in the chest the first time he'd earned it. And he didn't wish for the sound to ever stop.

"I think your mother is making fun of me, Hattie."

She looked up at Vienna. "Are you making fun of Daddy West, Mommy?"

"What? Me?" She pressed a hand to her bodice as she shook her head. "Never." But her green eyes still sparkled with amusement.

West affected a sigh as though surrendering. Then, mindful of not jostling Hattie, he reached out to snag Vienna's wrist with one hand and tickled her in the side with the other.

"No, no, no," she protested as she tried wriggling out of his grasp, her shoulders shaking with fresh laughter. "You know I'm ticklish."

He grinned. "I seem to recall that fact, yes." West tickled her a second time.

"You have to give her a kiss now, Daddy West," Hattie said, her entire expression brimming with delight. "'Member? Mommy says if you tickle someone, you have to kiss them, too."

Vienna smiled, but West could see it was slightly forced. "That's just a little game for you and me, Hattie. Daddy West doesn't have to...to kiss me."

"Yes, he does." Hattie's brow was scrunched in consternation. "If I tickle you, I have to give you a kiss on the cheek. An-and if you tickle me, you have to give me a kiss on the cheek." She pointed her thumb at herself.

Still holding Vienna's hand, West sat up and gave a slow nod as if he were thinking the matter over. "Seems only fair," he heard himself admit aloud.

His heart started hammering at his ribs. What was he doing? Why had he agreed with the little girl? But he knew the answer at once. The idea of kissing Vienna, however foolish, had been on his mind ever since he'd caught her after her fall off the ladder. Seeing her courage and dedication in caring for her daughter and making her laugh with such abandon this afternoon had only entrenched the notion further into his mind.

"Yep, it's only fair, Mommy," Hattie repeated as she crossed her arms.

Tugging her hand free of his, Vienna used it to tuck her hair back into its coif. "I suppose it is only fair." Her almost panicked look belied her words.

"Give her a kiss on the cheek, Daddy West." The little girl pointed from him to Vienna.

How could he refuse her or his heart in that moment? He leaned forward at the same time Vienna did. For several heartbeats, nothing else in the room—or the world—existed, save for the two of them, as he placed a kiss against her smooth cheek. Hattie's cheer of approval sounded far away as West eased back to peer into Vienna's fathomless green eyes.

As wonderful as kissing her cheek was, he very

much wanted to kiss her lips, too. Would she approve or be angry with him? He supposed it was only natural, with them being married and spending so much time together, that his feelings would start to move beyond friendship now and then. But that didn't mean Vienna's had followed.

West rose to his feet. As he did so, he felt certain he saw the briefest flash of disappointment cross Vienna's face. Had she been hoping for a real kiss, too?

"Thank you for the kiss, ma'am." He pantomimed tipping his hat, which sent Hattie tipping over onto her side in another fit of giggles.

Vienna gently righted her daughter on the bed. "I'd better get her settled for her nap. There's lunch still waiting for you at the back of the stove." She scooted the pillows down for Hattie.

"Thanks," he said, smiling at her, then at the little girl. "Have a good nap, Hattie girl."

West gathered up his socks and left the room. A whistle naturally slipped from his lips as he made his way downstairs. Hattie was fully on the mend, the ranch was nearly ready for guests, and Vienna hadn't looked displeased after his kiss on her cheek.

After collecting his plate, he sat at the kitchen table. Each day he felt a little more like this place was theirs. He saw less of Chance's influence on Vienna, too. Creating a home here had clearly been the right thing to do for all of them.

"Did she go down all right?" he asked when Vienna came into the kitchen as he was washing his dishes.

She shot him a bemused smile. "It took a little bit. She couldn't stop talking about your puppet show."

"I'm glad she enjoyed it." Truth was, he'd probably

enjoyed it as much as Hattie. If not more. Making her and her mother laugh had become a priority of his and he'd been more than successful today.

Vienna took his clean plate from him and dried it with a towel. "Did you perform shows like that for your sisters?"

"A few times," he acknowledged with a nod.

His younger sisters, especially, had enjoyed his attempts to make them laugh. He'd like to think he would have done the same as an uncle to their children. The thought threatened to dissipate the enjoyment he felt this afternoon, so he set it aside.

"It was very sweet of you to do that for Hattie." Vienna put the plate in the cupboard.

West grabbed the towel to dry his utensils. "I'm glad I could help," he said before adding, "She's important to me, too."

"I can see that." Vienna turned to face him as he handed her the clean utensils. "And I hope you know how much I appreciate it. Although I am sorry she coerced you into giving me that…that kiss." Her face pinked before she spun away from him to put away the fork and knife.

He waited to speak until she peeked at him over her shoulder. "I wasn't coerced, Vienna." It was the truest thing he could say without revealing more.

"Weren't you?" Her eyes sparked with challenge as she gazed back at him. And possibly hope? "Oh, there's a letter for you in the parlor, by the way. It came today, from Howard Eaton."

West debated staying and talking or going and reading his letter. His eagerness to know the contents of

Howard's missive won out. "Hopefully he wrote to say he's found guests for us."

"I hope so, too," Vienna called after him as he headed for the parlor.

If the letter did contain good news, then West would be hard-pressed not to march right back into the kitchen and kiss Vienna properly this time.

Covering her heated cheeks with her hands, Vienna was grateful for a few minutes alone in the kitchen, while West read his letter. Not that she'd minded his teasing, even when it escalated into him tickling her. It had been nearly as welcome and wonderful as his kiss to her cheek had been.

Except the warmth she'd observed in his brown eyes, both here in the kitchen and earlier upstairs, filled her with equal parts elation and confusion. If West wanted to keep things friendly between them, and nothing more, than why had he looked as if he might kiss her for real? Why had his voice held a note of seriousness when he'd confessed that he hadn't been strong-armed into kissing her cheek?

Maybe she was only seeing what she wanted to see. Vienna sighed and lowered her arms to her sides. Given her own growing feelings for West—feelings that went beyond friendship—she was probably imagining things in his voice, eyes and demeanor that weren't actually there.

The realization brought a prick of regret—and a sudden longing to tear up the weeds that continued to invade her garden. Moving toward the back porch, she paused. West hadn't returned to the kitchen yet. Curious, she walked down the hall and into the parlor. She found him seated in front of the cold hearth, his head in his hands.

"What's the matter?" she asked, stepping closer, alarm pooling in her stomach.

West's head jerked up. "Just pondering Howard's letter."

"Which said?"

He glanced toward the other chair where the open letter sat. "He…um…hasn't been able to secure any guests for us yet."

"Oh." Her dread morphed into disappointment. And then fear. "What will we do, West, if he can't find anyone who wants to come here?"

Rising to his feet, he threw her a smile, but she knew him well enough to know it wasn't genuine. "We'll figure something out." He picked up the letter and stuck it back in its envelope. "We will," he repeated. Though it sounded as if he needed to reassure both of them and not just her.

"How long do we wait?" They'd have to pay back their loan, whether they ended up with guests or not.

West tucked the letter into his pocket. "I think we ought to wait another three weeks, at least, before we give up on Howard finding someone for us."

"And if we still have no one scheduled to come?"

"I'll travel back east myself if I have to," he said, his gaze determined, "to drum up business."

She crossed her arms, hating the idea of her and Hattie here alone. But if West's leaving meant securing the guests they needed, then she would endure it, somehow.

"I won't let you down, Vienna. Not again."

He touched her arm briefly, his expression resolute, and then he marched outside before she could respond.

Before she could tell him that she didn't doubt his determination or his ability to help. Before she could ask what he'd meant about not letting her down, again.

Five days later, a wrangler from the Running W brought the news that Maggy had gone into labor. Vienna thanked him for bringing her the message and promised she would drive over within the hour. She didn't want to miss the birth of her dear friend's baby.

She found West working on the bunkhouse they'd agreed to build near the guesthouse. It would be similar to the "dude pen" at the Eatons' ranch and would provide housing for any bachelor visitors. They'd both thrown themselves into work around the ranch since receiving the disappointing news from Howard. The renewed focus had kept Vienna's attention where it ought to be—on the ranch, and not on what West may or may not feel for her.

As she observed him, he paused in his hammering to cough. Was he getting sick?

"Are you all right?" she asked as she approached.

West straightened and whipped around. "Fine. Just a little cough."

"Would you be able to watch Hattie for me? Maggy is in labor and I'd like to be there for the baby's birth."

He nodded, his mouth lifting with a smile. "Of course."

"I'll wake her up from her nap and have her come out here with you, if that's all right."

"She can hand me nails like she was doing earlier."

And loving every minute, as evidenced by her daughter's particular displeasure at needing to stop to take a nap today.

"Wonderful. I'll go get her." Vienna started back toward the house, then turned around. "Are you sure you aren't getting a cold? You were out in the rain, too, West."

He shook his head. "No, I'll be fine. Do you want me to hitch up the horses to the wagon?"

His stubborn insistence reminded her of Hattie's, but she decided to keep that amusing fact to herself. "That would be great. I'll be right back."

She collected her hat and gloves before waking Hattie. The little girl didn't need any prodding to get out of bed after hearing she was to help West again. Vienna led her outside, where West had the wagon and horses ready and waiting.

"I don't exactly know what time I'll be back," she said as he helped her onto the wagon seat. "Supper is simmering on the stove, though, and Hattie needs to be in bed by seven."

West swung Hattie up and onto his shoulder. "Supper on the stove and bed at seven. We can remember that, can't we, Hattie girl?"

"Yep." She cheerfully waved to Vienna. "Bye, Mommy."

Vienna smiled, grateful to know she could trust West to take good care of her daughter. "Bye. I'll see you both later."

The drive to the Running W didn't take long, though in her excitement to see Maggy, Vienna had urged the horses to move quicker than normal. As she strode onto the porch and up to the front door, she realized this place no longer felt like home as it had for three years. It was the HC Bar that felt like home now, with her and

Hattie…and West. She pushed aside that last thought to knock on the door. Edward answered it right away.

"Vienna!" His tired expression brightened into a smile as he stood back from the door. "Come in, come in. Maggy will be quite relieved that you're here."

She entered the house, her gaze moving to the staircase. "How is she?"

"Doing well. The doctor thinks the baby will come this afternoon."

Vienna arched an eyebrow in surprise. "So soon?" she asked as she removed her hat and gloves.

"She's been in labor since late last night." Which explained the lines of exhaustion on the man's face. "Go on up. She's in our room."

Giving him an encouraging smile, Vienna headed up the stairs and down the hallway. She knocked softly on the correct door. Someone murmured, "Come in."

She slipped inside the room. "Hello, Maggy." Her friend was sitting up in bed, her face paler than normal but glowing with determination.

"Vienna, you made it!" she said in a winded voice. "And just in time."

Squeezing her eyes shut, Maggy reached out a hand toward Vienna. The doctor stood on the opposite side of the bed and appeared to be laying out his instruments on a clean towel.

"Dr. Cartfield." Vienna acknowledged the man with a smile as she clasped her friend's hand in her own. He'd been the one to attend her at Hattie's birth.

He smiled back. "Mrs. Howe."

"She's not…" Maggy opened her eyes and frowned at the doctor. "She's…Mrs. McCall now," she panted. "Vienna married West McCall."

"Ah, my apologies, then, Mrs. McCall."

Vienna shook her head. "That's all right." She was still getting used to the idea herself.

At that moment, Mrs. Harvey entered the room carrying a large pot. "Here's the hot water, Doctor." She set it down on the bureau and turned to Vienna. "Good to see you, love."

There was no chance to say anything else. Maggy cried out, squeezing Vienna's hand in a viselike grip, and several minutes later, the doctor announced the baby was coming. Mrs. Harvey assisted him, while Vienna kept a tight hold on her friend's hand and whispered words of reassurance—just as Maggy had done with her.

Less than a half an hour later, the baby's first cries echoed through the room. "It's a girl," the doctor declared.

Maggy's entire expression radiated happiness as tears spilled onto her flushed cheeks. "A girl," she repeated in awe. "I have a daughter."

Vienna squeezed her hand, then moved out of the way. Tears of happiness filled her own eyes. How precious the blessing of birth was and how wonderful that, like her, Maggy now had a daughter, too.

As the doctor finished seeing to Maggy, Mrs. Harvey helped get the baby cleaned, swaddled and safely into her mother's arms. "Have you and Mr. Kent settled on a name yet?"

"Liza." Maggy gazed lovingly down at her daughter.

"After Edward's sister?" Vienna asked as she assisted Mrs. Harvey in tidying up the bed and the room.

Her friend nodded and touched the sleeping baby's cheek. "Liza for her aunt and May for her grandmother.

That was my mother's name." Vienna could well identify with the wistfulness of Maggy's expression. She had also felt a keen longing for her mother after Hattie's birth.

"I'll send Mr. Kent in," the doctor said once he'd gathered up his things.

Vienna followed Mrs. Harvey from the room as Edward rushed inside, his expression elated. It brought a small wave of sadness to her that nibbled at the happiness of the occasion. Chance hadn't been around when his daughter had been born, and even if he hadn't been in prison, Vienna wouldn't have wanted him there. But she couldn't help wondering what his reaction might have been at seeing his child, though it likely would have been no more than the flat pretense of excitement he'd expressed in the letter he had sent her in response to the news.

West would surely be as ecstatic as Maggy's husband at the birth of his first child.

Her cheeks scalded with heat at the errant thought. She needed to get her hands and mind busy with something else. Mrs. Harvey, thankfully, welcomed her help in putting together supper for the Kents and the staff. Vienna spent the next few hours, happily cooking and talking with Mrs. Harvey. She'd missed spending time with her. But when Mrs. Harvey's questions turned from the dude ranch preparations to how things were going with West, Vienna just as eagerly excused herself to take supper up to the Kents.

She didn't plan to linger long after delivering the meal, but Maggy offered to let her hold the baby. And Vienna couldn't resist. After she'd settled into the rocker in the corner, she accepted the warm bundle

Edward placed in her arms. Little Liza looked as if she might inherit her mother's rich red hair.

"She's beautiful, you two," Vienna said softly.

How well she could remember the awe she'd felt when she'd held Hattie for the first time. But the sweetness of this moment with Liza was cut short by the reminder that Vienna wasn't likely to experience such a precious time again. Hattie was no longer a baby. And Vienna's marriage to West was in name only, which meant she would have no other children.

Fresh tears swam in her eyes, but not for the reason Edward and Maggy would likely think. Why was she feeling grief over something she'd agreed to, had wanted even? Why did the thought of not being a mother all over again fill her with such sorrow?

She had so much in her life to thank the Lord for— her own beautiful daughter, a safe home and a kind friend to be her spouse and business partner. And yet, Vienna couldn't fully flatten the yearning growing deep inside her as she handed back the baby, bid the Kents and Mrs. Harvey goodbye, and drove home under a glorious sunset-stained sky.

It wasn't a pining she could really name, either. Just a feeling that whispered that what she'd once thought she hadn't wanted might very well be the very thing she wanted, after all.

Chapter Fourteen

When West woke the following morning, he felt as if he'd been struck by one of the boards he had hammered into place on the bunkhouse. His head and body ached, and his cough had gotten worse. He attempted to sit up, but the room tipped dizzily around him. Lying back down on the bed, he rolled onto his side and shut his eyes, telling himself he'd rise in a few minutes—once the aching stopped and the room stayed put.

The creaking of the door jerked him awake sometime later. "West?" Vienna stuck her head inside the room, her brow lined with concern. "Is…is something wrong?"

"No." He shook his head as he slowly sat up. "What time is it?"

She pushed through the door, ignoring his question for one of her own. "Are you sick?"

"I'll be fine, Vienna."

Her eyebrows jerked upward in obvious disbelief. "It's after eight in the morning and you're still in bed."

"It's all right, really." He went to stand, but his legs didn't seem to want to cooperate. As he sat back down, dread pulsed through him, along with his heart rate, at what should have been a simple matter of rising from the bed.

They couldn't afford for him to be sick, not now— not when the animals needed tending, and the bunkhouse needed finishing, and the furniture they had ordered for the guests would need to be unloaded from the delivery wagon and put inside. Not to mention what Vienna would think of him if he failed to help her, to be useful.

"You've got a fever," she said as she placed her hand against his forehead. The coolness brought him a measure of comfort until she lowered her arm. "Which means you need to stay in bed."

His concerns increased and threatened to swallow him whole. He had to keep working, keep helping, keep staying busy. Because while God might still like him even if West didn't always do what He wanted, his fellow human beings wouldn't. Including any guests who came to the half-ready dude ranch.

"It's just a little—" A full-throated cough cut off his own words.

Crossing her arms, Vienna leveled him with a look he'd seen her give Hattie—one that told him she wasn't giving in. "As I said, you need to *stay* in bed, West."

"What about the animals? Or the bunkhouse?"

She gently pushed him back against his pillow, and he let her as the light-headed feeling returned. "We'll figure something out. Hattie was only down for a couple of days. You'll likely be the same."

A couple of days confined to his bed? She might as well have said a couple of weeks. "Vienna," he protested as she settled the quilt against his chest. Almost as if she'd recognized before he did that he was starting to feel chilled.

"Get some rest." She moved toward the door, where she paused to throw him a smile she likely meant to be encouraging.

But as she shut the door behind her, he didn't feel encouraged. He felt exhausted. Shutting his eyes, he offered a quick but heartfelt prayer, giving voice to something he hadn't thought he ever would do again. He asked God for what he wanted—a speedy recovery so he could get back to doing what he needed.

Judging by the angle of the light coming in through the curtains, West guessed it was early afternoon when he finally woke up again. It took him a moment to realize the pounding he heard wasn't inside his own head. The noise was coming from outside. He carefully rose to a sitting position, relieved when he didn't feel as dizzy as he had that morning. Getting onto his feet proved harder. He was panting by the time he stood and shuffled to the window.

West braced himself against the window frame and parted the curtains. Across the yard, he could see a figure in a split skirt kneeling on top of the bunkhouse roof as she hammered the shingles into place. Wasn't Vienna afraid of heights? She'd certainly grasped his hand in a death grip when they had ascended the ladder to view the ranch from the roof of the guesthouse. But there she was, working away as if she'd been scaling roofs all her life.

He tapped on the glass to get her attention, but it was evident she couldn't hear him over the sound of her hammer. Feeling as chagrined as he did proud, he returned to his bed. The few minutes on his feet had drained him of any energy his long nap had given him. He also felt too warm for the quilt. West threw it off to the side, but it wasn't long before he was pulling it over himself again.

Sometime later, a knock to the door stirred him to wakefulness. "Think you can eat a late lunch?" Vienna asked as she entered the room with a tray. Hattie followed in her wake.

"Are you sick, too, Daddy West?"

He wanted to deny it, but his entire body would have rebelled at the lie. "Looks that way."

"Do you want me to give you a puppet show?" the little girl asked as she scrambled up onto the end of the bed.

West managed to crack a smile. "Not now, Hattie girl. But thank you."

"Maybe tomorrow," Vienna told her daughter before setting the tray across his lap.

He frowned. Surely he would be up and about tomorrow, especially if he stayed in bed all day today. And one look at Vienna told him that's exactly where she intended for him to stay.

The warm bread and soup tasted good, even on this summer day. As Hattie chatted to him about playing with the cats earlier, Vienna went to the window and opened it. Fresh air filled the room. Though he hadn't eaten breakfast, West found he couldn't stomach much of the lunch, however good it smelled and tasted.

"Are you finished?" Vienna asked him as she came to stand next to the bed.

West nodded. "Thanks."

"Come on, Hattie." She took the tray from him. "We need to let Daddy West get some more sleep."

Had she intended for her daughter's nickname to slip from her own lips? Whether she had or not, he still liked hearing Vienna say it. Or maybe it was the tender way she was looking at him right now. It made her saying the name all the sweeter.

Hattie pouted, though she followed her mother. "Try to get some more rest," Vienna said, balancing the tray against her hip as she gently steered her daughter out the door.

"You going back up on the roof?"

She turned. "How did you know about that?"

"I heard the hammering." He motioned toward the window. "I thought you were afraid of heights."

Her face flushed, but her eyes glinted dark green with determination. "It's a good thing you only built the bunkhouse to be one story. I've been able to handle it."

"I don't doubt that." She was capable of far more strength than she gave herself credit for. A worm of uneasiness uncurled inside West at the thought. Had Vienna only accepted his plan and his hand in marriage because she didn't believe herself up to the task of running a ranch on her own?

She smiled at his compliment, unaware of his troubled thoughts. "Thank you, West. Don't worry about a thing. Please just rest so you can get better."

He didn't put up any protest this time, not even to himself. As the door clicked shut and he settled back beneath the blanket, he vowed he would be better by morning. He had to be. If not, he feared Vienna would realize she didn't really need him, after all. Then what would he do? He couldn't compensate for his guilt over her unhappy marriage to Chance if Vienna no longer required his help.

Even in his ill and feverish state, he recognized his concerns stemmed from more than making restitution. He hated the idea of someone else—someone he'd come to care a great deal for—no longer finding him useful. He'd lost one family; he wouldn't give up a second one without a fight. If that meant crawling around on his hands and knees because he was too sick to stand, he would do it. He would do whatever he had to in order to do the work they wanted—needed—him to do.

By suppertime, Vienna was more than exhausted. She'd seen to the animals, hammered half the shingles into place and finished sewing her second set of curtains for the guesthouse bedrooms. Thankfully there was enough soup left over from lunch so she didn't have to prepare another meal.

She gave Hattie some scraps of material to play with in the parlor, then took a tray up to West. He was sleeping when she ducked inside. Not wanting to wake him, she set the tray of food on top of the bureau. Was he still feverish? She probably ought to check.

Or was she simply looking for another excuse to touch his face?

Blushing, she marched to the bed and placed her hand against his forehead. It still felt warm to the touch; possibly even warmer than earlier. He'd probably appreciate a cool cloth. Vienna left the food for now, and after checking on Hattie, she wet a cloth in the kitchen sink and wrung out the excess water.

West didn't appear to have stirred in her absence. Pushing aside a lock of his black hair, she placed the cloth across his forehead. His expression immediately relaxed. She meant to leave then, but instead, she found herself staring down at him.

He was still as handsome as the day they'd first met, though he looked older. Not that age had diminished his good looks. If anything, he'd grown handsomer with age and familiarity. Except he wasn't just her friend anymore or a fellow worker at the Running W. West was now her husband.

The yearning she'd felt after attending Liza's birth yesterday rose sharply inside her once more. Was it possible that West might one day feel more for her than the sort of caring that came with being friends and business partners? Did Vienna even want more than that?

She stepped back and folded her arms tightly against the swirl of emotions such questions inspired. She wouldn't soon forget, if ever, the consequences of falling in love with someone who wouldn't or couldn't love her back. She could well recall the loneliness and anguish of feeling her own love die when faced with her husband's indifference and abuse. If she let her heart have sway toward West, she could very well end up in a similar spot within her second marriage.

But even as that possibility made her heart speed up with fear, Vienna reminded herself that this time was different. West did care about her and Hattie, and she knew without a doubt that he would never lift his hand in anger against either one of them. They were safe there, with him. And she needed to be satisfied with that.

Resolved, she slipped out of the room and softly closed the door—on West and her vain longings for more between them.

West wanted to be angry the next day when he woke to the discovery that he was still sick. But he was too miserable and dog-tired to feel much beyond the aches and pains and fever. Once again, his petition for what he wanted had been ignored. He wasn't any better—in fact, he felt slightly worse.

Frustration and vulnerability rolled through him at not being well enough to sit up or stand, but he was powerless to do anything other than stew. Even the muted light from between the curtains hurt his head. He covered his eyes with his arm, though even that action left him peaked.

He drifted in and out of consciousness, only waking when Vienna brought him a little something to eat or a cool cloth. She even managed to keep Hattie from coming into the room.

His sleep was peppered with bad dreams—ones in which Vienna coldly turned away from him as Lucile once had for not helping. He kept trying to pick up a hammer, but each time, the thing seemed to weigh as much as an anvil and he couldn't lift it, even with both hands.

West woke with a start to semidarkness. It had to be after midnight. A lamp burned low on top of the bureau and shone onto Vienna's blond hair as she slept in the rocking chair. She must have moved the chair from her room to his after putting Hattie to bed. Apparently to keep vigil over him.

At the sight of her, her beautiful face relaxed in

slumber, her watchful care evident, a measure of peace washed through him, eroding his misery and anger. He felt marginally better, at least for the moment. It wasn't just a change in his attitude, either. He thought he felt less fatigued and sore.

As if she'd sensed his wakefulness, Vienna suddenly sat up. "You're awake."

"So are you." For the first time in two days, he didn't have to struggle to smile.

"How do you feel?" she asked as she stood and approached the bed.

"A bit better."

Her fingers settled onto his forehead. "I think your fever broke."

"Good. Then I can get back to…" He let his words trail out as she stepped back and folded her arms. "Why are you frowning like that?"

One eyebrow rose. "Because you're still sick, West."

"But you said my fever broke."

She sat beside him, her expression compassionate. "Yes, it did, and that means you are on your way to getting better. You're not fully there yet, though."

He didn't need to hear her say any more. West could read her prognosis in her eyes. Another day in bed was what Dr. Vienna would order. Well, he was sick and tired of being in bed after two solid days of doing nothing but that. He'd show her that he was made of tougher stuff, too.

Sitting up, he scooted to the opposite side of the bed and set his bare feet on the floorboards. His breath whooshed out faster than normal, but he didn't feel light-headed. Only tired.

"What are you doing, West?" Her tone held an annoying note of patience.

"Going to check on the livestock."

She didn't react as he stood and wobbled a moment on his feet, beyond folding her hands in her lap. "The animals are fine. Hattie and I took care of them after supper."

"Still…" West searched his muddled brain for some excuse—any excuse—to escape the four walls of his room. He needed to prove he was closer to being better than Vienna thought. "I…I left my tools outside the other day."

"They'll be fine until morning when *I* will put them back in the barn."

He made it to the bureau and managed to wrest open the top drawer. "What if it rains?"

"There was a clear sky at sunset tonight."

Grunting instead of arguing with words this time, he pulled a shirt from the drawer. He slipped his arms into the sleeves and began to button it overtop his pajamas. "I'll just double-check."

She sat there, saying nothing more. Instead, she watched as he grabbed a pair of trousers and socks next.

"Do you mind…"

He meant to ask her to wait in the hall while he changed, but his good intentions weren't the only things petering out. His energy was draining from him like water through a sieve. He steadied himself with a hand on the bureau, the pants and socks tumbling from his grip. The enormity of the task ahead of him—getting dressed and retreating outside—crashed over him. Defeated, he sank into the rocking chair.

Wordlessly, Vienna came over and picked up his clothes from off the floor. She tucked them back into their respective drawers, then knelt in front of him.

"West, look at me."

Her hand came to rest on his knee, making it impossible for him to ignore her presence. Not that he really wanted to anyway. He just couldn't bear to see the impatience in her eyes when he looked at her.

Finally, he pulled his gaze to hers. It wasn't exasperation he saw there, though. It was gentleness, empathy and kindness.

"I know you hate staying in bed, and I don't blame you one bit for not wanting to be there." She offered him a sweet smile. "But you're sick, and the only way to get out of bed sooner is to take care of yourself."

Her words rolled reassuringly through him. As much as he wished it otherwise, she was right. He was still sick, fever or not, and his petition to recover quickly hadn't been granted.

"I don't want to let you down," he admitted in a low voice, covering Vienna's hand with his own. "All over again."

Her eyes widened in obvious surprise. Perhaps she didn't blame him as he blamed himself. He didn't see how that could be, but her next question confirmed it. "When did you let me down the first time?"

"With Chance." The confession scraped against West's dry throat as it left his tongue, but in its wake, he also felt a great unburdening. "I encouraged you to court him, Vienna. But if I'd known what he was really like, what he was capable of, I never would have pushed you in his direction." He glanced down at the floor. The weight of his guilt felt lighter, but it was still there.

Vienna's grip tightened on his knee. "West..." She paused until he looked at her again. "You are not responsible for Chance's choices. Or mine. I pursued a courtship with Chance Howe of my own free will and volition."

"I still feel like it's my fault," he said, shaking his head with regret. "I knew how vulnerable you were back then." He couldn't bring himself to mention that he knew some of her vulnerability had likely stemmed from him curtailing anything more than friendship between them. He'd had so little to offer Vienna in comparison with Chance. "I've tried to make up for it, and I'll keep try—"

She withdrew her hand at once. "What do you mean make up for it?"

"Well, helping you and Hattie, for one."

Her face seemed to drain of color. "Is that your reason for being here, then? You felt responsible for everything with Chance, so you decided to assuage your guilt by helping out his widow and daughter?" She shot to her feet and folded her arms against him.

"No." His head had begun to throb—both at sitting up and the abrupt turn in the conversation that he hadn't anticipated. "In part, that's why I wanted to help you. But that isn't the only reason."

She gazed at something across the room, her expression tight. "What were your other reasons?"

Hadn't they already gone over this when they'd first discussed their plan? "I needed a ranch, and you needed a home and someone to ward off unwanted marriage proposals."

"You're right," she conceded, falling back a step.

But West felt no triumph. "And also because we're friends, Vienna."

"Yes, we are friends, aren't we?" Why did the question sound laced with pain?

Shaking his head again, he stared down at his hands. "I'm sorry. I'm still not feeling well, and I've made a mess of things. Do you mind if we finish this conversation later?"

"Of course." She nodded once. "I can help you back to bed."

He allowed her to assist him onto his feet, and then he mostly managed to do the rest on his own. Once he was back in bed, he caught her eye. "Thank you for all of your help."

"You're welcome." Vienna moved toward the bureau. "Do you want the lamp?"

"No." He only wanted to sleep. Maybe then he could escape the questions over what he'd done and said that must have been wrong or why the light had gone out of Vienna's eyes.

The instant she left West's room and set down the lamp, the tears came. Vienna covered her mouth with her hand to stifle any noise. As the salty moisture ran down her fingers, she slid to the floor.

West had largely married her out of obligation, as a way to atone for his guilt. No wonder she'd overheard him tell Alec that love wouldn't be a factor in this marriage of convenience. It was an arrangement between friends—nothing more, nothing less. She'd known that, both when West had proposed the idea in the first place and when she'd finally agreed to it.

Vienna had been more than happy to keep things uncomplicated between them, too, as they went forward, creating a dude ranch and a home. So why did she feel as if her heart had been broken all over again?

Because I've fallen for him a little more each day.

The truth of that thought sent another splinter of pain through her chest. Resting her head back against the wall, Vienna shut her wet eyes and drew in a shaky breath. It wasn't just that she'd come to care for West as more than a friend. She'd foolishly hoped he was beginning to feel the same way. But she'd been wrong—again. And ridding herself of such hope would likely prove to be as painful as the realization that tonight her fledging hope had died.

Chapter Fifteen

The next two weeks passed in a tiring but satisfactory whirlwind for Vienna. Keeping busy helped ease the ache inside her heart. And while she had to divide her time between caring for Hattie, the ranch and West, she'd still finished the curtains for the guesthouse, experimented with simple meals West could make over a fire on pack trips, and overseen the delivery of the new furniture. Edward and several of his men had come over to finish the bunkhouse as well as help Vienna get all the furniture set up.

Vienna could tell it bothered West to watch others doing the tasks he'd expected to do. But he hadn't fought her again on staying in bed. Instead he'd been the model patient. He'd dutifully stayed in his room and had even helped keep Hattie entertained, while everyone else worked. Eventually he was able to walk up and down the stairs and eat meals at the table without looking so pale, but there were still noticeable lines of fatigue on his face when he came into the kitchen most evenings.

They hadn't revisited their conversation about the

past, and Vienna wasn't sure if she felt more relieved or troubled by that fact. She wanted to better understand West's guilt and why he'd encouraged her toward Chance in the first place. But to bring it up again would only be a painful reminder that, at least for him, their relationship had been founded on need, not want. And that wasn't going to change, no matter how much she wished it were different.

Vienna did miss their shared evenings in the parlor, though. They'd fallen out of the habit while West had been sick and Vienna had been busy around the ranch. She missed those nights of sitting in front of the fireplace and talking. But maybe the routine wasn't meant to last anyway. Once they had guests at the dude ranch, they probably wouldn't have the time or the privacy to keep meeting in the parlor like that. If they ever did get guests…

Shaking her head, she finished putting away the clean supper dishes. She needed to trust that God would heal her freshly wounded heart and that the ranch would thrive, however and whenever that might be.

A sound at the back porch had her turning in time to see West step inside the kitchen. "Animals are all set for the night."

Even knowing he'd only married her out of obligation, her heart still tripped at the sight of him. "Thank you."

"Is Hattie in bed?"

Vienna nodded. The kitchen was set to rights, too. Which meant perhaps they could talk tonight. "Would you maybe…" She had to push the question out her suddenly dry lips. "Well, I thought maybe we could talk, in the parlor. Like we used to."

"I'd like that, I really would, Vienna."

His brown eyes shone with a sincerity that made her pulse quicken even more. Could he have missed their nightly talks, too? Even if it was only as friends, she would welcome the time together.

"But," he added, throwing her an apologetic smile, "I can't tonight. I've got to be up real early tomorrow."

Her hopes tumbled to the floor and shattered, but she did her best to maintain a curious demeanor rather than a disappointed one. "Oh? Something important?" She couldn't think of anything that needed to be done first thing tomorrow morning.

"It's pretty important, yes."

When he didn't offer any further details, she nodded. "Then I'll say good-night."

"Good night, Vienna."

His gaze softened as he studied her a moment. It wasn't the first time she'd noticed him looking at her like that, either. There had been several times the last few days when she'd noticed him watching her in a new, almost affectionate way.

But it's only because we're friends, she firmly reminded herself.

She feigned interest in wiping the table, though she'd already wiped it earlier, until West left the kitchen. Then she dropped into a chair. She felt as tired and worn-out as the tattered, damp rag she clutched in her fist. It was exhausting trying to keep her own emotions in check and not read into West's actions things that weren't there. Hopefully they'd have guests soon— that would give her something else to focus on. Because with only the three of them on the ranch right now, she was struggling not to think about West all the time, and it was already more often than her poor heart could handle.

The next morning she woke to the smell of something cooking on the stove downstairs. *Strange*, Vienna thought. She must be dreaming. Reaching out to ensure Hattie was still asleep, her hand touched only empty blankets. She scrambled to a seated position to find she was the only one in the room. Where had Hattie gone? Had the little girl wandered off again?

Adrenaline pulsed through Vienna as she hurried out of bed, threw on her robe and pattered quickly down the stairs. Perhaps she ought to wake West first. But before she could spin back toward the stairs, the sound of laughter floated down the hallway from the kitchen. She moved toward the sound, relief and confusion battling inside her.

When she reached the kitchen doorway, she stopped short at the sight in front of her. West was working over a pan at the stove, while Hattie stood on a chair beside the table. A large bowl sat in front of her, along with a pile of eggshells.

"Hello, Mommy," her daughter said, waving. Her sleeves had been rolled back and Vienna's apron was triple tied around her waist. "Daddy West is teaching me how to crack the eggs."

Turning away from the stove, West waved to a chair with his spatula. "Have a seat."

"What are you…?" She sank into the chair, shaking her head in bewilderment. Maybe she was still dreaming. Except the smell of flapjacks was mouthwateringly real. "Why are you…?"

Hattie grinned at her. "It's your birthday, Mommy!"

Her birthday? Vienna's gaze jumped to the calendar nailed to the wall. With how busy she'd been, she had completely forgotten. But West hadn't. This must have been why he'd declined talking in the parlor last night, the reason he had to get up extra early this morning.

"I didn't think you could cook," she said, even as he set a heaping plate of flapjacks in front of her.

His eyes flashed with amusement as he poured maple syrup onto the stack. "I most certainly can. You just never asked." He threw her a grin, then turned to Hattie. "Are the eggs ready for scrambling, Hattie girl?"

"Uh-huh." The girl lifted the bowl and passed it to him.

Vienna took a bite of flapjack. "This is good, West. Really good, actually."

"Thank you, ma'am." He pretended to tip his hat to her before pouring the egg mixture into another pan.

She forked several more bites. "How come you didn't say anything when I told you about the camping meals I've been trying out?"

"Figured you enjoyed doing that," he said with a shrug. "And while I can cook, most of what you came up with is still better than what I know how to do."

Vienna gave him a pointed look. "*Most* of my cooking is better?"

"There are a couple of dishes I specialize in." A minute or so later, he expertly hoisted the pan and shoveled a portion of eggs onto her plate. "Breakfast happens to be one of them."

She couldn't argue there. "Then perhaps we ought to share breakfast duties."

"Me, too! I can help," Hattie exclaimed as she sat down. West got the little girl a plateful of breakfast before Vienna could even move.

When they'd all eaten, Vienna stood to do the dishes. But West blocked her way to the sink. "No dishes for you today."

"Oh?"

She couldn't think of a clever rejoinder. Not with West standing so close that she could see the lighter ring of brown to his eyes and smell the pleasant scent of soap on his freshly shaved face.

"As the birthday girl, you have the entire day to yourself."

Vienna fell back a step as much in surprise as to put some distance between them. "Which means?"

"No dishes, no cooking, no chores." He ticked the items off on his fingers.

A soft smirk leaked past her lips. She could hardly visualize an entire day not busily spent taking care of everything and everyone. "What am I going to do, then?"

"You can play with me," Hattie said, twisting on her chair to look at Vienna.

West nodded. "There you go. You can play with Hattie, or work in the garden, or read a book. But no regular chores."

"Daddy West is a bit bossy, isn't he?" She directed the words at Hattie, but she kept her gaze locked on West's.

His lazy grin sent her stomach tumbling with flutters. "Comes from working around stubborn wranglers for years."

"Are you insinuating that I am stubborn, Mr. Mc-Call?" She leaned slightly toward him.

He matched her stance, his gaze dancing with pleasure. "If the shoe fits, Mrs. McCall."

The fluttering became a swarm of butterflies dancing inside her. It wasn't just from hearing West call her by her married name, either—he'd said it before. It was the way he spoke it now, in a low voice, and the way he was looking at her that made this time feel different.

"All right, then," she conceded, sweeping past him to put her dishes in the sink. She hated how breathless she sounded. "I will not lift a finger to help today."

Hattie clapped her hands. "Hurray! I get to help Daddy West."

"Yes, you do, Hattie girl." He tousled her bed-head hair as he returned to his seat.

Tears of gratitude sprang to Vienna's eyes as she paused in the kitchen doorway. *Thank you*, she mouthed when West glanced over at her. Hopefully he sensed that she meant appreciation for all of it—the breakfast, his kindness to her daughter and his thoughtful birthday gift.

The smile he sent her way as he mouthed *you're welcome* said he understood. It also had her wishing she could go back to standing close to him again. She held back, because Vienna wasn't sure she could do so without breaching the distance to kiss him. And regardless of the intent yet affectionate way West had looked at her just now, kissing him would be a grave mistake.

Once more shoring up her determination to maintain their friendship and not try for anything more, Vienna headed back upstairs to get ready for the day.

* * *

West tiptoed across the floor so as not to wake Hattie. After shutting the door partway, as she liked it, he breathed a tired sigh of relief. Getting the girl to settle down and take a nap had proved far more difficult than he'd expected—and it didn't help that he could be so easily cajoled into reading her one more story. Especially when she looked up at him with those large, green eyes and asked, "Please, Daddy West." But three stories and a few lullabies later, the little girl was finally asleep.

Back downstairs, he cleaned up the remnants of lunch. He was glad to see that Vienna hadn't done it while he'd been putting Hattie down for her nap. Which meant she was probably out working in her garden again. After her initial reluctance, Vienna had seemed to settle in and enjoy her birthday.

West had been thinking for more than a week about what to give her as a gift. She'd done so much around the ranch while he'd been sick and had helped nurse him, too, and he'd wanted her to know her efforts hadn't gone unnoticed. A new dress or hat would likely have been appreciated, but he'd wanted to give her something special. Once he'd come up with the idea of giving her a day off from her usual work, he could hardly keep his plans a secret, especially last night when she'd looked so hopeful as she had asked him to join her in the parlor. He'd hated the blatant disappointment he'd seen in her eyes at his refusal, but West had hoped she would forgive him when she understood why he had declined her invitation.

She had appeared to do just that—to have forgiven him this morning—if the brightness in her green gaze and the pure joy in her smile were any indication. If only her overjoyed response had been directed at him personally and not just at his gift.

He shook his head at the foolish thought as he put the clean dishes away and scrubbed the table. There might have been times this last week when he'd thought he'd detected something more than kindness or friendship in Vienna's gaze. But any gratitude or compassion toward him on her part was likely a direct result of his being on his feet again and able to help her. Only West seemed to recognize that she didn't need his help as much as she probably thought she did. She'd handled the final preparations for the dude ranch well enough on her own.

Hopefully not too well, he thought with a frown, tossing his rag on the sideboard. He still hoped to be needed here, to feel as if he were a full-fledged partner in their dude ranch venture. *And possibly something more?*

He pushed aside the notion. Vienna didn't seem to want anything more from him than friendship and help. And he hadn't wanted anything more, either. At least not until the other night when he'd confessed his guilt over encouraging her toward Chance. His admission had brought back memories he'd set aside—of how he'd fallen in love with Vienna back then. How it had taken every bit of willpower he'd possessed to step back and allow another man to win her heart.

This time there was no competition from another man, but West wasn't sure Vienna's heart was available for winning anymore. Not after all she'd been through, and not when she and Hattie only needed a man around who was honest, responsible and dedicated—nothing more.

Forcing a whistle to his lips, he headed outside. He still had a couple of shelves left to hang in some of the guest bedrooms. Movement in the garden drew his attention. Sure enough, Vienna knelt among her plants and flowers. He switched directions, suddenly eager to talk to her, just the two of them.

"Enjoying the day?" he asked as he approached.

She shaded her eyes to peer up at him, her mouth lifted in a full smile. "It's been wonderful. Thank you, West." She glanced at the house. "Is Hattie sleeping?"

"Yep."

Her eyebrows lifted in mild surprise. "That didn't take you long."

"What can I say?" He crouched down next to her and plucked up a nearby weed. "I am a man of varied talents."

She laughed. "So I've learned." Clipping some flowers with her scissors, she added them to the pile on the cloth beside her. "What else is there I don't know about you? Are you an aficionado of romantic poetry? Or an accordion player in secret?"

"Afraid not," he said, settling on the ground. The shelves could wait. "I think by now, you know everything about me."

The instant the words left his mouth, he knew they weren't entirely true. Vienna seemed to know it, too. She gave him a long glance, then returned to her flower clipping. West wondered if she meant to say something more or not. Maybe he'd tackle the shelves, after all.

Before he could climb to his feet and make his exit,

she spoke. "There *is* something I don't know. Something I've wanted to know for a long time."

"All right." He sounded casual enough, but inside, his heart began thrashing around. What did she want to know?

Vienna sat back on her heels, her expression earnest. "Why did you encourage me and Chance?" She lowered her gaze to the blooms in her hand. "Back then, I'd thought that maybe you…"

"Had feelings for you?"

Her chin whipped up. "Yes," she half whispered.

"That's because I did." He feigned interest in the road and the piece of grass he tore free from the ground. Anything to avoid seeing the possible hurt or condemnation in her green eyes.

He heard her breath exhale in a slow whoosh as if she were gathering the courage to say something. "Why didn't you tell me that?"

"I wanted to…" How much she might never know. "But if I had, then you might not have given Chance a fair shot."

From the corner of his eye, he saw her shake her head. "I—I don't understand."

"I wanted you happy, Vienna." Tossing aside the piece of grass, he finally looked at her, silently pleading for her to understand. "I knew how important a home was to you, even back then. What did I have to offer? A foreman's wage and no house. I thought that, at least with Chance, you would have a ranch and a home right away."

Silence met his words, though the play of emotions across her face was as easy to read as if she'd shared them aloud—confusion, consternation, regret and acceptance.

"You didn't give me a choice," she said at last.

He hung his head. "No, I guess I didn't. And I'm sorry for that. But I thought I was doing the right thing. The thing that would bring you the most happiness."

"I should've known." West wasn't sure if she was talking more to herself or to him. "It made no sense at the time, but it does now."

West regarded her warily. "Can you see why I blame myself for how Chance treated you? If I hadn't stepped aside, believing I knew what was best for you—if I'd told you instead what I really felt for you…"

"I can see it, yes. But as I said before, you're not to blame, West. Each of us made choices." She rested her hand on his sleeve. "I could've chosen to ask why you pushed me toward Chance. And I could've chosen not to marry him."

Things might have turned out differently if they'd each made different choices, including Chance. But just because things hadn't worked out as West or Vienna might have wanted didn't mean they hadn't worked out properly in the end. After all, it was he who was married to her now.

"Thank you for telling me all of that, West." He could tell she meant the words, but she still withdrew her hand from his arm after saying them and fiddled instead with the scissors in her lap. "Actually, there's something I…I need to tell you, too."

Before he could ask what it might be, someone called to them from the direction of the road. It was the postman. West climbed to his feet to greet him. After they'd exchanged pleasantries and briefly discussed the fine, dry weather, the man handed West a letter. The return address was the Custer Trail Ranch.

"It's from Howard," he told Vienna after the post-man departed.

She stood, her expression as anxious and hopeful as his must be. "Do you think he secured some guests for us?"

"I hope so." West tore open the envelope and pulled out the letter. He skimmed the opening paragraph, searching for news about their potential guests. Then he found it.

Alec went home for a visit the other week, and while there, he was able to drum up interest in your dude ranch among his friends and their fam-ilies. Expect your first twelve guests to arrive on the eighth of September. Congratulations, West!

"Well?" Vienna stepped closer. "What did he say? Do we have guests?"

He dropped the letter to his side, his shock giving way to elation. "We have guests."

"We…" Her eyes widened.

West grinned at her. "We have guests," he repeated.

Covering her mouth with her hand, she shook her head in disbelief.

"We have guests, Vienna. We actually have guests coming in eight days."

She gave a startled laugh. "Eight days? Will we be ready?"

"We're practically ready now," he said, tossing the letter into the air. "And we're going to have guests!"

Too full of jubilation to just stand there, he lifted

Vienna off her feet and swung her around as he'd done outside the bank all those weeks ago. She laughed, the sound every bit as joyful as the news itself.

"How did they do it?" she asked when they stopped spinning. Her hands remained wrapped around his neck—a fact West didn't find unpleasant in the least.

He tipped his head in the direction he'd excitedly flung the letter. "It was Alec. He went home and talked to his friends and their families."

"That was rather noble of Alec. To do that for us."

He peered down at her. "Are you wishing you'd married him instead?" He'd meant the question to sound teasing, but it came out more serious than he'd intended.

"Maybe." A playful smile lifted the corners of her mouth.

"But you didn't. You married me."

Her eyes resembled deep pools of green. "Yes, yes, I did," she whispered, drawing West's attention to her lips.

A faint thought in the back of his head made him pause. Vienna only wanted to be friends, and if she cared more for him than that, it was only because of how he'd helped her. But the reminder was lost when he noticed the smudge of dirt on her cheek.

"You have a little…" West lifted his hand to cup the side of her face. Using his thumb, he brushed away the dirt, though he couldn't help caressing her cheek a second time after the smudge was gone.

He fully expected her to retreat in the wake of such an intimate gesture, one that surely breached the bonds of their friendship. But Vienna didn't step away. Instead, she leaned into his hand and shut her eyes.

It didn't take longer than a single heartbeat for West to make a decision. He narrowed the distance between them and kissed Vienna on the lips. Their sweet familiarity filled him with wonder and delight—even the good news about their coming guests couldn't compete. West had kissed her once before, years ago, but as wonderful as that had been, that experience still paled in comparison with how right and amazing it felt to kiss Vienna now.

It was only later, after he stepped back and reluctantly left her in the garden so he could hang the shelves, that he questioned if he'd made a mistake in kissing her. It certainly wasn't in keeping with their plan to simply remain friends. Vienna hadn't seemed angry with him, though. Not during the kiss or afterward. Then a sudden thought had him grinning foolishly to himself for the rest of the afternoon.

He might have been the one to initiate the kiss, but Vienna had definitely and willingly kissed him right back.

Chapter Sixteen

Vienna tried concentrating on the conversation and the food surrounding her. After all, this occasion was in her honor. The Kents had invited her, Hattie and West to dinner to celebrate her birthday, even if it was a day later. But no matter how enjoyable she found the talk about the baby or how delicious Mrs. Harvey's cake tasted, Vienna couldn't keep her thoughts or her gaze off West.

Yesterday had been one of the happiest days she'd experienced in a long time. It hadn't just been having an entire day without work, either. There had also been the news about the guests, then her and West's wonderful kiss in the garden, and an evening spent talking with him in the parlor as they ate corn he'd rummaged up from somewhere and popped over the fire.

She smiled down at her plate at the march of happy memories through her mind, including West's confession yesterday about having had feelings for her in the past. Vienna had nearly told him before the postman's arrival that she *still* had feelings for him, ones that went beyond friendship. But she was secretly glad she'd been interrupted.

While she guessed West wouldn't have kissed her if he wanted to simply remain friends, she couldn't ignore the possibility that, for him, their kiss may have only been the outcome of a thrilling moment. A rush of emotion inspired by the realization that their plans for a dude ranch were indeed moving forward. West hadn't kissed her again or taken her hand in his, though Vienna couldn't help noticing he seemed especially happy since yesterday. Was that because they were going to have actual guests or was it because of her? She wanted to ask him, and yet she feared the answer.

"Vienna?"

She whipped her chin up to find everyone watching her, including West. Blushing, she shook her head. "I'm sorry. Did you ask me something, Maggy?"

"Do you want to come up and see Liza?"

Vienna nodded with genuine eagerness. Before she could push back her chair, West hopped up to help her. "Thank you," she mumbled, once more aware of Edward's and Maggy's gazes. Mrs. Harvey had already taken Hattie to the kitchen, stating, "This way the grown-ups can talk."

Vienna followed Maggy out of the dining room. Her friend threw her a searching look as they started up the stairs, but Vienna ignored it. She asked Maggy about how the baby was doing. It was the perfect way to deflect any questions from her professionally inquisitive friend. Maggy chatted happily about Liza and how big she'd grown as they made their way down the hallway.

Inside the nursery, Maggy lifted the sleeping baby from the cradle. Vienna moved closer for a peek. "She

has grown." She smiled at Maggy who beamed with
motherly pride.

"Do you want to hold her?" Her friend tipped her
head toward the rocking chair in the corner of the room.

"Yes, please."

Vienna settled into the rocker and Maggy passed the
baby to her. The sweet scent of baby powder wafted
over her as she cuddled Liza closer. "I think she's going
to have hair every bit as red as her mama's when she
grows up."

"Which is fine by me," Maggy said, taking a seat on
the rug. "As long as she inherits her father's patience."

The baby yawned, then blinked blue eyes up at Vienna. "Hello there, little Liza. I have been completely
remiss in coming to visit you and your mother." She
shot Maggy an apologetic smile. "Things have been
so busy at the ranch, what with Hattie and West both
sick. But still, that's no excuse."

"You're forgiven. Speaking of West, though…" Vienna didn't miss the interested gleam in Maggy's blue
eyes. "Has something happened between you two?"

She shrugged and pretended to be busy adjusting
Liza's blanket. "No."

"Really? Because neither of you ate much tonight
and you couldn't seem to stop glancing at each other."

"Oh?" Maggy's statements were true for Vienna, but
she hadn't noticed West behaving in a similar manner.
The possibility that he might have been had her heart
traitorously thrumming faster.

Maggy leaned back on her hands and regarded Vienna for so long that she shifted nervously in the rocking chair. No wonder her friend made such a good

detective. One probing look from Maggy Kent and the culprit was ready to spill everything.

"You've kissed him, haven't you?" she finally exclaimed in a loud voice as she sat up straight.

Vienna glanced at the door. "Not so loudly, Maggy."

"Sorry." But the full smile that lifted her mouth held no trace of remorse. "I knew it. I just knew it."

Vienna sighed—there'd be no dodging her friend's curiosity now. Not unless she fled the room, which would only confirm whatever Maggy was thinking. "What did you know?"

"That you and West would eventually fall in love."

Staring out the window, Vienna shook her head. "It isn't love. It was just…one kiss."

"But you do love him, don't you?" The gentleness in the question made it nearly impossible for Vienna to feel angry at Maggy for asking it.

She directed her gaze down at the baby in her arms. The longing she thought she had repressed rose sharply inside her once again. "Yes," she half whispered.

"Then it's perfect." Maggy scrambled up onto her knees.

Vienna leaned her head back against the rocking chair. "How is that perfect? West made it very clear that love wouldn't factor into our relationship. I'm right back where I was years ago, Maggy—in love with a man who doesn't love me back."

"He may have said that," her friend conceded. "But you aren't where you were before, Vienna."

She frowned at her. "Why not? How is this time different than the last?"

"Because West isn't acting like a man who is trying to push you away again."

Maggy stated the words with such sureness and finality that Vienna couldn't stop the seedlings of hope she'd already torn up from sprouting all over again. "Has he said something to Edward?"

"No." Maggy shook her head. "And he doesn't need to. I saw the way he watched you during supper." She reached out and touched Vienna's sleeve. "The way a man watches the woman he loves."

Could that be right? Did West feel more than friendship for her? Standing, Vienna placed Liza back inside her cradle. "What do I do?" She hadn't exactly meant to ask the question aloud, but she was grateful that she had. She trusted Maggy's advice.

"Tell him how you feel."

"Just like that?" She spun around to face her friend. "I go up to him and say, 'You know, West, I think I've fallen in love with you, even more so than the last time. Do you think you might possibly feel the same way?'"

Maggy laughed, but it wasn't unkind. "That sounds more like something I would say, but, yes, that works."

"Maybe after three years, your boldness is rubbing off on me," Vienna said with a wry smile.

Coming to stand next to her, Maggy linked her arm through Vienna's. "And I believe your sweetness and motherly instincts are rubbing off on me."

Vienna squeezed her arm. "You really think I should say something to him?"

"I do." Maggy released her and moved toward the cradle. "I need to feed the baby, but I'll make some excuse for Edward to come upstairs if you want time alone with West right now."

Her cheeks flushed at the thought of sharing her heart with him. She needed time to calm down, to decide what she wanted to say. "No, that's all right. I'll tell him tomorrow."

"Will you?" Maggy pinned her with a stern look as she lifted Liza into her arms.

It was Vienna's turn to laugh. "I will."

"In my experience," her friend said as she took a seat in the rocking chair, "it's better to say something sooner than later."

Vienna moved toward the door. "I'll tell him. I will. Thanks for the birthday meal…and for the advice, Maggy."

"My pleasure. For both."

Returning downstairs, Vienna was almost relieved to find the dining room empty. The men were probably outside. She'd have to wait until tomorrow, after all. But her pulse kicked up with trepidation at the thought of finally revealing her heart to West.

What if Maggy was wrong? Vienna might lose West as her friend, even if she would still have him as a business partner. If Maggy was right, though… Fresh hope bloomed within her like a summer flower in the sunshine and this time she let it.

Right or not, she didn't want to be timid about her own feelings any longer. It was time to share them with West—and pray she'd have the courage to embrace them or let them go once and for all.

West wiped his sleeve across his damp forehead as he studied the envelope in his hand. Who would be sending him a telegram? The messenger hadn't given him any clue, other than saying he had a message for Mr. McCall.

Maybe it was from Alec, he reasoned, confirming

that the dude ranch would be ready for the guests coming their way.

He glanced at the house, debating whether to open it now or wait until after he'd eaten supper. Vienna had mentioned this morning that she had something she wished to discuss with him when Hattie went to bed. So perhaps he ought to wait to read the message until after that.

Starting for the house, he paused, his curiosity getting the better of him. If the telegram was from Alec, West would want to share its contents with Vienna right away. He made a quick decision and opened the envelope. The first thing he noticed was that it was addressed to *Westin McCall*. Alec never called him that. Those who did, with the exception of Lucile, West hadn't seen in over a decade. And that sent his heart thudding with dread, even before he read through the short missive.

FATHER IS DYING. STOP. HE WANTS TO SEE YOU. STOP. PLEASE COME AS SOON AS YOU ARE ABLE. STOP. WILL WIRE MONEY IF NEEDED FOR TRAIN TICKET HOME. STOP. YOUR LOVING SISTER CORDELIA. STOP.

Questions and emotions swirled through him, making West feel as if he'd been caught in a dust cyclone. His father wanted to see him? It seemed impossible—both that the great Lawrence McCall could be dying and that he was willing to bury the hatchet because of it.

The words *loving* and *home* rankled. West didn't

consider any of his family particularly loving in their choice not to have contact with him. And Pittsburgh hadn't been his home for years. The ranch was his home now, with Vienna and Hattie. The realization brought a smile to his mouth, but it froze in place when he realized what his family was asking of him. They wanted him home—as soon as possible—and yet, his place was on the ranch, especially with guests arriving in five more days. He couldn't up and leave Vienna right now. While he might feel some obligation to his father and the family he'd been born into, West had a family here, as well, and they needed him, too.

But his father was dying. If West hoped for any sort of reconciliation between them, he would have to hurry to Pittsburgh and hope he didn't arrive too late. He glanced down at the telegram again and felt the familiar pull between what others wanted for him and what he wanted.

Pushing out a sigh, he stepped onto the back porch and headed into the kitchen. Vienna and Hattie were already seated at the table, and the little girl was saying the prayer. West removed his hat and shut his eyes as he listened.

"Bless me and Mommy," Hattie said. "And Daddy West and all the horses and the cows and the kitties…"

It wasn't the first time he'd heard Hattie pray. He'd listened to dozens of her prayers since he'd come to the HC Bar. However, tonight, hearing her innocent voice plead with the Almighty for him and Vienna and the animals, something deep inside him stirred with emotion and brought a film of tears to his eyes.

With this little girl and her beautiful, strong mother, West felt accepted. They didn't expect him to be anything other than what he was—a cowboy, a rancher, a husband and a father.

"West?"

He opened his eyes to discover the prayer was over and the pair of them were watching him. "Smells good," he said as he joined them at the table.

"Did the postman deliver some mail?" Vienna nodded at the envelope he still clutched in his hand.

Shaking his head, he set the telegram on the table and deliberately placed his hat over the top of it. There'd be time enough to discuss its contents once Hattie was asleep.

He tried to keep up a cheerful demeanor and maintain his end of the conversation, but he did a poor job of both, judging by the questioning glances Vienna kept throwing his way. Once they'd finished the dishes and Vienna excused herself to get Hattie into bed, West felt relief that he no longer had to pretend.

After slumping back into his chair, he removed the telegram from beneath his hat. Its contents hadn't changed, no matter how much he wished they had. Of all the rotten timing… If only the news had come sooner than now or later, in another month. But any sooner and he would have still been sick in bed, and much later, he might not have been able to get away.

"All right. What's the matter?" Vienna took a seat across from him.

He attempted a smile, but it felt more like a grimace. "You had something you wanted to say first."

"It can wait," she said, her cheeks coloring. "I'd like to know what's bothering you. And don't try to deny it, West. I can tell when something is on your mind."

He didn't see any point in arguing what was the

truth. "A messenger delivered this." He slid the telegram across the table toward her.

"It's a telegram." Her confused gaze rose to his as she picked up the paper.

Nodding, West waited for her to read the message. A soft gasp slipped from her lips, but he wasn't sure which part she found most startling. Or maybe it was the entire thing.

"I'm so sorry." She shook her head as she lowered the telegram, her expression sorrowful. "Do you want to go and see your father?"

West shrugged and fiddled with the brim of his hat. "To be honest, I don't know. A part of me does and another part of me feels angry that it's only now that he wants to make amends."

"I don't blame you for feeling that way at all." She set the message back in front of him. "There's a risk involved either way. If you stay here, you likely won't see your father again in this life. But if you go, the reunion with him and the rest of your family might not be what you hope."

He wasn't surprised Vienna had so succinctly articulated his own thoughts. Resting his elbows on the table, West pressed his forehead into his palms. "What do I do, Vienna? We have our first guests coming in five days, but if I wait until after that, he might not be there."

"I know."

"It will take me two days to get to Pittsburgh, which only leaves me one full day there before I'd need to head back."

She scraped back her chair and stood. "It's still enough time."

"Then you think I ought to go?" He lifted his chin to look at her, mild panic churning in his gut at her determined look. Did she no longer need him or his help?

Vienna gripped the back of the chair. "Family is important, West. This may be your only chance to make peace with your past. We'll be fine until you get back."

"Will you miss me?" He wasn't exactly sure what had compelled him to ask. But he needed to know he still had a place here.

Her green eyes softened. "Of course I'll miss you," she admitted quietly. Then with greater volume, she added, "So will Hattie."

"I'll miss you, too. Both of you." Any lingering fears melted when she returned his smile. "You sure you'll be all right until I get back?"

She nodded. "There will be much more to do when the guests arrive, and you'll be home then."

Home. West climbed to his feet, feeling relieved. He could do this—they both could. "Since most of our guests are coming from the Pittsburgh area anyway, I can join them on their train ride here." He gave her a long look. "I'll be with them, Vienna."

"I trust you."

He couldn't think of a greater compliment than that. As they regarded each other silently, words lodged in his throat—how much he would truly miss her, how much he'd enjoyed their kiss the other day, how much he wanted them to be a real couple.

That last thought startled him. Was that really how he felt about them now? He wasn't entirely sure, and he didn't want to say something until he knew for certain what he wanted. There'd be time enough on the long train ride east to consider his feelings and how best to share them later.

"I guess I'd better go pack."

Vienna trailed him down the hallway. "Will you leave first thing in the morning?"

"Yep." He paused on the stairs as he suddenly remembered something. "Did you still wish to discuss whatever it was you wanted to talk about?"

He thought she shook her head a little too quickly, but he might have imagined it. "There will be time enough for that when you get back. Right now, you need to pack, get some sleep, and in the morning, we need to get you on a train."

Chapter Seventeen

By the time West reached Pittsburgh, he felt turned inside and out and so tired he was sure he could sleep for a week straight. The fuzziness in his head from the cold he'd thought he'd shaken had returned, too. He scrubbed at his eyes as he stepped off the train, unsure who would be there to meet him at the station. He'd sent a wire ahead of himself, to let his sister know when he'd be arriving. The swarms of people and noise pressed in on him, overwhelming and smothering. The collar of his Sunday suit choked his neck, and he wished he was wearing his old cowboy hat instead of the bowler he'd purchased. It wasn't the first time on his journey that he missed the familiarity and openness of his home out west.

"Westin!"

He turned toward the feminine voice to find a stylishly dressed woman pushing through the crowd toward him. Strands of dark brown hair, as curly as his own, framed her face beneath her feathered hat. Cordelia looked older than he remembered, though still as pretty and poised as she'd been more than ten years ago.

West wasn't sure how to greet his sister. Would she act formal and distant? Or pleased to see him? But when Cordelia reached him and clasped him in a tight hug, he warmly returned the embrace.

"Look at you, baby brother," she said, stepping back and adjusting her hat. "You look old."

He grinned as memories of their old banter returned to his mind. "Why, thank you, Cordy. You're looking well-aged yourself."

"Cordy," she harrumphed, though her brown eyes danced with pleasure. "I haven't heard that nickname in far too long." She linked her arm with his, then glanced with raised eyebrows at his single suitcase. "Is that all you brought?"

He could well recall the numerous pieces of luggage she and their mother and sisters had insisted on bringing on every trip, no matter how short. "Yep, this is it."

"Very well," she said with a frown. West wasn't sure if it was his Western vernacular or the simplicity of his baggage that bothered her. "The auto is waiting for us."

It was West's turn to be surprised. "Auto? Father owns an automobile?"

"Nonsense. You know how old-fashioned Father is." She began tugging him toward the exit. "The automobile is for me and James to use."

Cordelia chattered away about her husband, James, their two daughters and their son. She hardly paused to let West comment. By the time they reached the automobile, his ears were ringing.

"You don't have to put on a good face for me, Cordy," he said as he settled in the back seat beside her. His sister sniffed and turned to look out the open side of the vehicle as the driver pulled away from the station. "Who says it's for you?"

The rebuke, though spoken softly, still had the power to sting. West wasn't the one who'd stayed and watched their father age and become ill. "How is he?" he finally asked.

"We've said our goodbyes twice already, thinking he wouldn't live to see morning." She gazed at him with tear-filled eyes. "But I think he has been holding out for your return, Westin."

He glanced at the buildings they passed, nearly all of them unfamiliar to him now. "How did you know where to find me?"

"Lucile." He sensed Cordelia watching him. "She told me that she ran into you while she and Walter were in North Dakota. She said you were at the ranch with a pretty blonde woman."

When he made no comment, she continued. "I was happy to hear you'd moved on from Lucile's rejection. For what it may be worth, I never thought she was right for you."

"That's not what Father thought." He faced her again, the old hurt poking at him anew. "And none of you saw fit to contradict him, at the time."

Cordelia flushed, but she kept her chin tilted upward. "I may have acquiesced to Father's demands on some things, Westin. But that doesn't mean I never formed my own opinions on your choices." Her next words were barely more than a whisper, "Or wished I could have written to you."

"Why didn't you?" he couldn't help asking.

She studied her gloved hands. "I wanted to, so many times. There are still half a dozen letters that I started to write you tucked inside my desk drawer." Her gaze held a hint of pleading when she looked at him. "And I wasn't the only one, Westin. But James still works for Father. So I had to choose—my husband or my brother."

"I...I didn't know, Cordelia." He shook his head. "I just assumed you all felt the same, and agreed that I was no longer part of the family."

A wave of sadness and fatigue descended over him. Resting his head back against the seat, he shut his eyes. Did his mother and younger sisters feel the same as Cordelia? Had they also wished to stay in touch with him but hadn't wanted to cross Lawrence to do so?

"How have you been all these years?" she asked, her tone full of sincerity.

He opened his eyes and smiled at her. "I've been well."

"And you're in Wyoming now?"

West nodded. "I—we—are starting a dude ranch there."

"Oh, Westin, isn't that what you always wanted to do?" She smiled at his nod. "And by 'we,' I assume you mean you and Alec."

A flush heated his neck. "No, Alec is still at the Custer Trail Ranch in North Dakota, though he might be leaving there soon to do something else."

"So who is your partner, then?"

He feigned renewed interest in the scenery outside the automobile. "A friend," he hedged, not ready to divulge any more information just yet. He was still trying to understand his feelings for Vienna—he didn't need them being questioned or overly scrutinized by his sister. He was grateful when Cordelia didn't press him for a more specific answer.

"I'm sure the moment my little Jamie meets you that he is going to want to live out west, as well." She gave another sniff of amusement. "He's already infatuated with anything to do with cowboys."

West didn't miss the note of fear behind her words. "What would you do if he did wish to live that sort of life?"

"I…" His sister lowered her chin. "I don't know, to be honest. I can't imagine him living so far away, and yet, I want him happy, too. I suppose that's what every parent wants for their child—to know that they're happy, but also to be certain they are safe. It's challenging when those two goals seem to be in opposition."

Reaching out, he took her hand in his and squeezed it. "I look forward to meeting him, Cordelia. To meeting all of them. And I promise not to share too many wild tales of Western adventure. He still has a lot of growing up to do. Maybe he'll want to do something different."

"Thank you." She squeezed his hand back, then straightened her shoulders. "You'll be staying with Mother and Father."

Alarm shot through West as he released her hand. "Is that wise?" He'd been hoping to stay at her house or with one of his other sisters.

"Of course. Besides, it isn't as if you'll be there all alone. Anita and Lydia are there now."

Would his younger sisters be as welcoming as Cordelia? "Are either of them married?"

"They both are," she answered with a smile. "Anita married the son of one of father's old partners and has a daughter and a son. And Lydia shocked us all by marrying a successful department store owner. They have one daughter."

He chuckled. "I remember Lydia always did enjoy shopping, even as a little girl."

"Yes, she did. You'll likely meet her and Anita's families tomorrow."

Four nieces, two nephews, and two brothers-in-law to meet. West shook his head again in surprise. Life hadn't stopped moving forward, even with him gone.

"Here we are."

Peering past his sister, he caught a glimpse of the Queen Anne–style mansion where he'd grown up. It was enough to send his heart thrashing about inside his chest. He let himself out as the driver helped Cordelia from the car. Then with his bag in hand, he faced the house. It looked as cold and formidable as the last time he'd stood here, viewing it from the sidewalk. He remembered how his sisters had gathered at the large parlor window, their noses pressed to the glass, as they waved goodbye to him. His mother had stood behind them, her cheeks wet with tears. A lump settled in his throat at the memory and he coughed to dislodge it.

"Are you coming?" Cordelia paused halfway up the walk.

West straightened his hat and forced a nod. "I'm right behind you."

She didn't bother to knock on the imposing front door. Cordelia simply let herself in, calling out, "Mother, we're here."

After shutting the door behind them, West set down his bag and hat and faced the grand staircase. More recollections crowded his mind. Times when he'd sailed down the banister, only to be soundly scolded by his father for such ungentlemanly behavior. Maybe that was another reason West had chosen the profession he had—as a cowboy or rancher, he could still be a gentleman but without all the formality and rules he'd known as a child.

Two grown women rushed down the stairs. West registered the familiarity of their faces before they simultaneously threw their arms around him. "Westin, you're home!"

He eased back with a laugh to get a good look at them. "I think I'm in the wrong house, Cordy," he teased. "I don't recognize these two women at all. I'm expecting two girls in braids."

Anita arched dark eyebrows at him, but he could tell she was trying not to smile. "You aren't exactly young and spry yourself anymore."

"But as charming as ever," light-haired Lydia said, hugging him again.

Over their heads, he caught sight of another figure descending the stairs, far more demurely than her daughters. "Mother?"

"Westin? Is it really you?" She paused on the last step, her hands rising to cover her mouth.

He'd never thought he would see her again, and now his mother stood before him. West crossed the entryway toward her. "It's me, Mother."

She wrapped him in a hug, the well-known scent of her perfume encircling him, too. "Oh, my boy. My boy. You're home."

The welcome reception from all of them pushed back at the dread that had become a rock in his stomach the last hundred miles or so on the train. But as much as West appreciated the chance to see them and recapture some of the warmth he remembered from the past, he wasn't a boy anymore, and this wasn't his home. Like the four of them, he, too, had lived a life of his own—away from here.

"How…how is he?" West asked with a glance toward the ceiling as he released her.

Tears glittered in his mother's dark eyes. "The doctor says he likely won't make it to the end of the week."

"We believe he's been waiting for you," Lydia piped up from behind.

He turned to find his sisters eagerly watching him. It wasn't difficult to read the hope in each pair of eyes— hope that finally their family would be reunited. But what if they were wrong? What if their father didn't want to reconcile as much as reprimand West one final time?

"Would you like to see him now?" his mother asked.

West forced himself to nod and follow her up the stairs, though inside he felt like a goose headed for the chopping block. He spied new furnishings, paintings and knickknacks, but everywhere he looked he also saw the shadowy wisps of memories.

His father's room was shrouded in semidarkness, the curtains drawn tight against the summer evening. A single lamp burned on a nearby table and its glow only reached the foot of the bed. At its head lay an unmoving figure with a face as white as the sheet that covered his chest.

"Lawrence?" West's mother leaned over the figure. "Dearest, Westin has come. He's here."

The voice that replied didn't sound like the strong, bellowing one West well remembered. "Westin?"

"Yes, Lawrence. Westin is here." His mother stood back and motioned for West to take her place.

His lungs tightened with anxiety as he approached the bed. "H-hello, Father."

The sunken eyes that gazed up at him looked nothing like his father's. Neither did the thin, wasted lines of the man's aged face. But the hand that reached for West's and gripped it with surprising strength was familiar. How often had this same hand clasped his shoulder during a moment of correction or offered him a hearty handshake in a rare moment of pride?

"Westin," his father said hoarsely. "You are back."

He shot a confused look at his mother. Did his father think he was back for good? "I'm here, yes. I wanted… wanted to see you."

"Sit."

Grabbing a nearby chair, West took a seat. "I was sorry to hear you're sick, Father."

"Not sick." Lawrence gave a slight shake of his head. "I'm dying."

West glanced down at his lap, unsure what to say.

"I didn't know if you would come."

West nodded slowly. "At first, I wasn't sure I would, either." It was the most honest exchange he could recall between them.

"I told your older sister…" His father exhaled a heavy sigh as if his earlier admission had robbed him of the energy to keep speaking.

Resting his elbows on his knees, West leaned forward. "You told Cordelia what?" he prompted.

"That she was foolish to send for you."

Cold trepidation ran through him. Had he wasted

his time in coming all this way? "So you didn't wish to see me?"

"No," Lawrence barked. "I wanted to see you, but…" He turned his face away. "I knew you wouldn't come back to…to take my place."

West didn't bother to hide his shock. A glance over his shoulder revealed that his mother had slipped from the room, leaving him and his father alone.

"You hoped I would come back and take your place at the bank? That's why you wanted to see me?" Frustration sharpened his tone and strangled his fear. After all these years, his decisions and the life he'd created for himself still weren't acceptable. Still weren't good enough for Lawrence McCall.

His father shut his eyes. "Of course I wanted that… it's what I always wanted." Another heavy sigh eased from his pale lips. "But I knew it was foolishness to think *you* would want that. Still, Cordelia thought you ought to have a chance to decide for yourself…before I hand everything over to James."

The surprises were coming almost too quickly to register in West's mind. Cordelia had cared enough about him to see if he wanted to take over his father's company in lieu of her husband? He thought back to what she'd said in the automobile. *I had to choose— my husband or my brother.* She'd chosen the former in the past, but this time, she was willing to let West decide for all of them.

"You don't want that, do you?" His father faced him again, all of the fight gone from his expression.

West studied his hands. Even dressed in his best suit, he didn't feel like a businessman. And yet, he knew his next words could potentially either restore his family to him for good or reopen the chasm between them.

Family was important, and being back here, he realized how much that was the truth, how much he had missed them—all of them. But bowing to his father's wishes this time would come at an even greater cost than the one he'd paid when he'd walked away years before. He had more than himself and his dreams to think about now. There was Vienna, his wife, and Hattie, his daughter. And their friends and the guests to the dude ranch.

"I recently acquired a ranch," he said quietly. "A beautiful spread with a house and a barn and plenty of pasture."

When his father made no comment, West continued. He described the guesthouse, the bunkhouse, the livestock. Then he went on to talk about Vienna and how he'd married her so they could run the ranch together. He told his father about Hattie and the day she'd been lost and how he couldn't have been more scared if she'd been his own flesh and blood. He talked about teaching the little girl about horses and life on a ranch and how he hoped she would come to love the land as much as he did.

"It's not an easy life." He shifted on the hard chair as he gazed about the room. "Just like with anything, it requires hard work, but it's a life I've come to love."

West bent forward again, hoping he could help his father understand. "There's hardly been a day over the last ten years when I haven't thought about all of you, and I'm sorry I didn't do more to try to make amends. But I have my own family to consider now, too." He swallowed hard, then said simply, "And my place is with them."

"Then there is nothing more for you here," Lawrence intoned in a weary voice.

West's breath rushed out on a tide of sorrow as he hung his head. He might feel peace as far as his decision was concerned, but it still hurt that his father wouldn't choose to see or understand him.

"Apparently," his father mused, "you have achieved everything I truly wanted for you…somewhere else."

Jerking his chin up, West gaped at him. "What do you mean?"

"You have become a man, Westin. An honorable and dedicated man, through hard work and effort, exactly as I would have wanted for you here." His brown eyes shone brighter and his face looked less ashen. "I never doubted it would happen. I knew from the time you were little that whatever you put your mind to… you would accomplish. You are much like me, though it may pain you to hear me say that." He gulped in air several times before continuing. "I had hoped…to steer that determination and hard work toward finance and eventually politics…but I knew even then that it wasn't meant to be. Don't you think I saw the way you watched those cowboys…the first time we visited the Custer Trail Ranch?"

West was startled to see his father's mouth lifting at the corners. "I didn't think you'd noticed."

"Ha." Lawrence gave a rumbling laugh. "I knew in that moment that no bank or money or political position could compete with riding a horse over unfettered land."

What was his father saying? "Then how come you

fought me on it? How come you encouraged me to court Lucile?"

"Because…I didn't want to lose you. I didn't want to give up on my dreams for us." His father gripped the sheet between his hands.

"Why tell me this now?"

Lawrence smiled fully at him this time. "You talk with the same pride about this ranch and family of yours as I used to of banking and all of you." The smile drooped from his face after a moment, leaving a strained expression in its wake. "I had hoped you would come…not to take over, Westin, but so I might ask for your forgiveness. I have realized these last few months…that I no longer wish to live in…in disappointment and regret."

Scooping up his father's hand in his, West willed back the threatening tears so he could say the words they both needed to hear. "Yes, I forgive you, Father." His own statement resounded through him, as loud as thunder in its truth and as soothing as a salve to his past hurts. "Can you forgive me? For staying away so long?"

"Yes, Westin…I forgive you, too," he whispered as he clasped West's hand tighter. "I had my lawyer… come over last week. To change my will…to its original wording. You'll find your inheritance…has been restored."

A jolt of surprise shot through West. If he was to have his inheritance again, he and Vienna could pay off their loan right away and possibly have enough left over to buy more livestock or add on to the house much sooner.

"Wait," West said as the rest of his father's words caught up with him. "You had your lawyer change your will last week? How did you know I would even come?"

"I didn't, not for sure. But I never stopped hoping... that...you...would..."

His father's grip slackened, and his eyes fell shut.

"Father?" When Lawrence didn't stir, West jumped up in alarm. "Father?"

His mother, who must have been waiting outside the door, rushed into the room. "It's all right," she reassured as she drew close. "He's only sleeping. Talking wears him out, even more so than eating. And he's done precious little of both the past few days."

"I'll let him rest, then." He squeezed his father's hand, then set it back down on the sheet. "Good night, Father. I...I love you."

Their meeting had been nothing like he'd expected, but he knew he'd made the right decision in coming. As he turned to go, he thought he saw one corner of his father's mouth lift briefly. It may have only been a trick of the lamplight, and yet, West felt certain his father had heard him. And that the half smile was his father's way of saying, "I love you, too, son."

"I miss Daddy West."

Hattie's exaggerated pout nearly made Vienna laugh. She might have done just that, if she hadn't been missing West so much herself.

If she hadn't been sure of her feelings before, she knew them now. She loved West—as far more than a friend.

As soon as he returned, Vienna would tell him that she wanted a real marriage. But what if he didn't want that, too? Her heart thumped faster beneath her blouse at the possibility until Vienna squared her shoulders. If West didn't want a real marriage, then she would eventually buy him out of his part of the ranch, hire others to manage the guests' activities and the livestock, and see if her marriage to him could still be annulled at that point. Because, now that she knew her own heart, she didn't think she could bear to be around him the rest of her life and remain only friends.

"Is he going to come back, Mommy?"

Her daughter's question drew Vienna's focus back to the conversation. Kneeling on Hattie's side of the bed, she shifted her stance on the hard floor. "Of course he's coming back."

"But my other daddy didn't." The little girl's green eyes reflected childlike concern and innocence.

Vienna pushed out a sigh. "That's because your other daddy went to Heaven, Hattie. And before that..." She searched for the best way to explain. "Before that, he made some bad choices and he had to face the consequences of those choices. That's why he didn't live with us before he died."

"Did he love me? Like Daddy West does?"

Her daughter's face blurred with Vienna's tears. How grateful she was that West loved her daughter as his own.

For a moment, Vienna reconsidered saying something to West about her feelings. If he didn't feel the same way and they had to call an end to their partnership and their marriage, Hattie would be devastated. But she mentally shook her head at the thought. She couldn't keep living and pretending that she felt only friendship for him—not when she wanted something more. Even if he didn't return her feelings, though, she knew West would still try to be a part of Hattie's life.

"Your other daddy didn't understand much about love, Hattie." She clasped the girl's tiny hand between her larger ones. "But I imagine he understands better now that he's in Heaven and that he does love you. Does that make sense?"

Hattie nodded sagely. "Does Daddy West understand about love, Mommy?"

"Yes," Vienna said, her own hopes on that score beating in time with her pulse. "I believe he does."

Snuggling down into her covers, her daughter yawned. "I know someone else who loves me," she murmured.

"Me," Vienna answered.

"Not just you, Mommy. God loves me, too."

She had to clear her throat in order to reply. "You're right, sweetie. God does love you."

And He loves me, too, Vienna thought with sudden clarity. *He's been walking right beside me, whether I feel brave or not. He's been taking care of me and Hattie this whole time.*

"How did you get to be so grown-up?" Vienna asked as she stood and kissed Hattie on the forehead.

The little girl smiled with obvious pride. "My mommy and daddy teached me."

It was the first time Vienna could recall Hattie referring to West as her daddy without using her full title for him. As Vienna picked up the lamp and left the room, she couldn't help hoping her daughter's words would prove true. That she and West could be a couple, that the three of them could be a family—in more than name only—from now on.

Chapter Eighteen

After leaving his father's room, West wandered down to the parlor. Out of habit mostly, from his evenings with Vienna. Cordelia glanced up from the book she was reading when he walked into the room.

"Where are Anita and Lydia?" he asked as he took the chair opposite hers.

She tucked her bookmark into her page and shut the book. "They went to sleep."

"Aren't you tired?" He leaned back against the chair, feeling suddenly exhausted himself.

His sister rubbed her finger across the book's cover. "A little. But I want to be awake…just in case."

West nodded in response as he stared at the cold hearth. His thoughts went to Vienna and Hattie— again. He could picture Vienna at home listening to Hattie's bedtime prayers and putting the little girl to bed. Then she would likely go back downstairs to the kitchen or into the parlor. An intense desire filled him to be there with her.

Now that he and his father had mended things, he couldn't wait to return home. And not just to accompany their guests to the dude ranch, either. He wanted to be there with his family…with his wife.

"Did you love James, before you married him?"

Cordelia looked momentarily surprised at the question, and then her expression softened. "Not like I do now." She set her book on the side table. "I liked and respected him, certainly. But I also knew it was as much a business arrangement as a marriage, since James had just begun working for Father."

A business arrangement. West could well identify with that. But he also understood the part about liking his intended. That's how he'd felt about Vienna even before their marriage.

"So when did that change?"

His sister's gaze turned thoughtful. "I couldn't pick one defining moment. It was the result of a thousand little ones, all added up together. Then one day, as we were putting the girls to bed, I looked across at him and I realized how much I loved him."

West sat forward in his chair, his hands loosely clasped in front of him. He and Vienna had certainly experienced their own share of a thousand little moments, including their kiss on her birthday. His mouth lifted at the remembrance. Kissing her then had felt even more right and natural than it had seven years earlier. He wanted to keep kissing her, and making her laugh, and working beside her, and raising Hattie together.

And having children of our own.

He jerked upright at the errant thought. Was that really what he wanted? A real marriage and more children with Vienna? His heart beat in time with his answer—*yes, yes, yes*. West didn't want to just be friends with Vienna anymore or a husband and father in name only. He wanted more—he loved Vienna and he wanted to go on loving her for the rest of his days.

"What has you smiling over there?" Cordelia asked, her eyes narrowing with curiosity. "And why all the questions about love?"

Rising to his feet, West crossed to her chair and kissed his sister's cheek. "That, my dear Cordy, is a conversation for another time. But thank you for sharing what you did." He paused at the door. "Thank you for sending that telegram, too."

"Are you glad you came?" She looked relieved but also a bit doubtful.

He smiled fully at her as he nodded. "I'm very glad."

His cough returned sometime in the night, along with the soreness in his head and muscles. Which meant West was already awake and collecting a drink of water from the kitchen when he heard the distant sound of weeping. He rushed upstairs to find his mother and Cordelia at his father's bedside.

"Is he…" West looked at his father, who appeared more still than he'd been earlier.

His sister, eyes red, nodded. "He's gone."

Remorse rocked through him, stronger than he'd expected, but he felt peace, too. He'd been able to forgive and be forgiven, and their last words to each other had been full of love and understanding.

The next few hours, after Cordelia woke their other two sisters, brought a whirlwind of activity—contacting the mortician, planning the details of the funeral, and West explaining again and again why he couldn't stay until then. By late afternoon, he felt dizzy each time he stood. Hopefully it was only because he'd slept very little since leaving Wyoming. He couldn't be sick again. The guests to the ranch would be more than a little concerned about their planned holiday if he showed up at the train station tomorrow feverish and coughing.

"Westin, you don't look so well," Lydia said at dinner.

He dropped his napkin alongside his plate. "It's West."

"What did you say, Westin?" his mother asked.

Shaking his head, though he regretted the action at once, he pushed back his chair and stood. "I believe I'll head to bed."

He was relieved when no one protested the early hour. If he could sleep from now until morning, he would surely be fit and ready for the return journey home.

Vienna could hardly contain her nervous energy. She kept rising up and down on her toes, her eyes peeled toward the approaching train. In a few minutes, the first guests to the dude ranch would disembark. Still, that wasn't the only reason for her excited fidgeting and racing heartbeat. West would be among them, as they'd planned, and she couldn't wait to see him. Would he care if she embraced him in front of everyone? Or should she save her eager greeting for a moment alone later? If they got a moment alone.

The past three days she hadn't had much time to think, let alone have a private conversation. Not that she wasn't grateful for the help of the Kents and Mrs. Harvey. A couple of wranglers from the Running W had helped polish all the horses' tack until a person could almost see his reflection in the shined leather. Maggy and Edward had kept Hattie busy as they helped clean the house and guest quarters, while Mrs. Harvey had assisted Vienna in the kitchen, preparing some of tonight's supper and other things for future meals that could be kept cold in the icebox.

Now everything was ready. There were flowers in every room, the table in the dining room was set for supper, the beds were ready for weary travelers to fall into, and Edward and Maggy had volunteered the use of their wagon, in addition to Vienna's, to help carry the guests to the ranch. The only things they were waiting on were the visitors—and West.

The train settled to a stop amidst the screech of brakes and the hiss of steam. People began to get off. Most of them headed away from the station or were greeted by those waiting, but a small crowd began to form in the center of the depot. These had to be their guests.

Vienna started toward the knot of people, her gaze darting between them and the train cars. West hadn't appeared yet—he was likely helping some of them with their luggage. Her heart thudded rapidly as she drew closer to the guests. She didn't know what to say to them, and she felt relief that West would soon step out and handle the introductions.

When she reached the fringe of the group, she blew her breath out slowly. Any moment now West would hop off the train, send a grin her way and take charge. But a minute dragged into two and he still hadn't alighted down the train steps. What was taking him so long?

"Do any of you know who's supposed to be meeting us?" a young man asked those around him.

The group erupted into murmurs. "Someone from the HC Bar Ranch, I suppose," an older woman said, frowning.

"I think his name is McCall," another added.

Vienna threw a panicked look at the train. No one else seemed to be getting off now. Where was West? Had she missed him? She glanced over her shoulder at the Kents' wagon, but the only ones waiting there were still just Maggy, Edward and Hattie.

"Do you think they forgot us?" A man in a bowler hat looked around, his expression concerned.

Vienna was going to have to take charge herself, though everything in her was telling her to bolt the other way. To rush back to the ranch and never leave it again. She hadn't felt this inadequate or shy in a long time. What if she said or did the wrong thing? What if she embarrassed herself or West? On the other hand…if she did leave, she would have no way to pay back the bank's loan. They might never have any other guests, either, if word got out about her failure with these people.

With her ears pounding with the sound of her own pulse, she climbed onto a nearby bench and loudly cleared her throat. The crowd turned in her direction, twelve pairs of eyes trained on her.

"My sincere apologies for the delay," she said in a voice that sounded nothing like that of a timid woman. "I'm Vienna Ho—" She shook her head. "Vienna Mc-Call. I recently remarried and it's still a challenge to remember my new last name."

Several chuckles and smiles rewarded her honesty.

"Let me be the first to welcome you to Wyoming," she continued. "We are looking forward to hosting you at the HC Bar this week." Stepping back down onto the platform, she pointed at the two wagons. "If you'll gather your luggage and follow me, we'll get everyone situated for the drive to the ranch."

Any triumph she felt at her accomplishment diminished as she neared the Kents' wagon. "Where is Daddy West?" Hattie asked, her brow furrowed and her green eyes large with sadness.

"I—I don't know, sweetie." Fresh worry spiked through Vienna as she glanced back at the train, willing West to suddenly appear. But there were no other passengers left, except for those preparing to board the train. "I guess he decided to stay in Pittsburgh a little longer."

Edward frowned as he straightened away from the wagon. "I would have thought he'd send a telegram then."

The conversation was cut short as the guests required assistance with getting themselves and their luggage into both wagons. There was no room left over in either vehicle by the time they had everything and everyone in place, but the guests good-naturedly squeezed in close together.

"Mind if Liza and I ride with you?" Maggy asked. "Hattie can stay with Edward."

The unshed tears clogging Vienna's throat made it next to impossible to reply. She simply nodded, more than grateful to have Maggy's support. After Edward helped them both onto the wagon seat, she clucked to the horses and drove away from the station.

Vienna mustered up enough courage and energy to

point out several of Sheridan's more prominent buildings and the Big Horn Mountains in the distance. But
aside from that, she was grateful that the guests didn't
seem to expect her to talk. Instead, they happily chatted among themselves, exclaiming over this and that.

Unfortunately, that left no distraction for Vienna
from the confusion and fears that threatened to over-
whelm her. Why hadn't West come home? Was he all
right? Did he regret his life out west after being back
in Pittsburgh? She swallowed hard, but the lump in
her throat wouldn't loosen. Soon tears were stinging
her eyes, and she had to blink them away in order to
see the road ahead.

Surely she couldn't do this, couldn't see to these first
guests completely on her own. What was she supposed
to do with them tomorrow, when the group expected
to do more than sit at her table and eat?

I can't do this, God, she pleaded silently. *I'm not
brave enough or charismatic enough or...or...rancher
enough for this. Not by myself, anyway...not without
West.*

All of her old insecurities, ones she'd thought she
had buried with Chance, roared back to life inside her.
How often had he scolded her for saying or doing the
wrong thing? Or reminded her that she was too weak
and timid to handle making important decisions or nav-
igating social situations with poise and strength? Her
hands began to shake where they gripped the reins, and
her chest tightened with her shallow breaths.

West had been wrong about her—she hadn't possessed some hidden strength all these years. She
wouldn't ever possess real courage or fortitude. Instead, she would always be timid, shy, bashful Vienna.

Who couldn't be relied upon to handle such a monumental job on her own.

A memory nibbled at the edges of her consciousness, trying to make itself heard over the clamor of her own panic. Something West had once said…about bravery.

Bravery isn't the absence of fear, she remembered him saying. *Think of Daniel… He trusted God was with him and that likely gave him the courage to face his fear and still move forward.*

Trust God, face the fear and move forward.

Relief so profound washed through Vienna that she had to fight to stay seated and not slump to the floorboards at her feet. If bravery wasn't the absence of fear, then she could be brave. She *had* been brave.

She thought back over the last few months and all she'd done, though it had been frightening at times. Agreeing to start a dude ranch, marrying West and acknowledging her true feelings for him, if only to herself. All of those were things she'd feared initially, but she had felt that fear and moved forward. And she hadn't done it alone, either. Yes, West had helped her greatly, and so had Maggy and Edward. But most important, so had God.

What had Hattie reminded her of the other night? That God loved them both and was watching over them. Because she knew that truth, Vienna could do this.

"Are you okay?" Maggy touched her sleeve.

Vienna nodded. "I am." And she meant it. She was still concerned about what had happened to delay West and she felt disappointed that he wasn't there now, but she was equal to the task ahead of her. At least, she and God were, together.

"I'm sorry West didn't make it back on time. If you need anything at all…"

She smiled fully at her friend. "I know, and I appreciate that, Maggy. More than I can say. But I think I'm going to be all right. Even without West here right now."

"That a girl." Maggy returned her smile as she bumped Vienna's shoulder with her own. "You are an amazing, strong woman, Vienna McCall, and I'm proud to call you my friend."

Tears filled her eyes again, only this time they were tears of gratitude and hope. "Thank you. I've learned a lot of that from you."

"Maybe." With a shrug, Maggy adjusted the blanket around her sleeping baby. "But I really only reminded you of what was there all along."

Urging the horses to pick up their pace, Vienna laughed. "I think you're right, Maggy. And best of all, I can finally see and believe that for myself."

Chapter Nineteen

The ride from Sheridan to the HC Bar had never felt so long to West. He urged his rented horse from the livery to pick up its pace, but the animal clearly didn't sense his rider's desperation or share his urgency to reach home. Even the beauty of the pinking sky failed to fully breach West's anxiety.

After resting, he no longer felt as ill as he had the night his father had passed away. But his health had come at a terrible price. Instead of only sleeping until the next morning, he'd awoken to near darkness and the awful realization he'd slept an entire day. And missed his scheduled train. He wouldn't be returning to the ranch with the first group of guests as he'd told Vienna he would.

Fresh apprehension brought a bitter taste to his mouth. What had Vienna done in his absence? Had she sent the guests away? Worse still, what did she think of him?

That he loved her and wanted a full marriage with her was no longer a question in West's mind—an assurance that had grown, along with his fears, the entire journey home. But could she love him, especially after he'd failed her? He hadn't done what she'd wanted, and he wasn't sure his rushing back now would be enough to convince her that she still needed his help. That she still needed him.

West hung his head, his chin nearly touching his shirt. He'd done more than think about Vienna on the long train ride. He'd also prayed. At first, he'd been loath to ask God for what he wanted—to still have a chance with Vienna. After all, most of the things he'd wanted hadn't come in the way or time that he'd hoped. But as he thought back over the last ten years of his life, he'd begun to see things differently, more clearly, than he ever had before.

If God had immediately granted his petitions to be reunited with his family when West had prayed for that years earlier, he might not have come to Wyoming or even met Vienna. Or had the chance to start a dude ranch with her and be married to her. God, in His infinite and loving wisdom, had delayed granting that blessing in West's life to give him time for blessings far greater than those he'd hoped for.

Once West had realized that, he'd humbly asked God that if possible he would like to have his heart's desire this time. But if not, he would trust in Him. The peace he'd felt in finally petitioning Heaven for what he really wanted and surrendering the timing and outcome had eased some of his inner unrest. At least until the train had pulled to a stop in Sheridan.

"Please, Father," he whispered again in a choked voice as he lifted his gaze to the sunset sky. "If possible, don't let it be too late for Vienna and me. Help her hear me out and help me know how I can make this up to her."

The sight of the HC Bar's archway sent his heart beating double-time. Would Vienna refuse to speak with him? Would he find the place devoid of guests? Or would they be standing around bored and annoyed, after a day of nothing to do but hang around the ranch?

He tugged on the brim of his cowboy hat, grateful he was back wearing his regular clothes instead of the stiff suit and bowler hat. His suit was folded neatly inside his bag and he'd given the hat away to a man on the train. He didn't need it at home.

A group of young adults stared curiously at him as West rode past the corral where they were watching some of the horses. Which meant Vienna had brought the guests here, after all. He felt a glimmer of pride, but it was quickly swallowed up with concern. Would he need to smooth their ruffled feathers, regarding their unproductive first day on the ranch, after he attempted to smooth Vienna's?

But as he rode closer to the house and outbuildings, the people West saw moving about the yard or sitting on the back porch in the rocking chairs didn't look displeased. If anything, they looked content, as if they were fully enjoying themselves.

Confused, he dismounted and led the borrowed horse into the barn. A man, leaning on the door of one of the occupied stalls, turned to look at him, then smiled.

"Westin McCall, how good to see you again," he said, sticking out his hand. "Oh, sorry. Your wife told us you go by West now."

He eyed the man a moment before recognition

dawned. "Mr. Ashton!" The gentleman had been a client of his father's bank before West had left home. "Good to see you, as well." He shook the man's hand.

"How is your father?" Mr. Ashton asked. "I heard he was ailing."

West cleared his throat to dislodge the lump of grief there. "He passed away, actually."

"I'm sorry to hear that. He will be missed."

"Thank you. I'm grateful I was able to be with him at the end."

Mr. Ashton waved a hand at the stalls. "Fine ranch and family you have here, McCall."

West nodded in appreciation. He was relieved Ashton didn't look bored or discontented with the accommodations. Swallowing hard, he pushed the question he needed to ask from his mouth, though he wasn't sure he wanted the answer. "How has your stay been so far? I sincerely apologize for not being here yesterday for your arrival."

"No worries," Mr. Ashton said. "Your wife has been the perfect hostess, and Mrs. Ashton and I had a most delightful ride this afternoon."

Had they taken the horses out by themselves? "Did just the two of you go for a ride?"

"Oh, no." Mr. Ashton hooked his thumbs in his belt loops. He sported one of the largest belt buckles West had ever seen. "Your wife took all of us out."

Vienna had taken them on a ride? West gaped in surprise at the gentleman, who thankfully didn't seem to notice.

"We had a delicious breakfast," Mr. Ashton continued, "followed by a demonstration from your charming wife on how to milk the cow and care for the horses.

After that we went on our ride. Such beautiful country you have here." The man smiled. "We had a wonderful picnic lunch by a stream and then returned to get a little rest before supper. I'm hoping you might take some of us fellows fishing tomorrow. Mrs. McCall said there's good fishing if we head toward the mountains."

West arranged his face into a casual expression to hide the shock he still felt. "Fishing tomorrow? Of course."

"Very good. I'll see you at supper, McCall."

He waved as the man exited the barn, and then he dropped his arm to his side. Everything had gone well, even with him absent. West wasn't sure if he ought to feel grateful or flat-out worried. If Vienna no longer needed him...

Shutting his mind to the too-familiar rut of negative thinking, he quickly unsaddled the horse and brushed him down. If he hurried, he might be able to catch Vienna in the kitchen for a private moment before supper. His heartbeat sped up again as he crossed the yard, exchanged greetings with the guests seated on the back porch and entered the kitchen.

"Daddy West!" Hattie hollered with a grin.

When she ran toward him, he caught her and tossed her in the air before giving her a hug. "Hattie girl. I've missed you."

"I've missed you, too. And so has Mommy. She told me."

Was it true? Had Vienna missed him? Or at least up until yesterday when he'd failed to show up as he'd promised. He forced his gaze to Vienna, who was pulling something from the stove. "Hello."

"Hello," she echoed. She didn't appear angry, especially when she smiled at him.

Hattie put her small hands on either side of his face and turned his head so he was looking at her again. "How come you didn't come yesterday?"

"About that... I'm sorry I wasn't here." He meant the words for both of them. Glancing toward Vienna, West found her watching them. "I got sick again and slept through the train's departure, but that isn't an excuse. I said I'd be here and I wasn't."

The little girl wriggled to get down, so he set her on her feet. "That's okay, Daddy West. I forgive you."

A feeling of warmth spread through his chest at Hattie's sweet, sincere words. He only hoped her mother would be as forgiving.

"Hattie," Vienna said, "why don't you go put the forks on the napkins like I showed you how to do yesterday?"

Her daughter grinned. "All right."

She scooped up the forks and skipped out of the room. Leaving him and Vienna momentarily alone. Uneasiness brought a chill sweeping through him, in spite of the warm room. Removing his hat, West stared down at it. The sounds of Vienna moving about the kitchen filled in the sudden silence.

"I'm sorry, Vienna," he said without lifting his gaze. "My father passed away the night I arrived in Pittsburgh. There was a lot to do after that, and I guess I pushed myself too hard. But I didn't think I was so ill that I would sleep clear through an entire day."

The noises around him stopped. "If you were feeling even a part of what you did the other week, I'm surprised you didn't sleep longer than that."

West looked at her in surprise. "Then you aren't… angry?"

"Surprised and worried but not angry." Her eyes glowed dark green with sincerity. "And I'm sorry about your father. I'm glad you were able to see him one last time."

He dipped his head in a nod. "Me, too. We…we came to an understanding." He wanted to tell her about his inheritance, but fear pushed the words back down his throat. Would she feel obligated to ask him to stick around if he told her that he had the money to pay off their loan?

"That's wonderful, West. I'm so happy for you." She smiled at him as she began pulling rolls off a pan and placing them in a towel-lined basket.

Hattie scampered back into the kitchen. "I did the forks, Mommy."

"Thank you. Will you do the spoons next?"

As Hattie left the kitchen again, West looped his hat on the back of a chair and went to wash his hands at the sink. "It sounds like things have gone really well here."

"I hope so."

He shot her a glance over his shoulder. "Mr. Ashton said you took everyone on a ride."

"I did, yes."

Grabbing a towel, he wiped his hands dry. "I'm impressed, Vienna."

"Thank you." Her cheeks flushed pink. "It wasn't as scary a task as I once thought it would be."

"What did you do with Hattie?"

She paused in removing the rolls to give him a smug look. "I took her with me. With those riding lessons you've been giving her, she did fantastic and she really enjoyed the experience."

"Well, Mr. Ashton had nothing but good things to say about being here so far." He crossed to the table and began to help her put the rolls in the basket.

Vienna shrugged, but her expression shone with happiness. "I'm glad to hear it. It hasn't been easy, but I've managed and the guests have been gracious."

He was proud of her. She'd finally seen how capable and strong she could be. But where did that leave them? If she didn't really need his help anymore, did she still want him there?

"You brought the guests here, cooked delicious meals for them, and took them on an enjoyable ride." He forced a light chuckle. "Looks as though you can handle all of this rather well on your own. Maybe you don't need much help, after all."

She glanced up at him. "What are you saying, West?"

"I…"

They both reached for the same roll. West didn't let go and neither did Vienna. The feel of her fingers against his felt wonderfully familiar. Thoughts swirled around his head, moving too quickly to grab hold of. He brought his gaze to hers. She was kind, beautiful and strong. And he loved her. He loved her with all of his heart. But could she possibly feel the same, especially now?

"All done, Mommy," Hattie said as she trotted back into the room.

Vienna startled beside him, pulling her hand from his. "Wonderful. How about you go pick some flowers from the garden? For the table?"

"But there are already flowers on the table." The little girl looked curiously at each of them in turn. "And I'm hungry, Mommy."

Picking up a roll from the basket, her mother handed it to her. "Here, you can eat this while you collect a few more flowers."

"Okay." She took a bite out of the roll and exited the kitchen for the third time.

Vienna faced him, her expression expectant but also slightly worried. "What were you saying?"

He focused on the rolls as he spoke. "My whole life I thought if I did what others wanted, they would like me—love me, even. But I also feared if I stepped out of line, the love would stop." West hated the vulnerability he felt at confessing something so private, and yet, he knew it was necessary to be honest with her. "When I went against my father's wishes and Lucile's and was cut off from my family, it just served to reinforce that belief. I didn't do what they wanted and so they stopped caring. Up until recently, I even believed God felt that way."

"Is that still what you believe?" she asked. Then to his surprise, she stepped toward him and placed her hand on his arm.

"Sometimes." He studied her lovely face. "I know I didn't do what you wanted yesterday, Vienna, and I hope to make it up to you. Because I—I love you. Not just as a business partner or a friend, but as a husband loves a wife." Her green eyes grew twice as large and he heard her quick intake of breath. "And I'd like to know if you might love me, too, and if you think you still…need me?"

West had never felt more exposed than he did in that moment. Would she agree or ask him to leave like his family had all those years ago?

"You love me?" she said in a soft voice as she rested her hand alongside his jaw.

He nodded, his heart thumping with hope at the tenderness in her expression and her touch. Until she spoke again.

"The truth is I don't need you, West. Like you've told me before, I am capable and strong. And if I let Him, God will magnify that strength even more."

Disappointment knifed through him. He tugged Vienna's hand away from his face and fell back a step. "You…you don't need me?"

"No, but I want you."

He frowned down at the floorboards. "If that's true, then maybe you can buy me out—"

"West?" She drew closer to him again. "Did you hear me?"

"You said you didn't need me."

Why was she smiling at him? "Did you hear what I said after that?"

Had he? Once she'd revealed she didn't need him, he hadn't bothered to hear much else. What had she said? Something about God magnifying one's strength and about her wanting…*wanting him*?

"Wait. Did you say you don't need me but you want me?"

Vienna laughed. "Yes."

"Does that mean…"

She lifted both her hands and cupped each side of his face, like her daughter had earlier. "It means I love you, too. As a wife loves a husband. And that's because of who you are, West McCall. Not because of what you do or don't do for me or Hattie. I love you for you."

No words had ever sounded sweeter to him, nor could he ever recall feeling more love for a person than he did right now for Vienna. Best of all, she loved him back—simply because he was himself.

"Then will you marry me, Vienna Harriet McCall?" he asked as he placed his hands on her aproned waist.

Her eyes sparkled with pleasure. "I believe we're already married, Mr. McCall."

"But I want to do it properly this time. In the church, with Hattie and our friends there."

She leaned into him. "I would be honored to marry you all over again."

"Mommy? What are you doing?"

They both glanced at the doorway, where Hattie stood watching them. She no longer held a roll in her hand but a fistful of flowers.

"I am about to kiss Daddy West," Vienna declared with a full smile as she peered at West again. Then she pressed her lips firmly to his. A joy he'd never imagined experiencing filled him head to toe.

Hattie giggled as her mother eased back. "What are you going to do now, Daddy?"

If he thought his happiness couldn't be added upon, he would have been wrong. Hearing the little girl simply call him "daddy" solidified the perfection of the moment.

Gazing at Vienna, he grinned. "I'm going to kiss your mother back, Hattie girl."

And that was exactly what he did.

Two weeks later

Similar to how she'd felt before her first and second wedding ceremonies, Vienna had flutters in her stomach. But today they didn't stem from nervousness. They were tremors of excitement and anticipation. In a few minutes she would become Mrs. Vienna McCall—for the second time in a matter of months. Only today she knew without a doubt that West loved her as much as she loved him.

"You look stunning," Maggy exclaimed, turning Vienna toward the floor-length mirror.

Her long, white gown hugged her waist before flowing to the floor. Ms. Glasen, Sheridan's most accomplished dressmaker and a friend of Maggy's, had created the beautiful gown. In her hands, Vienna held a bouquet of late-summer roses.

"What about me, Ms. Maggy?" Hattie asked.

Maggy took Hattie's hand and guided her forward to stand beside Vienna. "You look absolutely beautiful, too, Hattie. Daddy West will be in awe of both of you."

The little girl beamed into the mirror and swished her fancy dress from side to side.

A knock at the door quickened Vienna's pulse. It must be time. "Come in," she called as she turned away from the mirror.

Alec, who'd told them that he wouldn't miss their second wedding ceremony for anything, poked his head inside. "The pastor says he's ready." He smiled at Vienna. "However, I don't know that West is ready. One look at his beautiful bride and he's liable to get tongue-tied."

"Thank you, Alec," Vienna said, blushing with pleasure at his compliment. "We're ready, too."

She followed her daughter and Maggy out of the small room and stopped at the entrance to the chapel. From the back, she could see the church was nearly full. The guests included their friends and neighbors as well as her aunt and cousin and West's mother and sisters. It seemed no one wanted to miss the wedding this time.

For a moment, she felt a twinge of sadness that her parents and brother wouldn't be among those seated. But as Edward stepped up beside her to lead her down the aisle, Vienna reminded herself that they were likely aware of today's importance in her life and were smiling down on her with approval.

The organist started playing as she and Edward walked down the aisle. Vienna had purposely waited to look at West until this moment. When her eyes met his, he smiled with such radiance that it nearly stole her breath. He looked incredibly handsome in his new three-piece suit, which had been a gift from his family. This handsome, wonderful, kind cowboy was about to become her husband—again.

Soon she was standing next to West, her hand tenderly clasped in his, as the pastor began the ceremony. There was none of the panic or sweaty palms she'd experienced when they'd been married by the judge. Today she felt as if she were lit from the inside out with joy and peace.

Several chuckles echoed through the church when the pastor asked if "you, Westin McCall, take Vienna Harriet McCall to be your lawfully wedded wife?" And then again when he asked if Vienna McCall took

Westin McCall as her lawfully wedded husband. But Vienna didn't mind their humor over her and West marrying each other again. This second ceremony was important to them and their little family, though they were grateful to share the special day with others.

Once the pastor pronounced them man and wife, West didn't wait for the directive to kiss the bride. To Vienna's great joy, it wasn't a kiss on the cheek that West gave her as he had in the judge's chambers. Instead he drew her close and kissed her on the lips, bringing more delighted laughter from the guests and happy tears to Vienna's eyes.

West grinned at her as he stepped back. "I plan to keep doing that every day," he said in a voice low enough that Vienna was sure only she could hear.

"Just every day?" she countered, raising her eyebrows at him. "Surely we can justify every hour or so now that we're married for real this time."

His deep laugh followed them down the aisle and out the church. Then, with Hattie tucked between them, they drove the Kents' buggy back to the Running W, where a party was being held in their honor.

Hours later, after the delicious food had been eaten, congratulations accepted and she had danced with West, they headed home—just the two of them. Hattie was staying the night at the Kents' and the relatives were staying at the hotel in nearby Big Horn. The quiet of twilight settled like a blanket around them as Vienna scooted closer to West on the buggy seat.

They hadn't gone far when he stopped the buggy and presented Vienna with a long kiss. "Are you happy, Mrs. McCall?"

"I am." She rested her head against his shoulder as

he started the buggy moving forward again. "Though at this pace, we won't be home until morning."

"Already tiring of my kisses?" West teased.

Vienna lifted her chin to look at him. "Never." When his brown eyes shone with fondness, she lifted herself off the seat and placed her own firm kiss against his lips. "Are *you* happy, Mr. McCall?"

"More than I can say." He settled a kiss on her forehead as she snuggled closer. "Did you decide yet if you want to take our guests next week on their first ride, while I make their supper?"

She smiled, both at the question and the reminder that their dude ranch was proving to be successful. Their first group of guests had talked enough about their wonderful experience at the HC Bar with their friends that she and West now had guests scheduled for the rest of the month and well into October. And with West's inheritance restored to him, they had paid off the bank loan and were already making plans for what else they wanted to add to the dude ranch.

"What would you say if I *did* want to take them on their first ride?"

West glanced at her, his expression serious. "I would say they're in for a real treat. Though my supper may slightly pale in comparison with yours."

"Only slightly?" She poked him in the ribs as he laughed.

"Is that what you want to do, then?"

Vienna reached out and pulled back on the horse's reins, stopping the buggy. "What if we did it together? Both the ride and preparing supper?"

"Together?" he echoed before nodding. "I like the sound of that."

"So do I," Vienna whispered. Then tugging on his lapel, she kissed him again as the stars shone with approval overhead.

* * * * *

If you missed Edward and Maggy's romance,
be sure to go back and get swept away with
THE RANCHER'S TEMPORARY ENGAGEMENT.

And don't miss these other Western adventures
from Stacy Henrie:

LADY OUTLAW
THE EXPRESS RIDER'S LADY
THE OUTLAW'S SECRET
THE RENEGADE'S REDEMPTION

Find other great reads at www.LoveInspired.com

Dear Reader,

After reading a fascinating article about the history of dude ranching, I knew I wanted to make that a part of Vienna and West's story. Thankfully they didn't complain!

The Eaton brothers—Howard, Alden and Willis—who were originally from Pittsburgh, are credited with operating the first dude ranch near Medora, North Dakota, in the 1880s. The tale is that a guest suggested the brothers charge people room and board to come visit, and the idea of the dude ranch was born. Howard Eaton is said to have been the one to coin the word *dude* in reference to their guests who came from back east to visit the Custer Trail Ranch. And he did, in fact, take guests on pack trips to Yellowstone National Park. The descriptions of the ranch as well as its numbers and buildings are based on accounts of the place in 1901.

Visitors to the Custer Trail Ranch weren't mail-order cowboys; a lot of them could ride well. However, they did tend to dress more extravagantly than regular cowboys. The idea of traveling back east to recruit guests and needing references from them is also true. The story about Teddy Roosevelt, who was a friend of the Eatons, and his robber bedfellow is supposedly true, as well. In 1904, the Eatons left North Dakota and moved their dude ranch to Wyoming. Their ranch is still in existence today.

It wasn't until 1904 that Golden Hair, from the story of the three bears, was named Goldilocks. Also, of interesting note—for years, the tale was meant as a cautionary one to children about not snooping about where they shouldn't.

Having already set one story in the beautiful countryside near Sheridan and the Big Horn Mountains, I was excited to set another there. I also enjoyed giving Vienna and West, two secondary characters from my last Love Inspired Historical *The Rancher's Temporary Engagement*, their own happily-ever-after. It was a lot of fun to write their marriage of convenience story, as well.

My hope is that, like West, readers will also realize God doesn't love us just because we do what He wants. He loves us unconditionally. I also hope that, like Vienna, readers will recognize their own inner strength and abilities, and that with God that strength can be magnified.

I love hearing from readers. You can contact me through my website at www.stacyhenrie.com.

All the best,
Stacy

We hope you enjoyed this story from
Love Inspired® Historical.

Love Inspired® Historical is coming to
an end but be sure to discover more
inspirational stories to warm your heart
from **Love Inspired®** and
Love Inspired® Suspense!

Love Inspired stories show that
faith, forgiveness and hope have the power
to lift spirits and change lives—always.

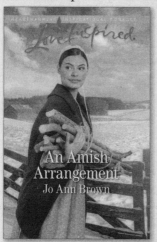
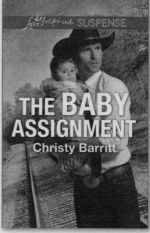

Look for six new romances every month
from **Love Inspired®** and
Love Inspired® Suspense!

Get 4 FREE REWARDS!

We'll send you 2 FREE Books plus 2 FREE Mystery Gifts.

Love Inspired® books feature contemporary inspirational romances with Christian characters facing the challenges of life and love.

FREE
Value Over
$20

Her family's future in the balance, can Clara Fisher find a way to save her home?

Read on for a sneak preview of
HIS NEW AMISH FAMILY by Patricia Davids,
the next book in **THE AMISH BACHELORS** *miniseries,*
available in July 2018 from Love Inspired.

Paul Bowman leaned forward in his seat to get a good look at the farm as they drove up. Both the barn and the house were painted white and appeared in good condition. He made a quick mental appraisal of the equipment he saw, then jotted down numbers in a small notebook he kept in his pocket.

"What is she doing here?" The anger in his client Ralph's voice shocked Paul.

He followed Ralph's line of sight and spied an Amish woman sitting on a suitcase on the front porch of the house. She wore a simple pale blue dress with an apron of matching material and a black cape thrown back over her shoulders. Her wide-brimmed black traveling bonnet hid her hair. She looked hot, dusty and tired. She held a girl of about three or four on her lap. The child clung tightly to her mother. A boy a few years older leaned against the door behind her holding a large calico cat.

"Who is she?" Paul asked.

"That is my annoying cousin, Clara Fisher." Ralph opened his car door and got out. Paul did the same.

The woman glared at both men. "Why are there padlocks on the doors, Ralph? Eli never locked his home."

"They are there to keep unwanted visitors out. What are you doing here?" Ralph demanded.

"I live here. May I have the keys, please? My children and I are weary."

Ralph's eyebrows snapped together in a fierce frown. "What do you mean you live here?"

"What part did you fail to understand, Ralph? I… live…here," she said slowly.

Ralph's face darkened with anger. Paul had to turn away to keep from laughing.

She might look small, but she was clearly a woman to be reckoned with. She reminded him of an angry mama cat all fluffed up and spitting-mad. He rubbed a hand across his mouth to hide a grin. His movement caught her attention, and she pinned her deep blue gaze on him. "Who are you?"

He stopped smiling. "My name is Paul Bowman. I'm an auctioneer. Mr. Hobson has hired me to get this property ready for sale."

Don't miss
HIS NEW AMISH FAMILY by Patricia Davids,
available July 2018 wherever
Love Inspired® books and ebooks are sold.

www.LoveInspired.com

Looking for inspiration in tales
of hope, faith and heartfelt romance?

Check out **Love Inspired**® and
Love Inspired® **Suspense** books!

New books available every month!

CONNECT WITH US AT:

Harlequin.com/Community

Facebook.com/HarlequinBooks

Twitter.com/HarlequinBooks

Instagram.com/HarlequinBooks

Pinterest.com/HarlequinBooks

ReaderService.com

Love Inspired®

LIGENRE2018